GRANT'S

Heat

SHARK'S EDGE: BOOK FOUR

ANGEL PAYNE & VICTORIA BLUE

GRANT'S *Heat*

SHARK'S EDGE: BOOK FOUR

ANGEL PAYNE & VICTORIA BLUE

WATERHOUSE PRESS

For David and Kadin.

Thank you for seeing me through this challenge.

*Knowing the two of you are always there
gives me the courage and peace of mind to
concentrate on getting well.*

I love you dearly.

—SS

For Tom.

*The heat's never too crazy for you,
and I'm so damn grateful.*

—Angel

CHAPTER ONE

GRANT

"So, as you can see, Mr. Twombley, this property is quite a steal. It won't stay on the market long. If we don't make an offer in the next day, someone else will."

I followed my real estate agent from the hallway into the master suite of the fortieth-floor condo of the downtown Los Angeles neighborhood. This was the only room with which I was really concerned, but Charlene didn't need to know that. I liked the woman enough to have worked steadily with her for the last five years, but she didn't know much about me on a personal level. I had every intention of keeping it that way.

Char kept on chattering. Something about floor-to-ceiling something or other. I tuned her out while venturing into the en suite bathroom. Typically, the bedroom and bathroom were the only two rooms I used in most of my places, so I focused on what mattered here.

Marble slab counters topped sleek gray cabinets, and matching marble tiles lined the walls of the oversized shower. My six and a half feet made most shower enclosures uncomfortable, so this plumbing masterpiece had me sold on the condo quicker than any of the other features Char had droned on about thus far. Give me a luxurious bathroom, and I was a happy boy indeed.

"Let's put in an offer as soon as you can draft it."

"Excellent, Mr. Twombley," she purred. "I had a feeling you'd like this place."

"But I want to come in at thirteen percent under asking."

Just as swiftly, her shoulders sagged. But I didn't feel a second of compunction about being the confidence murderer. Charlene Jackson and I had closed at least twelve deals together, and she argued with my initial offer every single time. By now, I expected her diligence—but in hopes of saving us both some time, I held up my hand to stave off her ensuing protest. Not that it stopped her. "You heard me," I said firmly. "Can we make one offer where you don't argue with me first?"

"Grant . . ."

I just stared, waiting for her to continue.

"I just think it's a bad number," she persisted.

"You already know that won't change my mind."

"You're risking driving them from the table by lowballing them."

"I understand you feel that way. And that is the offer I want you to make. Write it up and send it over so I can sign it." I scrolled through my phone blindly to signal the conversation was over. The agent let out a frustrated sigh while she packed up her briefcase at the kitchen island.

"This was a great find, Char. Good job." Turning a full circle, I took in the airy space one last time before concluding, "I don't have anything in this neighborhood but was looking for something around here." When she didn't respond, I looked up to see she was still pouting, stuffing things into her designer bag. "That's a nice bag, by the way."

"Really?" She visibly warmed, her green eyes sparkling in the late-morning sun that shone through in the eat-in kitchen's windows. "You like it?"

"I do." I meant it, which came as a small surprise, since that wasn't my original intention. The goal had simply been to get this woman over her snit. Getting Char to revel over her latest handbag or shoes was like setting out catnip for the neighborhood's stray tabby.

The woman stroked the leather with a gentle hand, gazing at the thing like the parent of a newborn. "Thanks so much," she crooned. "Today's her debut."

I chuckled. "Her? Handbags have a gender now?"

"This one just feels like a she." Char looked adoringly at the bag again. I didn't dare ask if the accessory had a name.

Before leaving, I gave my agent a quick peck on each cheek. "Thanks again," I said. "Being here in downtown is going to help me out in a lot of ways."

Most notably with my demanding responsibilities for Sebastian Shark.

Who, as one of the people on the planet who knew me best, would probably roll his eyes at learning I was planning to purchase my seventh residence.

My best friend was also the owner and CEO of Shark Enterprises. He loved to lecture me about smartly spending my money, but the man hadn't gone from gutter rat to Fortune 500–lister *without* knowing the value of every dollar he made. Now, just as we'd watched each other's backs on the playground, we looked out for each other on the corporate battlefield.

Being his right-hand man and COO at Shark Enterprises was a lot of damn work, especially now that Sebastian's namesake skyscraper was starting to rise from the ground in the financial district, but my daily responsibilities also meant lofty paychecks. I had the financial freedom to add to my residential real estate collection whenever I damn well felt like it.

I didn't plan on stopping for a while, either. Currently, my goal was to have ten properties. Maybe I'd stop there; maybe I wouldn't. The plan was that I would never be far from home. My therapist had a field day with the topic, so I tried to steer clear of it altogether. I knew all the fucked-up reasons behind the bizarre need and driving desire to amass residences the same way other people collect vacation-spot shot glasses or truck-stop hot sauces, but again, I couldn't see the benefit of examining it all too intimately.

Right now, I needed to worry less about places to have my mail forwarded and more about where I was supposed to be in less than thirty minutes.

I headed out into the overcast January morning to where Sebastian's driver, Joel, was waiting to make sure I made the meeting on time.

Once in the back seat of the town car, I pulled out my phone to catch up on all the incoming messages I'd missed during the property tour with Charlene.

But the moment the device came to life, a different message caught my eye instead. Like a magnet to metal, my gaze was drawn right to the text from one feisty, smart-mouthed, ill-mannered, and quick-witted little package named Rio Gibson. On my screen, however, she simply showed up under one name. Blaze.

The nickname had settled in while she and I worked together at Abstract Catering's prep kitchen in Inglewood. The little catering company, co-owned by her and Sebastian's fiancée, Abbigail, wouldn't be little for too much longer. Abstract was on a major upward trajectory in the catering scene in Los Angeles and the surrounding area. They had paid their dues for the success in spades, especially during that grueling month last summer when Bas had been forced to hide Abbi away at an estate in Twentynine Palms. There were some mean, still unidentified enemies, messing with him, and he'd been terrified about his woman being next on their hit list.

Subsequently, Sebastian hadn't taken any chances with the people closest to her either, so I was the one assigned to Rio's personal protection detail. Which, in turn, meant a lot of grueling hours on my feet in a sweltering industrial kitchen, where we prepared lunches for businessmen and women who'd scarf the food down behind their desktop computers while taking meetings or attending webinars. I knew from firsthand experience there were days the food we toiled over making all morning was barely tasted. The next day, we'd turn around and do it all over again.

I opened the text thread with Blaze.

Want to meet for lunch after deliveries?

Meeting with (Shark emoji) at the Edge's site. Someplace near there? You okay?

Of course I'm okay. Just figured you're missing me.

How about the Bunker Hill Steps? Text when you're on your way?

Will do.

I tried to play it cool, but I could feel a grin tugging at my lips. Yeah, I guess I had missed her. We'd spent so much time together in that hellfire kitchen, and then, as quickly as the assignment started . . . it stopped.

Rio Gibson was the kind of woman who got under your skin. She was abrasive as hell when you first met her, but after a few days, we'd found an easy rhythm around one another, and I actually looked forward to seeing her each morning. She was considerate, funny, and smart as hell. All wrapped up in a sexy, spitfire package.

"And here we are, Mr. Twombley," Joel called over his shoulder while he pulled toward the curb. "That was the lightest midday traffic I've seen in years."

Of course it had been. While I was happy to have set up an impromptu meeting with Rio, I could kick myself for not getting anything work-related accomplished on the drive.

"Thanks for the lift, man," I said to Joel, sliding across the seat to exit at the curb in front of the bustling construction lot.

"My pleasure. Just text when you're done. I'm assuming you and Mr. Shark will be heading back to the office from here?" Joel asked.

"Not sure what Bas has going on, but I won't need a ride from here. I'll tell him to let you know, though."

I shut the car's door and went in search of my best friend. We were scheduled to meet with the superintendent and two foremen at the Shark's Edge job site.

It had been nearly four months since Terryn Ramsey, Sebastian's former administrative assistant, had committed suicide here. There'd been a lot of scuttlebutt about some foremen walking off the job, but we were too far into the project to lose key players. If even one of these men quit now, we would be set back weeks while we selected replacements, and the project timeline—as well as the budget—would take a major hit.

I met Bas in the security team's trailer, where we donned hardhats and safety vests, and then we were escorted to the superintendent's trailer across the massive property.

The building's foundation had already been poured, and tons of steel beams had arrived on-site earlier in the week. Pride radiated off my friend, his usual intensity giving way to a subtle smile, as we crossed the uneven ground in the all-terrain vehicle the workers used to navigate around the job site.

"Mr. Shark! Mr. Twombley!" The rotund superintendent shook our hands in turn when greeting us at the narrow door of his makeshift office. "Great to see you, gentlemen. You boys need to start leaving your fancy shoes in the car when you come down here, though. I keep telling you every time I see you."

"You do, Jerry, you do," Bas teased back, slapping the man on the back as he ushered us inside.

"Things are looking great, Mr. Nash." I motioned over my shoulder toward the early stages of the structure. Even in its skeletal state, the Edge was captivating to look at. "This building is going to be amazing."

Jerry harrumphed with a good-natured grin. "Got my eye on that bonus. The wife wants to take a Caribbean vacation. Her sister goes on a cruise every year, and that's all we hear about for two months after she gets back." His smirk fell as he rolled his eyes dramatically.

Bas and I feigned answering laughs together. "Well, keep up the good work, and you and Mrs. Nash will be hosting your vacation picture slideshow before you know it," Bas encouraged.

"And how's your beautiful lady?" Jerry returned. "When is the baby due again?"

The contentment glowing from Bas turned into a full light show of happiness. "Abbi is due May twentieth," he supplied. "And she's doing great. The morning sickness has finally calmed, so we've got a bit of a break."

Another commiserating chuckle from Nash. "Yeah, well, wait until you have to witness the delivery. That's just stuff you can't unsee. You know what I mean?"

"I'm trying not to think about it."

"Wise man!"

The two men laughed and then bumped shoulders. I just stood there, never feeling more out of place. On the other hand, I couldn't have felt more grateful. I'd never imagined there'd be a guys' club I didn't want to belong to until Bas's life began being taken over by baby-daddy dribble.

"All right, all right." Jerry flopped unceremoniously into a creaky old desk chair and then motioned for us to take seats as well. "Enough small talk. Let's get down to why you came by. I know you two suits have a lot more important things to do with your day. How can I help you, gentlemen?"

Sebastian leaned forward and planted his elbows on his knees. "I'm just going to shoot straight with you, Jerry. I have a feeling you're the kind of guy who appreciates that sort of thing. Am I right?"

"Well, you got me pegged, Mr. Shark. Guess I'm pretty easy to read." Jerry's stomach visibly vibrated as he chuckled.

I looked on, almost wanting to shake my head and congratulate Bas for recruiting another member to his fan club. My friend's chameleon-like approach never failed with the working-class man—or woman, for that matter. It was kind of awe-inspiring.

"Nah, it's not that," Bas told the guy. "People forget where

I came from. Where we came from." He gave me a fraternal shoulder knock with his own. "Thing is, Grant and I have been busting our asses since we were teenagers to build this business into what it is today. We both know what it means to put in an honest day's work."

Jerry nodded thoughtfully. "But you didn't come all the way over here just to tell me that."

Sebastian didn't bump me anymore, but the glance he tossed at me was just as impactful. "No," he finally said. "We didn't."

"So again, how can I help you?"

Sebastian looked at me again, wordlessly bouncing the metaphorical red playground ball into my square. I didn't need further cue to take over point on the conversation.

"There's been a rumor that some of the construction management team is talking about walking off the job. Bas and I figured we better come down and see if you knew anything about it. If that's true, then the follow-up is obvious. What can we do to prevent that from happening?"

"Well." The man was back to punctuating with a lot of heavy breath, only now the humphs matched how he shifted uncomfortably in his seat. "I'd be lying if I said I hadn't heard anything. Just some grumbling, mostly, from some of the guys . . . about pulling chocks. But it's hard to take it seriously, you know? A lot of these guys are as bad as hens clucking in a hen house."

"What's the problem?" I surged to my feet. "Why do they want to walk? And why this late in the game?"

"It's ridiculous." Jerry shook his head, now seeming embarrassed to have to be the voice behind the complaint.

"Not if there are real concerns," Sebastian retorted,

pinning his stare to the man. "Come on. Level with me, Nash. I try to be fair to all my people. There's always a solution, as far as I'm concerned."

But still, Jerry waffled. He laughed then and stroked his meaty hand from his beard to the back of his neck. The man had a hard time maintaining eye contact while saying, "They're ... uh ... well, they're saying the job site is cursed."

"Cursed?" I repeated in question. Surely I couldn't have heard him correctly.

"Stupid, right?" Jerry fought to form a full laugh. "But there was the body ... your assistant, picking here of all places to off herself. That came right after all the gossip about Viktor Blake coming after you for God knows what. Some were saying the guy has ties to Russian mobsters." The big man paused, giving an uneasy sense the next sentence was going to be a doozy. "Then some of the guys were saying your woman had gone missing for a month ... "

"She wasn't missing," Sebastian said through clenched teeth. "She was with her family on the East Coast. Not that it's anyone's business."

"I mean no disrespect, Mr. Shark." Jerry held his hands up in front of his round torso. "I told you, they're like a bunch of hens. I just want to get this job done—on time and under budget. That's how I land my next gig."

"Yeah. Okay, okay." But Bas glared at me as he muttered it, with fury rolling off him in waves.

Damn it.

When I finally thought I'd gotten him over his obsession with Viktor Blake, this bullshit was stirring it up all over again.

"So how serious is the problem?" I leveled. "Are we going to lose men, or is this just 'clucking' too?"

"Because I have no problem handing out pink slips," added Sebastian.

"*Bas*. Christ."

"What? I'd rather stay ahead of a rising tide."

I refrained—barely—from clocking him in return. That would only make shit worse at this point. The guy had turned a hundred and eighty degrees in attitude from where he started. Bringing Abbigail into the conversation was a game changer.

Fortunately, Nash seemed to sense that as well and just moved on. "Of the two foremen in question, one is seriously looking for other work, and the other is just playing follow-the-leader. He's too comfortable here. Unless something falls into his lap, he won't leave."

"Fine," Bas snapped. "What about you, Jerry? Are you going to up and leave?" Bas leaned forward again, hands clasped between his spread knees. "Just level with me, man. I need you to ante up and give it to me straight. Right here. Right now."

"No, Mr. Shark. You have my word." Jerry held his hand up in oath. "I'm going to be the man handing you the keys to the front door of this finished building. Right on time, like I promised I would when you gave me this job in the first place."

Bas pulled in a long breath through his nose. Fortunately, the nod with which he finished spoke his belief in the man's solemn vow. He stood up to shake Jerry's hand, and I followed his lead. I gave him my business card and asked him to keep me posted on any developments with the potential deserter, though I sensed Bas would have the man separated from the company by the end of the workday. It was probably for the best.

At least that was what I told myself.

When we were back out on the street in front of the job site, I turned to my friend and tried to get a read on his mood. He was tense and closed off, but I wouldn't be deterred.

"Talk to me, chief."

"Can you believe this shit?" He kicked a small stone, sending it flying into a nearby planter.

"It's pretty ridiculous," I agreed.

He booted another stone.

"Okay." I slanted a sideways grin. "I know your brain's unfolding at least three plots already. I'm hoping at least one of them has legal activities we can implement."

"That's the only one escaping me at the moment." Bas halfheartedly grinned back. "Impulsively, I want to fire them all and tell them to go fuck themselves."

"Buuuuttt . . . " I drew out the word, hoping he would fill in the following quiet with a more reasonable plan. Unfortunately, nothing but chirping birds and traffic noise took up the airtime.

"But what?" Sebastian looked up from his cell phone. "Joel's on his way. Are you heading back to the office?"

"No, I have another meeting close by. I'll walk. Thank you, though." I pulled out my phone to make sure the plans with Rio hadn't changed. I prayed, with more fervency than I should, that they hadn't.

"Who's your meeting with?"

Shit. Why didn't I have a fabricated answer ready? Oh yeah, because I wasn't used to having to lie to my best friend about my comings and goings. When I didn't answer right away, Bas grew noticeably interested.

"Twombley?"

I'd still been feigning attention on my phone and hoping he'd give up the effort, but I couldn't ignore his direct prompt.

Looking up from my device, I tried to seem casual. "Hmmm?"

"Your meeting?"

"What about it?"

"Who's it with?"

"My realtor. And before you say anything"—I held up my hand, just like I had a hundred times before when having this conversation—"I'm just looking. I have to keep her in the game, or she will get too busy with other clients to service my needs when I need her to show me something."

"Hey. You do you, man. I've got too much shit going on to babysit you too right now," Sebastian said, wholly frustrated and condescending. And frankly, pissing me off more than it probably should.

"Guess what, man? I don't need a babysitter. Never actually have. You've always made it your mission to be in everyone's business. And I love you for that. I do. But right now—"

"Whoa. Hold up," Bas interrupted. "Why did you just ruin a perfectly normal conversation with an 'I love ya, man'? And we're not even drunk?" He squeezed his eyes closed and raised his face toward the sky. "Jesus Christ." He dropped his head and pinched the bridge of his nose. "This day is just getting better and better. I need to go home and fuck my fiancée. That fixes all the wrongs in the world."

"Okaaaay." I managed a chuckle. "I'll take your word for it, man."

Thankfully, Joel pulled up at that moment, resetting Bas's brain into CEO mode. The man was off without another question about my meeting.

I quickly texted Rio that I was on my way. After a ten-minute walk, I was hiking up the sprawling steps at Bunker Hill.

When I finally reached the summit, there was a raven-haired pixie with the constant devilish gleam in her brandy eyes to greet me. As I gasped for air, she threw her head back, taking obvious delight in my distress.

"What's"—gasp—"so"—gasp—"funny?" I folded in half, gripping my knees while sucking in air through my nose. "Motherfucker, that's a lot of stairs."

She popped up on her feet while I straightened my stance. The top of her head only reached the knot of my tie since she was in one of the nineteen pairs of Chuck Taylors she owned. And yes, I'd counted and mentally cataloged them all.

"You, Mr. Tough Guy, getting so winded from a few steps." She cranked her head back to look up at me, so I went back down three of the shallow concrete steps to put us back to mutual eye level.

"This was your plan all along, you little brat," I accused, narrowing my eyes.

Wiping a tear from the corner of her eye, she asked, "What?"

"You're trying to kill me."

"Nah." Her elfin features sobered. "I like you too much to kill you."

She issued the last of it in a voice so soft, I could've been mistaken about what I'd heard.

"Maybe just hurt me a little, then?" I decided to fight fire with fire. As I added to the quiet taunt, I leaned slightly toward her, letting my register drop even lower. "Like a cat toying with a mouse?"

"Yeah. Maybe something like that."

Rio grinned and looked at where her slender fingers wrapped around the railing. Black nail polish tipped her delicate hands, bringing a dirty image to the forefront of my mind. I imagined that metal pole being my shaft instead . . .

And there was no going back.

My slacks became agonizingly tight in the crotch.

No. Bad Grant. Married woman.

At once, my logic—and my stomach—supplied the perfect subject. "Are you hungry, Blaze?" I inquired. "Have you eaten anything today?" The woman had a terrible habit of neglecting herself in favor of caring for others, and I called her on it routinely when we worked together.

"Yes, Daddy. Thank you." She wrinkled her nose at me in defiance. "But I am hungry, now that you mention it. I think there might be an empanada cart across the patio. Somewhere that way."

She pointed with one of those black nails, and my dick kicked up again. And now, the recognition was getting outright odd. Since when was Wednesday Addams nail polish a thing I actually liked? Easy answer: *never.* Goth girls just weren't my thing. Too much angst. Too much emotion, period. But Rio Gibson wasn't the quintessential goth girl. She had her own unique style in just about everything she did.

Her short ebony hair, for example. It was downright fascinating. I found myself staring at it when we talked. It caught and absorbed sunlight like a spectrum. Then, depending on the way she turned her head, it shone the rays back in different colors altogether. Sometimes scarlet or cobalt, other times the deepest chestnut or hint of violet.

"Is your hair naturally black?" I randomly blurted the curiosity as we walked across the deck. Jesus, I probably sounded like a smitten schoolboy, though at the moment, I didn't really care. Right now, I didn't want to think about what anyone else thought—except for the captivating human at my side, who tilted her head before answering. Likely, she was trying to figure out the same thing I was. What the hell had gotten into me?

"Yep," she answered simply and then completely changed the subject. "I'm buying. What would you like?"

"You'll do no such thing." I didn't lift my gaze from the small menu.

"Why? I can afford to buy you lunch, Grant."

"I'm sure you can. But I'm old-fashioned and a gentleman. And because I said so. Tell the woman what you want, please. Beef and a bottle of water for me, please, and whatever the lady would like." I motioned Rio to order with a sweep of my hand.

She huffed and rolled her eyes. And sure enough, my cock twitched yet again. Dear God, how I longed to teach this girl some manners—and to do it my way. A different definition of "the old-fashioned way." Over my knees. A paddle. My hand. A hairbrush, maybe? On her delicate bare ass ...

"Hmmm." I shifted my stance, applying damn near the same kind of discipline to my willful erection.

For fuck's sake. Settle down.

"Hmmm, what?"

"What?" I startled from my fantasy. Good thing too, since the cart was getting a line and the sweet old lady behind was pushing me off with a pointed glare. I paid her and then guided Rio to the side, where we could wait for our food.

"You said, 'hmmm,'" she pointed out, her eyes going big and curious. "So what were you hmming about?"

I blinked. Then again. Well, shit. She was clearly expecting an answer—to a comment I hadn't meant to voice aloud.

"These smell so good, don't they?"

My lying skills were really getting to stretch their wings today. Fortunately for me, Rio bought into the illusion this time.

"They do," she answered excitedly. "I think this was a good call. And thank you, Mr. Old-Fashioned Twombley, for treating me to lunch. Next time, it's on me. No arguing!"

"We'll see."

"Yes, we will."

"Hmmm."

She bit her lower lip and flashed me a cheeky grin.

I clenched my jaw and attempted a rebuking glower. But the woman was my glower killer. I simply couldn't be in a bad mood around her. Especially not now, as our order came up and the little lady handed our food over the stainless-steel surface.

We found an empty precast concrete table out of the way, in the shade of a large Angel's Trumpet. Though scientists had likely named the plant eons ago, it was a perfect fit for a planter in the center of the City of Angels. The hearty beauty clearly agreed, since even on this hazy afternoon it was showing off its drooping yellow horn-shaped flowers, some as large as my fist.

"This is a perfect little lunch spot," Rio declared after sitting down. "A secret little hideaway. I love how LA has all these gems tucked away for the people who dare to look beneath the surface."

"Me too."

But I was only half-invested in the response. I was *wholly* mesmerized by the sight of the woman as she unfolded the paper napkin and placed it on her lap, treating the paper square as if it were the most beautiful linen. The action was so unique in this background of casual business lunchers, college kids on laptops, and people walking their dogs.

In short, it was a typical weekday afternoon in La La Land. And I didn't want to be anywhere else except here, next to the girl taking dainty bites from her meal like the Queen of freaking England. She was constantly a revelation to me. A divine surprise.

"Have you lived in LA for a long time?"

"My whole life," I said freely.

"Wow." She popped up her eyebrows again. "A real California boy? Should've known those sun streaks in your hair were natural."

My cheeks ached from a fresh grin. She'd noticed my streaks?

"Damn straight they are," I supplied. "In all those years, I've seen the city go through so many changes. Some good, some not so good. But I love it here. I can't imagine living anywhere else." I cut into my lunch with the plastic knife, watching the flimsy cutlery yield to the crust.

"Do you travel a lot?" Rio asked, going with the finger food approach.

"For work, yeah." I gave up and picked up the doughy pocket too. "But not that much for pleasure."

"Why not?" she asked around a bite.

"It's not that much fun when you're alone, I guess?" How sad did that sound?

"Why are you alone?" She watched me thoughtfully.

I refrained—barely—from choking on my next bite. "Damn. You dig right in, don't you?"

"I guess I do. Sorry?"

I laughed. "When you say it like a question, it doesn't sound very contrite."

"Well, I'm not trying to be rude." She took a sip from her soda. "It's just my way, I guess." And then she shrugged her petite shoulders. "I've always been this way. I don't see the point of tap-dancing around a subject, you know? When people hem and haw, scrambling to be nice when being *direct* would do the job better, it drives me crazy. I want to yell, 'Oh my God! Say what you mean!'"

I let out another laugh, assuming she'd finish by doing the same. But when she simply took another bite and seemed to drift off in thought, I indulged the chance to take in her stunning profile. The woman's features never ceased to fascinate me. Those dark lashes framing such expressive eyes. Her chiseled cheekbones balanced by that full bow of a mouth. Her adorable short haircut surrounding such blatant feminine beauty...

Finally, I ripped myself free of her allure long enough to reply, "I can appreciate that." After thinking about it more, I nodded. "Yeah, I think my days would be a lot easier if people just said what they meant."

"See? I'm smarter than people think I am."

Now she did laugh, though she averted her gaze from my probing one.

"Do you think people don't find you intelligent?"

"Grant. Be serious."

I intentionally said nothing. Not a damn thing. I wanted Rio to give up and look at me, but she busied herself with her lunch like it was her job. And she was going to be the best damn empanada eater there ever was, by golly.

"Blaze," I finally uttered.

"What?" She verbally stomped on the final consonant.

"Look at me."

I purposely used *that* voice this time. Concluded it with a quiet, dangerous pause that left no room for confusion—or discussion. The combination accomplished its purpose. She snapped her head back up. Within seconds, she'd also locked her curious stare to mine.

"You are smarter than most of the overeducated jackasses I deal with on any given day. That's a fact, plain and simple. You're clever, creative, and witty. And Jesus, you're smart. No . . . you're wise. Like an old owl."

And here came her little slap back—in the form of a biting giggle. "An old owl, huh? Now don't you know how to flatter a girl?"

I quirked up one side of my lips. "Ah, she mocks. But did you know owls have superpowered hearing and were the Greeks' symbol of victory in battle?"

She ticked a finger in the air. "And swallow their prey whole."

"Well, there is that . . . " I only paused to insert half a laugh before pushing on. "The point is, whoever made you feel less than any of those things doesn't deserve the power you're giving him."

She dropped the last bite of her food into the plastic basket, swallowing so hard I could see her throat work to move the food down.

"Grant. Stop." She quickly shot to her feet. "And stop calling me Blaze," she mumbled while she shuffled her lunch trash together onto the red plastic tray and reached for mine, but I shot my hand out and grabbed her wrist to stop her.

"Sit down."

And fuck if she didn't drop right back down to the concrete bench next to me—almost making me wish I'd resisted my instigating move. Almost. I couldn't bring myself to full remorse when so much of my body was cheering me on for it. But damn, I'd pay the price for it later. Fuck it, my clamoring muscles and roaring bloodstream were paying the price now. If only the woman knew how her reaction called to a side of me she knew nothing about...

Yet.

No. Bad Grant. Married woman.

Maybe if I kept repeating it to myself, it would sink in. This little firestarter was off-limits. A complete no-fly zone. No matter how hot she made me burn inside, no matter how my temperature rose from just being beside her—like sitting too close to a campfire right after someone stoked the logs.

So, despite how Rio Gibson's body called to the dominant nature of mine, I had to behave. But there was just no way I could miss how her chest was rapidly rising and falling and her jaw kept ticking with involuntary pulses.

"I'm not finished yet."

I said it—dictated it—with quiet purpose. I took a long drink from my water bottle. And I never let go of her wrist. I couldn't will my own body to do the right thing and release her. Not yet.

"There's nothing left on your plate."

"Did you have enough? Are you still hungry?" I asked instead of addressing her comment.

She moved to pull her hand from my grip, and I let her. "Yes, thank you. I...I have to go, Grant." She pushed down another heavy gulp, destroying any believability in her determined tone. Still, she added, "Traffic's probably already picked up. If I don't get on my way..."

You can stay with me.

Screw the fact that I didn't yet have a place close by. I had a dozen downtown hotels already on speed dial in my phone. With any other woman also stored in that phone, those words and my panty-dissolving grin would have ensured my night was already cinched.

But Rio Gibson wasn't any other woman.

Nothing about her ever would be.

"Where did you park?" I forced myself to ask instead. "Do you have to go back to Inglewood now?"

"No. I'm just going to take the van home tonight and leave my car in the garage at the kitchen. I moved Kendall in there before I left, so she should be fine."

"Kendall?" I asked, frowning while following her in what I assumed was the direction of the parked catering van. "Who's Kendall?"

"My Fiat. Suits her, don't you think?" Her uncertain grin was entirely out of place. I'd never seen a spec of hesitancy on this woman's face since I'd known her.

"If you say so." I shrugged. I'd never really understood the attachment people grew to vehicles. I didn't even own one or care to, for that matter. I got back at least an hour of time every day by not driving myself. But hey, who was I to judge the folks who did? I was the guy who got day-long highs—sometimes longer—from purchasing real estate.

"Are you headed back to the office?" she asked. "I can drop you off on my way."

"I think I'm going to take the rest of the afternoon off."

As I said it, I seriously wondered what body snatchers had landed and taken over when I wasn't paying attention. I never casually took the afternoon off. But today, the call seemed right. Well, more so than the next thing that popped out of my mouth.

"Do you mind if I ride with you to Seal Beach?"

For a long second, her only response was a brow raised in curiosity.

"I have a house there," I explained. "I think I'll stay near the water tonight."

"Seriously?" she charged, screwing up her face. "Why would you own property in Seal Beach? I thought you lived somewhere near here."

"That might be true soon, but not currently. But back to the point. Why do you find it so hard to believe? You like Seal Beach enough to own a home there."

"Yes, but I'm married and hoping to start a family. It's much more of a family-oriented community. Not a bachelor's paradise."

"My place is on the Naples side of town, closer to Long Beach. The neighborhood happens to be very lively on the weekends. There are a lot of great shops and restaurants within walking distance."

"But we're still a few days away from the weekend."

I lifted a new smirk. "Oh, I'm sure I'll find something to entertain me."

She stopped after chirping the key fob to unlock the van. "Why am I thinking it's wise not to ask for details about that?"

I stepped over to open the driver's door for her. "Because you're smart, remember?"

As Rio moved in next to me, she showed no mercy with the uptilt of her incisive gaze. "Oh, I remember...like an old owl."

★ ★ ★

After another hour and a half in shitty freeway traffic, Rio dropped me off in front of my waterfront home. She let out a low whistle and a comment or two about not being worthy of my company before I closed the door and headed up the front steps. I really did like this place, and something about being near the water—and fine, within ten miles of her—made my nerves settle after the frustrating meeting earlier in the day.

A cleaning crew made the rounds to all my properties, ensuring no matter where I decided to lay my head each night, the place would be turnkey. I also made sure a list of staples were kept on hand in the pantry so I could at least have coffee in the morning before I left for work.

Loosening my tie, I opened the glass doors that led onto the deck and let the salt air fill the entire home. Yeah, this was the right call tonight. Maybe I'd work off a little steam with a friend—the way my cock had been fantasizing about for the last two hours.

I pulled up my favorites list on my phone and scrolled through the names, trying to decide who the lucky lady would be. There was a lot of pent-up energy bubbling through my system, and someone would be in for a long, rough, but thoroughly satisfying night.

CHAPTER TWO

GRANT

Three hours of sleep just wasn't enough. Not by far. I didn't bother to share that enlightenment with Sebastian, who was the only one on earth with enough balls to call me at four in the morning. And then, when I didn't pick up, to do it again. And again.

But as I slid my arm out from under the warm, sleeping woman beside me and flipped over to see what had my device skipping across my nightstand, I couldn't help but swear at the bastard beneath my breath. My eyes took a moment or two to focus on the screen, separating the text from the background, forming individual shapes that made sense as letters then words. Goddamn Sebastian and his nonstop mind—and his assumption that since he'd been struck by lightning at this hour, everyone else was part of the storm too.

The night foreman quit. Turned in
his two weeks at the end of shift.

I set down the phone on the mattress long enough to hunt for some clothes. I was drawing a blank on remembering where Cybil and I had stripped last night. We'd gotten busy as soon as she'd arrived and had eventually ended up in the bed, but between then and now, I'd banged her downstairs, in the stairway, and against a doorjamb in the hallway. Finding pants anywhere near the bed wasn't likely.

Instead, I grabbed my phone and went into the bathroom. After shutting the door, I finished my return text to Bas.

> *It's a little early for this, man. I'll see you at the office, and we'll come up with a plan. Be there by seven.*

Kick her out and make it six thirty.

I didn't bother with a reply to his comeback as I turned the shower on full blast and grabbed a towel from the stack in the linen closet.

Luxuriating in one of my massive showers was a daily indulgence that no one got to interrupt. I didn't pass it over this morning, either. Something about hot water beating down on my skin did things for my body and soul that nothing else could. There were five hundred points of interest there for my therapist to expound upon—half of which I'd already examined myself at one point or another.

Growing up was a shitty experience for me. Much like my best friend, I'd lived in poverty and, on most days, couldn't count on a meal in my belly or a roof over my head. Bathing was usually at the kitchen tap or, if my mother hadn't paid the water bill, a public faucet somewhere with the fear of getting caught and chased off. Going to school in dirty clothes or not having bathed for a few days, especially once puberty set in, I was always at risk of being "that kid" who smelled bad. Kids can be real assholes to one another, trust me.

Never again.

I remembered the day I bought my first bottle of salon shampoo like most people remember their first kiss. A defining moment, as those things were called. After that, it was the coordinating conditioner, styling products, and body wash. Now, that regime was expanded to the point that the daily shower lasted thirty minutes while I stood under six showerheads of pelting hot water, and a specialized heat lamp made sure I never got as much as one goose bump of discomfort. I let the water rush over my body until I felt like my skin would peel off my bones, grateful for every . . . single . . . drop.

The walk-in closet had a few suits hanging within it, none of which appealed to me today, but I didn't have much of a choice since I'd come here on a whim. Maybe I'd just grab a different tie from the stash I kept at the office. Problem solved.

Well, the first problem.

Now I had to deal with the woman still sleeping in my bed. I always dreaded the morning-after part of this bullshit. While most of the women I casually slept with, Cybil included, knew I wasn't interested in anything more, there was always that odd occasion when one of them forgot the rules. It didn't matter that the damn things weren't written rules. I was still clear about them. With everyone.

One thing was for certain though . . . Standing here in a snit about the issue wasn't accomplishing anything. With a deep inhale, I touched Cybil's exposed shoulder. "Hey. Time to get up."

"Mmmm." She rolled toward the middle of the bed instead.

I walked over to the windows and started flipping open all

the shutters, letting in the watery light of early dawn. "Rise and shine."

"Rise and what?" she moaned into the pillow.

"Time to go," I replied. "I have to get to work."

"Now?"

"Now. Come on, you need to go."

"Ugghh, Grant," she whined. "Can't I just let myself out? We just went to bed a couple of hours ago. Baby, you wore me out." She stretched lazily. "Daaamn..."

"You know how it goes with me. If you don't like it, don't answer when I call you." My tone was flat and firmly in asshole territory. "I've got to be out of here in ten minutes. I can call you a car..."

"Ah, such a gentleman." Cybil sat up, not bothering to cover her naked body. My bite marks covered half her chest. "But don't worry. I've got mine here."

"Great. I'll see you downstairs. Do you want a cup of coffee?" I offered. "I'll make you one to go."

"That would be great. Cream and two sugars, please."

In the kitchen, I called for a car to take me into downtown LA and got started on the coffee.

I'd just finished making us each a cup when she appeared in the kitchen, fully dressed, high heels dangling from her fingers.

"Here you go. It's hot. Be careful."

"Thank you. And thank you for last night. You can call me anytime, Grant. Even if you're a total jerk when waking a girl up." She smiled while taking a sip from the cardboard cup.

The car service app signaled that my ride was nearing the house. "Let's go. My ride's here."

I set the alarm, and we went out the front door. "Take care

of yourself." I gave Cybil a quick side hug, despite sensing she craved more. As I stepped toward the car, I hoped karma didn't strike me on the spot for my behavior this morning. Because even I knew I was acting like an asshole.

By the time I walked into Sebastian's office, it was just after seven o'clock. His assistant wasn't at his desk, and the interior door to his office stood wide open, so I didn't bother knocking.

"Good morning, sunshine."

"You're late," my best friend grumbled from behind his bank of computer monitors.

"By whose standards? Most people don't start work at six, my friend. That's only you." I made my way to his coffee bar. "You want a cup?"

"I told you to be here by six thirty. And no thank you. I'm on my third cup already, and my heart feels like it's going to explode."

"I was dead asleep when you texted me, man. I got here as quickly as I could. And I was in Naples, not downtown, so chill out." When my coffee finished brewing, I went and sat in my usual spot on his black leather sofa. Eventually he would come over to join me. He always did.

My best friend had a lot going on in his life at the moment. "A lot" barely scratched the surface in his case. He had a baby on the way. A fiancée who hadn't had an easy time with the pregnancy. Issues with various nations' governments *and* maritime pirates along Shark Enterprise's international shipping lanes. And now the issues with the crews at the construction site for the Edge, the building that had been his dream for at least a decade.

On top of that, the man was the definition of a control

freak. He always had been, even when we were kids. I'd never faulted him for the behavior. We'd both dealt with our physical and emotional scars in our own ways, and Sebastian coped by trying to control everyone around him.

"Well, first shit storms first," I said as Bas took the seat across from me. "I think I've already come up with a solution for the foreman issue."

"Yeah?" He folded one leg over the other. "Let's hear it."

"Your brother-in-law to be. Sean Gibson."

"What about him?" Sebastian narrowed his gaze. "I'm pretty sure the man already has a job. As a site foreman, if I'm not mistaken?"

"Yeah, but Rio has said on more than one occasion that he isn't happy there. The project is much smaller than the Edge, but with some proper training, I think he'd fit right in. We could move Mahoney into the vacant night position and start Gibson on the day shift. I'm positive he could adequately fill the position."

Bas rubbed a finger across his upper lip. I couldn't read his thoughtful mien one way or another. He didn't look completely thrilled about the suggestion, but he also hadn't shot the idea down, so I laid out the most obvious reason the man would be our right choice.

"He's your woman's brother, for Christ's sake. And essentially, he's qualified. You'd score major points with Abbigail by giving Sean the job."

At first, Bas still said nothing. After a long moment, he finally commented, "That is the most concerning thing I've heard you say in a long time, my friend."

"What?" I countered while he shook his head in obvious dismay. My face ached already from twisting with such unnatural confusion. "What do you mean?" I couldn't help but be affronted. "This is a great idea. What's your issue here?"

"My issue?" Bas volleyed. "Is how little attention you pay to the people around you. You want to know the only trait more prominent about the mother of my child than her stubbornness? Her pride. The version of the stuff comes from generations of Irish honor and dignity. Generations that include Sean Gibson. I'm not so certain the man would accept a job handout from his little sister's baby daddy for that reason alone."

"Well, according to his wife, he'd be more than qualified for the job. And they definitely need the money. So if you're telling me that some sort of ancient pigheadedness would get in the way of getting ahead financially and giving his wife what she wants most, the man's a bigger idiot than I thought."

"Why would you know that?"

"Know what?"

"All of it," he clarified. "His qualifications. Their financial situation." He shot up one brow. "Her fondest desires."

"Because..." As soon as I stabbed my stare out the window, I knew it was the wrong damn move. Fuck it. Too late now. "We still talk. She tells me stuff." I shrugged. Another crap move.

"What?"

"I've explained this to you before," I defended, louder this time. "She's lonely. We've become friends. I'm her friend, Bas."

"Hmmm."

"Hmmm what? Christ. Am I going to feel this way with you every time her fucking name comes up now?"

"Like what?" He was still so quiet. Too quiet.

"Like I'm on trial."

That was when he chuckled while keeping his eyes trained on me. "I haven't said a single thing, man. Yet there you are"—he gestured his index finger up and down my torso—"squirming like a worm pierced on the end of a fisherman's hook."

A low growl worked up from deep in my throat, but I willed the eruption back down. He and Elijah had hauled out my worst side before, especially when they relentlessly razzed me about Rio. I couldn't keep letting it happen.

"Let's just stay on topic here, shall we? We won't know if the guy is interested in the job if we don't ask him. Let's just make an offer and see if he bites." It was my turn to take a shot at the dick-in-a-vise commentary. "Or do you have to ask Abbi for permission first?"

Sebastian sat back into the chair and grinned. "I already see what you're playing at, Twombley." Then he gave in to an actual laugh, which irked me more than his smirk, and shook his head slowly. "But one day you'll understand, buddy. You'll open yourself to the possibility of love. Then you'll know that it's not a matter of 'asking permission' or even being pussy-whipped. It's about mutual respect and consideration for the person you're sharing your life with. It's about keeping the peace and harmony in the home you're building together."

Just when I thought my lecture was done, he added, "And you're a fucking idiot."

I prepped a scathing comeback, but as soon as I turned and pressed my back against one of the big glass panes, Bas's words sank in as if he'd dipped arrows in acid and then took direct aim at my chest.

Was he right? Was I a serious dipshit here? I compelled myself to think about it. I compared the vapid, carnal sex from last night to the delightful, incredible lunch I'd shared with

Rio just a couple of hours before. The two activities couldn't have been more different, physically and emotionally. And the way I felt after each was on opposite ends of the satisfaction spectrum too.

Well … fuck.

I needed a change in my life. Desperately. Yet I continued to keep the company of a woman I had no future with—nor could even dream of having. But that only made me want it more. I'd thought fucking Cybil into the mattress would exorcise my Rio Gibson demons, but it had only made them worse. At least tenfold.

I was so lost in that brood, I didn't notice Bas standing, circling around the furniture, and joining me next to the window. Together, we watched the citizens of our city bustle about their morning routines. Pedestrians dashed around cars both parked and moving. Metro buses lumbered along, stopping at different intersections. People clad in everything from maintenance uniforms to pristine business suits were rushing along to start their days.

Next to me, Bas was busy texting. After no more than thirty seconds, he declared, "Abbigail thinks I should give Sean a call."

"So did she give you his number?" I asked.

The guy bugged his gaze. "Hold up. You don't have the number to their house?"

Great. I already knew I'd be regretting this admission. "Well, yes, I do, but—"

"Then call it. Christ, what are you waiting for?"

I shrugged with exaggerated purpose. "Shouldn't he be off to work already?"

"You would know better than me, stalker."

"I'm not—" But I didn't finish...because I couldn't. If I were being honest with myself, Bas's accusation wasn't completely off base. Not that he cared about me keeping tabs on Rio because I was worried about her getting to the prep kitchen so early every day. "You know what?" I finally spat. "Fuck this shit. Seriously."

"Twombley." Sebastian threw his hands up. "Settle down, man. I'm just busting your balls. Just call Rio and get his cell number. Or text her. I don't care. Let's just get this ball rolling. I'd love to actually solve a problem before eight a.m. How good would that feel for a change?"

"Your fiancée would just as easily have her brother's cell phone number," I pointed out.

Sebastian started to say something, almost as though he was going to correct me on something, but he stopped short, seeming to think better of it. He got strangely quiet instead. "Just call her, would you?"

"Fine." As I grumbled it, I quickly hit Rio's nickname on my recent calls list. I held the phone to my ear, waiting for her voice to come over the line.

"Hey there, Tree." Her voice filled the line, its husk a bite and caress in one. "It's awfully early. What could you possibly want already?"

"Good morning to you too." I chuckled. "Hey, I won't keep you long. I know you're probably knee-deep in lunch prep."

"And you'd be correct," she joked.

"Could you shoot me Sean's cell number?"

"Sean? My husband?"

"Do you know another Sean?"

"Actually, I do. Several others, as a matter of fact. It's a pretty common name."

"Rio."

"What?"

"Text me his number, please."

"Dare I ask why?"

"A foreman spot is available at the Edge. The day shift. We want to make him an offer."

"Are you fucking serious?"

"One hundred percent serious."

"Oh my God." She finally released a giddy laugh that likely resonated out to the ocean. "Do you know what this could mean for us? What this could totally do for us?"

Now I was just grinning into my device. "I have a general idea, yeah."

I prepared my senses for the sunshine of her next laugh. Instead, I could practically feel her dead quiet. "Wait," she demanded. "What do you want in return? You have to want—" She blew out a rough breath. "Or maybe this is some sort of trick. Are you fucking with me, Grant Twombley? Because this would be one of the cruelest things you could possibly do."

I was the one whooshing out air now—in relief. "No, Blaze," I assured. "It's not a trick. The other guy walked off the job last night. We—Bas and I—both thought Sean would be a good fit, so we want to call him and talk to him. Preferably sooner than later."

"Got it. Okay. Okay. I'll absolutely text you as soon as we hang up."

"Thanks."

"Grant. Thank you so much. Thank you, thank you, thank you. And please, thank Sebastian too. I don't know how I'll ever repay you for this."

Oh, I could think of a lot of ways, Blaze.

I kept that part to myself. Deep, deep inside. My outward disguise was a roll of my eyes. "Rio . . ."

"I mean it."

I dragged in another long breath to relieve the pressure off my crotch as my mind's eye filled with all my fantasies of her "repayment." Visions that were definitely going to ensure my place in hell. They were stamping my permanent parking space this very moment.

Worth it.

A ride I'd willingly take at the end of my days . . . as long as fate promised me that the rest of them would be filled with the surety of Rio Gibson's happiness.

★ ★ ★

"Sean will be here at noon for a meeting," Bas announced after ending his call to the guy. "But at this point, I think the face-to-face is merely a formality. He seems eager to get started."

I nodded, tacking on a smug smirk. "Admit it, Shark. Even when you haul my ass out of bed in the middle of the night, I have the best ideas in the room."

The man honored my statement with half an eye roll before replying, "I'll have HR draw up a standard package, on par with the other foreman. It'll have healthcare, 401K, life insurance, all the usuals. I don't see how he could refuse."

"Agreed."

"Has Rio conveyed his biggest complaint with his current job?"

I hesitated to answer. For a long, *long* beat. For some reason, I felt like I was betraying her confidence, divulging information she'd shared in private conversations. Trying to play it off as though I were just digging through my memory and not struggling with my morality, I offered a pensive expression. "Well, I know the health insurance they have isn't covering the infertility treatment she wants to start."

"Yeah, Abbi's talked about that too. But our plan is top of the line, so that should be an easy sell. Anything else that you know of? Where is he physically working? Is the commute far?"

"I'm not sure. I do know that he pretty much has dinner and goes to bed because he has to get up early to get on the road. So yeah, he must be commuting at least a bit—though Rio's up early too, to get into the Abstract prep kitchen. It's a pretty shitty existence for a couple when you think about it."

It certainly wasn't uncommon for a lot of families in Southern California. Home prices were so high in most neighborhoods that most households had to have two incomes. Often, the areas that had higher-paying jobs didn't offer desirable neighborhoods as well, especially if couples were interested in having a family. Commuting became a necessary evil in the daily lives of most residents.

No wonder I was still single.

Elijah Banks strode into Sebastian's office. As usual, the man looked like he'd stepped out of a fashion magazine spread. Our lifelong friend was model good-looking, with his naturally tan skin and light hazel eyes that told a hundred stories before he spoke a single word.

"My man," I greeted, giving him a brotherly side-hug-handshake type of greeting we had perfected over the years.

Sebastian just curtly nodded from where he was perched on the edge of his desk, never one to be openly touched by another. It wasn't a matter of coldness or aloofness; Elijah and I both knew that. Being thrown around by an alcoholic father just did certain things to a person.

Thank God Abbigail had come into Sebastian's life. Before her, the man wouldn't even engage in physical relations with a woman unless he was paying her, and the circumstances were defined by a particular kind of control. Not that I faulted the guy—my own tastes ran the same way for a lot of the same fucked-up reasons—but in Bas's case, the dynamic was starting to shut him down instead of charge him up. It hadn't been pretty.

"Okay, let's focus here. Will you both be here for the meeting with Jacob Cole at ten?"

Elijah nodded. "Absolutely. Categorized as my first priority today, along with the interview you just invited me to." He looked up from his phone with a start. "With . . . Sean Gibson? Like, the guy who's married to Rio Gibson?" He swung his stare over to me. "Like, your Rio?"

"Jesus Christ," I muttered as Sebastian spurted out a laugh. "Not helping, man."

Bas kept it up, though, relentless with his mirth. "Yep. The same one," he said to Banks.

Elijah batted his stare between Sebastian and me. "Why do I feel like I've missed a page of backstory here?"

"Because you have," I retorted.

"Have a seat," Bas instructed him. "Believe me, you'll want to be on your ass when I fill you in."

"And while you're at it, I'm stepping out to get caught up in my own office." I scrolled through my calendar app, quickly checking on my upcoming schedule. Normally I'd have my entire day committed to memory by now. But spending the night buried in Cybil's pussy had thrown my attention way off—a predicament that piled vexation onto my irritation.

"I'll be back at ten for the meeting with Cole," I said, concentrating on modulating my shit to something more professional.

"Should be an interesting meeting," said Elijah. "I'm anxious to see the design changes Bas asked for, along with his breakdown of the city planning commission meeting from two weeks ago. If they had issues with the latest revisions, Cole should have those to present to us today."

"Right. I'm hoping like hell the parking structure plans were finally signed off on," Bas added. "That's been the biggest thorn in our sides so far."

"Right?" Elijah grunted. "I would've never guessed that was going to be the holdup on this project."

"Sounds good." I jogged confident nods at them both as I turned for the door. "I'll be in my office until then."

My own office was on the same floor as Sebastian's but on the opposite end of the building. As I approached my door, my assistant smiled up at me. Reina had been with me for seven years now, and she was top-notch at almost every single task I threw at her.

"Good morning, Mr. Twombley."

"Good morning, Reina. How are you this morning?"

"No complaints so far. Hot yoga, ancient grains, and kale smoothie are on board, so I'm ready to go. How's your morning so far?"

Yes, my assistant was a California girl, through and through. She had crystals hanging from every available place around her desk, smelled of patchouli at all times, and had just recently cut off the dreadlocks she'd cultivated for five years.

Thank God.

"Not too bad. I have a meeting back in the big man's office at ten, then another at noon, so I'm going to try to tackle that stack on my desk until then."

"All right. Let me know if I can help you with anything. Don't forget you have a two o'clock with the sea-container vendor, and the journalist from *LA Bachelor* will be here to interview you at three."

"I wish I had never agreed to that," I said, leaning against my door. "What good could possibly come of it?"

"If I remember correctly," my assistant answered warmly, "the feature is going to focus on local philanthropists, and they were particularly interested in the volunteer work you do with Second Chances. It will be a great way to get exposure for the organization and bring more awareness to the needs right here in our city. I know you didn't ask for my opinion, but I think you should do it." She held my gaze while she finished making her point.

"You're right. As usual. Thank you for reminding me not to be so selfish."

"Mr. Twombley." She shook her head. "You are one of the least selfish people around here."

Inside my office, I hung my suit jacket on a hanger on the back of the door. After sitting down at my desk, I stared at the pile of papers in front of me. The damn stack looked like it had doubled in size since yesterday, and I had zero motivation to get to it.

Lately, my motivation had been waning for a lot of things.

Even a buzz on my cell—which had me looking at a happy text from Char, confirming my offer on the condo had been accepted—had me reacting with a hollow sigh and a matching cavern in my chest. Closing the deal on that property should've had me close to hard, but right now?

Nothing.

I paced restlessly to the window. Although I didn't have the view Bas had from his office, I still had a decent vista to behold. But even that didn't bring me the peace I needed at the moment. Nothing seemed to.

It was unsettling.

Something in my life was shifting. Something in me. The shitty thing was, it was happening faster than I could cope with. It wasn't rational. Or, at this point, even identifiable.

When did this change take place? What caused the shift? Something that was a lifelong thrill didn't stop overnight. The last time I bought a property, I'd been higher than a kite. I went to Lulu's and fucked one of her regular girls until she cried from all the orgasms. But right now, even envisioning that did nothing for my dick—or the widening chasm in the center of my chest.

My interoffice phone line rang. I strode over to my desk in a few long steps, grabbing the receiver off the cradle. "Yes, Reina?"

"Ten-minute warning," she said briefly, indicating it was already time to return to Bas's office.

"Thank you. I'm on my way." Grabbing my suit coat, I shut off my office lights—no sense wasting energy and all that happy green horseshit—and headed over to Bas's office for our meeting with the architect for the Edge, Jacob Cole.

CHAPTER THREE

RIO

"Kitty? Here kitty, kitty, kitty." I bent down to peek under the rosebushes that lined my front patio. The little scamp usually hid under the shrubbery while the neighborhood kids played outside. At the moment, however, it was getting late, and the street was relatively quiet, so there was no reason for him to hide.

I made friends with the black-and-white stray two weeks ago when his crying caught my attention. On that first night, he was brave enough to trot right inside my front door when I opened up to see what was causing all the commotion. The tiny feline strutted across my welcome mat with his little tail flying high like the flag of his very own nation.

He owned me from that first moment, weaving in between my ankles, motor purring louder than should be possible from such a small body. Once I began putting food out for the little man, we were official. He was mine, and I was his.

"Robert?" I called before setting the little porcelain dish down on the patio. I went with the French pronunciation of the common name because my small friend had an air of sophistication about him that deserved a little flair. Sean still hadn't met him, but he would love him when he finally did. At least I hoped he would. Already, I couldn't bear the thought of having to say goodbye to the young fellow.

For the past two weeks, Sean had been working even longer hours than he had at his previous job. Now that he was hired on with the team at Sebastian Shark's project, the Edge, he was trying to make a good first impression. Apparently that meant a real investment of hours. *A lot* of damn hours. When I complained that I never saw him, he reminded me about the incredible salary increase he was given and the premium health insurance we now had.

Put in those terms, the long hours didn't seem so terrible. Plus, my husband assured me he was just staying after hours for the first month or so, trying to get acclimated to the new job site itself and get up to speed on the project.

Sean confided in me just after being hired that the Edge was more massive and high profile than he'd ever expected. For those reasons and a thousand more, the attention to detail was more serious than any other job he'd ever been assigned to. When he came home after his first day and told me he'd taken the position, he was so excited about what the opportunity meant for our future, and we dared to have hope again. We went to bed that night and had wild, passionate sex with all the faith in our hearts that we were putting the icing on our good-fortune cake and adding a baby to our precious family.

But now, I'd be lying if I said I wasn't lonely. Very lonely, as a matter of fact. Abbigail, my sister-in-law and business partner, had cut back her work hours at our catering kitchen by at least half. She was just beginning the twenty-fifth week of her pregnancy, and since she'd already had one scare from overworking, Sebastian insisted she scale back the time she spent on her feet. That was all a sensible—and necessary—plan, but my personal adjustment was tough. Not only did

I miss the help around the kitchen, but I also longed for the daily girl time with Abbi.

Basically I was left with no other choice but to hire some outside help until Abbi returned from maternity leave.

Enter Hannah Farsey, a graduate of Le Cordon Bleu but utterly uninterested in landing a standard job with a five-star restaurant. So far, the visionary young woman was working out like a dream. She arrived first thing in the morning and left after I took off for the noontime deliveries. The timing on hiring her couldn't have been more perfect. Since the big Greystone party, word about Abstract Catering had spread through the city's social elite faster than a brush fire during a Santa Ana wind. As a result, the day-to-day operations at Abstract Catering had changed more than Abbigail or I could have ever predicted.

In addition to the regular lunch deliveries Monday through Friday, our private VIP clients had increased by almost thirty percent—at exactly the same time Abbi dramatically cut her kitchen hours. The only problem was that all the newly scheduled events were taking place before baby Shark was due. That meant I had to assemble my fresh team and hope like hell we functioned as well as the old one. Hannah's arrival had been a huge help in that regard.

Scheduled events.

At that thought, tingles of excitement pricked me. The sensation was both thrilling and unwelcomed. It was a heady yet shameful combination of emotions from the way our business was finally taking off and ... well ... something else entirely.

There was a secret I had been hiding from everyone. A dark part of my psyche that I didn't like to examine for too long.

Something that was wrong with me. And by wrong, I meant disturbingly so. Not like having one toe that was longer than the others or eating pineapple on pizza. This was something worse. A terrible secret I'd kept hidden from everyone in my life, including my husband.

Especially my husband.

Until Grant Twombley barged into my world.

He'd stumbled into the middle of my personal problem on an exceptionally stressful day at the kitchen in Inglewood while we were prepping for the lunch deliveries. I had drifted off—the way I tend to do when I get lost in the darkness—and I had completely forgotten he was still in the building.

I thought I played it off well enough because he didn't say anything to me about it. Not at first. But later that night, he texted me and told me we were definitely going to talk about what he saw. Again, I tried to act like I didn't know what he meant, but that man—damn that man—had a way of making me do and say things I never imagined I would.

Something about how he'd approached me . . . the steady, imposing voice he used, the way he held himself with such confidence as he stood near me . . . I don't know what happened after that, exactly. Because my body seemed to just react to his. My senses were pulled toward him . . . commanded by him. I didn't understand it myself, but I ended up telling him things I'd never told anyone before—like the very first time I felt the rush in my veins from lighting a match. The sulfur-rich smell in the air when the little orange head swayed in the breezed and then snuffed itself out.

Or the way the end of my nose tingled, even then, just thinking about that smell. And still, he didn't judge me, wasn't angry or reproachful. He was patient and listened. Seemed to be ... understanding, maybe?

But that power he had over me—whatever it was—was unsettling. Unnerving. Unfathomable. There was a physiological reaction between my body and his ... a connection I could no more control than comprehend.

And only in the quiet solitude of my own thoughts would I admit that I had never experienced such an intense response with another man before.

Not even Sean.

I needed to stay clear of Grant Twombley.

That decision hit me like a ton of bricks while I watched Robert lick the little plate so clean, I wondered if he'd take up the painted-on pattern, too. Not a speck of mushy kitty food was left in sight.

"All right, big man, I think you got it all. I won't have to wash the dish at the rate you're going. Have some water while it's fresh."

I splashed my finger in the bowl to direct his attention there while I took the empty plate away, feeling guilty there wasn't more food for him to feast on. But I'd seen his beggar routine on our first date, and he conned me out of two full cans of wet food with those big round eyes. No way was I falling for his Oliver Twist bit a second time.

The sun was just about retired for the day, and the temperature had dropped significantly. It was too cold for the little guy to spend the night outside, and it was going to break my heart thinking about him all evening. I knew Sean wouldn't really want him in the house, but he wasn't here right now, and I was tired of sitting inside all alone when I could have a little lovebug curled up on my lap, keeping me company.

With a shrug, I made a command decision. I opened the

door wider and let the little rascal strut inside.

"We're going to have to set some ground rules, Robert."

He sat down on his little cat bottom and gave me his full attention.

"Well, what a good boy!" My praise lasted for approximately two and a half seconds. Right before Robert darted out of the room and made a beeline for my bedroom. There, he dived straight under my bed. I followed after him, refusing to be deterred.

"First of all, you may not sharpen your nails on the furniture." I made the announcement in the middle of the room. "Secondly, you only do your bathroom business in the cat box. Absolutely nowhere else in this house." I paused a moment, listening for any signs of mischief from under the bed, and then continued. "And finally, no licking your butt in front of visitors. It's just bad form, all around."

Even though the kitten had taken off in the middle of rule three, it made me feel good to get all that off my chest, as though I had some authority over someone or something. Maybe I would get out my art supplies to make a little sign and post it near his cat box so he could see the rules and be reminded they existed.

Jesus Christ. I was already acting like a crazy cat lady.

The next time he decided to grace me with his presence, I was watching TV from my favorite spot on the sofa. I snapped a few pictures of him with the camera on my phone and sent the two best shots to Abbi.

Surprise! It's a boy!
Congratulations, Auntie!

Only moments passed before she answered.

OMG! He's precious! What's his name?

> *Thank you! It's Robert. Pronounced*
> *Row-Bear, like the French would say it.*

I'm shocked my brother got a cat.

> *He doesn't know yet.*

Uh-oh. Riiiiioooo!!

> *He's going to love him. What's not to*
> *love? It's a kitten, for Christ's sake.*

True. True.

I finished the conversation to take an incoming call from Sean—but as I should have expected, he was only getting in touch to say he'd be working late. But the weird thing wasn't the call itself. It was my reaction to it. I tried to infuse my voice with disappointment because I was genuinely disappointed. I mean, I *think* I was.

What I *wasn't* . . . was surprised.

Yes, he kept saying this wasn't going to be permanent. These late hours were just because it was a new job and blah blah blah. But something deep inside my belly kept nagging at me—warning me, almost—that there was more to the whole situation than just making a good impression at a new job.

More . . . that I didn't want to know about.

"No," I ordered myself at once. "Stop it. Right this second."

My damn frantic brain had a way of running off down its own path when I had too much time to myself. Lately, all I had was time to myself.

So I spent the next hour making up stories as to why my husband might not want to be spending time with me. Completely normal behavior, right?

One. Maybe I was putting too much pressure on him to start a family. Maybe deep inside, Sean didn't really want to have a baby just yet. Maybe he saw what his sister and Sebastian were going through with her pregnancy, and it had caused him to change his mind, and now he was afraid to tell me how he felt.

Two. Maybe, for Sean, all the extra money we would have to spend on infertility treatments wouldn't be worth it.

Three. Maybe all the projects that were half done or needed to be done around the old house we owned were seeming like more significant priorities than bringing a child into the world. Which, if we were honest, would just continue to cost more money that we didn't have.

On a rare occasion when we had been able to sit down and talk and I dared to bring up the topic of starting a family, my husband swore he still wanted the same thing I did. All I could do was trust he was being honest with me.

But actions spoke louder than words, and to make a baby, people had to have sex. We were barely doing that these days. Sean and I used to have a legendary sex life. Now it was sad and almost embarrassing how infrequently we made love. Yes, there had been the exceptional I-got-the-job passion marathon, but after that, everything was vanilla and tedious and seemed more like a chore for Sean than something he just couldn't get enough of—like it used to be. Neither one of us was at an age that our libidos should be waning, either.

Of course, he always said he was just tired or stressed out because of work. I tried to be understanding, even sympathetic. I attempted to be the initiator, the aggressor, even the caretaker. But at some point...

I'd started to seriously consider possibility number four. Had Sean met someone else? Were his needs being taken care of outside our bedroom? I hated myself for letting teenage insecurities rear their ugly, useless heads, but I couldn't help it. Sean was spending more and more time away from me, and I couldn't keep ignoring what was happening to my marriage.

Robert jumped on my lap, purring while rubbing his face on my offered fingers. "Hi, sweet boy. I'm so glad you chose me. I think I needed you more than either one of us realized." The sweet sound of his vibrating body calmed my nerves, and I focused on that instead of letting my thoughts run off and turn down into the darkness. I didn't want to do destructive things— to myself or my property. Even worse, to other people's.

Maybe Grant was at his place a few neighborhoods away, in Naples. If I texted him and he just happened to be there and wasn't busy, he could stop by. He had told me to call him anytime I felt like I needed an outlet. Now was definitely one of those times—and there was no harm in one friend reaching out to another in a time of true need.

He'd also mentioned, at least a few times, about wanting to learn some of his favorite recipes that we made in the kitchen. I could offer to give him a private lesson or two.

There would be no harm in that.

"Good God," I groaned to myself. Could I actually hear the ridiculous things I was suggesting? To have that man come over to my house this late at night while I was home alone and feeling vulnerable? No harm in that? *Really*, Rio?

Of course not.

Because the only recipe that'd be cooked up in that situation was an old classic called Disaster.

Soon, my eyes grew heavy with exhaustion—and I was grateful for it. I needed to go to sleep and forget about Grant Twombley. While I was at it, forget about the shit show my marriage was becoming. Everything would look better after a good night's sleep. I had to believe it—though that also felt as realistic as thinking Santa would come down the chimney and leave me pretty turquoise boxes while I dozed.

Sean crawled into bed beside me sometime after eleven o'clock. I lay still as could be, pretending to be asleep after I smelled the beer on his breath, even from my side of the bed. So what the hell did that mean?

I hoped the answer was that he'd just knocked one back with the crew after clocking out and time got away from them all while they shot the shit at some watering hole. He wasn't dumb enough to drink more than one and get behind the wheel. Typically he was responsible and called me or paid for a ride, so I took comfort in that history and fell asleep fully.

The next morning, we went through our usual morning routines, acting like everything was fine. After a quick kiss at the door, we headed to our cars. Goodbyes and promises of coming home on time to spend the night together were shouted over the rooftops of our vehicles as we loaded up for the morning commute.

Instead of crying off the makeup I'd quickly applied, I vowed to stop feeling sorry for myself while I drove into the prep kitchen in the industrial section of a downtown suburb. A heavy dose of Def Leppard, and I was back on solid ground.

Despite the lighter than usual traffic—and still humming the chorus to "Hysteria"—I still arrived after Hannah.

Does the woman ever sleep?

The adorable blonde popped out of her adorable car, dressed in her adorable chef's jacket and pants, an adorable smile already in place. All at the very non-adorable time of four thirty.

"Morning!" she shouted before following me inside and waiting while I disengaged the security system. Then, like every morning, we set to work like drones in a beehive. There was too much to be done for operating at any other pace, and Hannah and I were a well-oiled machine.

Sometimes, that wasn't the case with Abbigail and me. I adored my sister-in-law, but Abbi and I often had conflicting ideas about how things should be done. We butted heads because we could. Since Hannah worked for me, she did what I asked her to do, with incredible skill and efficiency. She wasn't afraid to share her ideas or ask questions, but she knew when to back off if she sensed I was holding firm on something.

The lunch orders were finished and loaded in the van earlier than usual. By the time I navigated through the crisscrossing streets of downtown, traffic was still light. Even parking was easy at the first few stops in the financial district. I could count on one hand how often that had been the case.

While riding the elevator to the top floor of the Shark Enterprises building, I had a swarm of butterflies in my stomach—especially when noticing Grant's name was on the meal recipient list that day and Sebastian's wasn't. It was then that I remembered Abbi had an appointment with her obstetrician and figured her guy must be accompanying her to the doctor's office. He was very insistent on being at every single checkup, ultrasound scan, and lab poke she had.

She called him doting. I called him a control freak.

Tomato. Tomahto.

As the lift climbed, those thoughts made my mind wander—and my heart sink. What would it be like to finally have a baby growing inside my body? I wondered what kind of husband Sean would be to his pregnant wife. Would he still be so preoccupied with work? The *ding* of the elevator doors opening made me jump. Shit. I hadn't even noticed the car coming to a halt, I'd been so lost in my thoughts. I was driving myself crazy. I needed to reconnect with my husband in a big way.

If he'd just come home before I passed out every night.

But this bullshit had to stop. Sean didn't even know what I'd been putting myself through. I'd just kept faking a smile and insisting I understood—all while he was trying to earn more money so we could finally start a family. The dream we'd shared for nearly six years.

Six long years.

Maybe this was the madness I'd read about on the online support groups. Women repeatedly talked about the emotional turmoil their infertility problems caused in their marriages. I scoffed at them, of course. Nonsense like that wouldn't touch Sean and me. We were deeply connected, different from every other couple. They weren't strong like we were.

Right now, I felt anything but strong—or connected. To anyone.

But that wasn't true. I did feel connected. To at least one person.

And right now, fueled by my frustration, I power walked from the elevator to his office. But I was so preoccupied with my own recrimination, I nearly mowed the man himself down with the lunch cart just outside his door.

"Easy there, Blaze."

I snapped my stare up, directly locking my gaze with Grant Twombley's intense blue one. That damn deep, sexy timbre of his was like verbal crack, vibrating through my system and coming to rest right at the apex of my thighs. Like a deer on a dark country road, I stared as though the man were an oncoming eighteen-wheeler. I stood frozen in the position he found me—rendered immobile by the intensity of his light.

Finally—Jesus...finally—I said something. "Uh, hey." And ever so cleverly, too!

He grinned, probably knowing the exact sort of electrical storm he was causing inside my body. The tumult was likely written all over my face, spilling out the details of every circuit he'd shorted in my nerves and every synapse he'd fried in my mind.

"What's going on with you today?" he asked, as calm as if the air around him wasn't crackling with fresh energy.

I tilted my head, wondering if a churchlike glow was about to appear around his head, filled with stained-glass glory. Though no way would he be the angel in the scene. Did devils get stained-glass glory too?

"Rio?" He copied my tilt, looking at me as if a slightly different angle would give him a better clue. "Hey. What is it?"

Silly man. If only he knew he was both the affliction and the cure.

"Nothing!" I said too quickly. Probably a bit pissy too.

"Okay. If you say so." He took a step back, giving me some much-needed breathing room, and then turned to reach for the doorknob to his office. "Would you mind terribly?"

For a long second, I simply stared at him.

He just stared back.

I gave in to an open fume. The rage felt easier than continuing to deal with—which was basically having to deny—this unexplained, unfair thing that existed between us.

"Mind what, exactly?" I bit out.

"Bringing my lunch into my office, please." He finished with that cocky grin, keeping it pinned in place until I huffed and put all my weight behind the cart to get the thing moving again on the thicker piled carpet.

I passed by him and he didn't bother moving out of my way, so our bodies rubbed against one another in the narrow space of the doorway. Because of our drastic height difference, my face was level with his firm torso, and I could smell the expensive cologne he wore combined with the crisp cotton of his dress shirt. The little white buttons had pearly striations throughout, like the veins in a marble slab.

Grant's blue eyes sparkled with mischief in the artificial office light before roving over my body from the top of my head to the soles of my shoes. When I allowed my own eyes to crawl all the way back up to his, I could feel the heat building in my core. The middle of his throat bobbed as he roughly swallowed, and I focused on my own throat for a moment. It felt so dry and scratchy, and when my eyes finally locked on his mouth . . .

Holy God . . . his mouth.

Grant Twombley had the most sinful mouth. Full, sensual lips that seemed to be made expressly for a woman's pleasure. Hours and hours of pleasure. But not mine.

No. Not mine. Not. Mine.

"Where do you want me?" I gasped. Then, mortified at what just came out of my mouth, I all but shouted, "It! Your lunch. Where do you want your lunch, Grant?"

Fucking hell.

I shook my head while squeezing my eyes shut. Wishing for a cloak of invisibility seemed pointless and juvenile, but it was worth a try.

Who was I kidding? None of my wishes ever came true, no matter how simple or how complex they were. I was always left to clean up the messes I made for myself—proved by the moment I peeked out of one lid and saw Grant watching me with that damn smirk plastered on his mug.

So the invisibility thing was really a no-go.

"Okay, seriously. What's going on with you today, woman? You're acting crazier than usual." He smiled, and I knew his intention wasn't to be cruel with his words. I'd been called crazy most of my life. Most of the time, people said the word to sting. Most of the time, it did.

"Just tired."

"Bullshit." Grant crowded closer to me, but the catering cart was still between us. Those damn blue eyes, piercing icicles, carved at my carefully constructed layers of protection. "Am I your last delivery?"

I just nodded. I couldn't trust the sound that might come out of my parched throat in place of words.

"Sit with me." He walked over to the conference table, an impressive piece of furniture despite being much smaller than the one in Shark's office. He never looked back to see that I followed. Somehow, he just knew I would. Again, it was that voice—not the words. That ineffable pull between us.

Okay, so I also had the lunch he'd paid a ridiculously high price for. But his food could've been sitting out in the hall on a paper plate, and it wouldn't have mattered.

"Do you want iced tea with your lunch?" I had to say something to stop this train we were on from barreling any farther down the track. I had an intense feeling there was a bridge out—just up ahead—and people were going to get hurt if we weren't careful.

"Sure," he said, finally looking away for a moment to tend to his vibrating phone. "Do you have lunch for yourself? If not, we can share."

"I'm not really hungry. Don't worry about me."

A low growl emanated from the center of his chest. "Blaze."

"Grant, I'm serious. Cut the bossy shit. I had a late breakfast, and I said I'm not hungry."

"Then sit down and tell me what's really happening with you." He motioned toward the door with the fork he'd just unfurled from his napkin. "You just about jumped out of your skin when you came around the corner out there."

After one last scan to ensure he had everything he needed to enjoy his meal, I took the seat beside him at the round table. I rested my chin on my fist, waiting for him to have a bite or two of his meal. It gave me a perfect break for organizing my thoughts.

I certainly wasn't going to get into the struggle I was having with my physical attraction to the man himself. That left the chaos with my husband. But did I really want to open up about that? Somehow it felt like a betrayal to Sean. But why would talking to Grant, my friend, be any different from talking to Abbi? Or Hannah?

Maybe it would be better, actually.

Grant might have a unique man's perspective on the whole mess. A point of view that I'd yet to tap into with anyone else.

"Jesus, Rio." He chuckled.

I gave my head a little shake. "Huh?" I asked, focusing on him again, offering a sheepish smile. I had really wandered off in thought. "I'm sorry," I muttered. "My brain follows weird tangents sometimes."

"It's fine," he replied. "I just said that this is fantastic."

He held the bite of pasta a bit higher to draw my attention to the subject, then shoveled it into his mouth.

Christ. That mouth.

No. Do not go there again.

Beneath the table, I gouged my fingernails into my thigh through the thin fabric of my leggings. I had to stop day drifting, especially when the subject was Grant Twombley's beautiful lips, and the painful trick helped me regain my focus. In the past, this was a favorite trick to help me center my mind when the bad habit used to be so out of control, I'd end up miles from home and have no idea how I'd gotten there. Or worse, I'd find myself—

"Blaze." Grant's voice was low and commanding, completely interrupting my thoughts.

"What?" I shouted back. Totally unnecessary but sticking with the new angry-not-aroused tactic.

"Stay with me, girl." He pushed his lunch plate to the side and leaned over until his face was just inches from mine. "Come on, Rio. Tell me what's gotten into you."

I refrained—barely—from rolling my eyes. "Damn it, I already told you—"

"And I already said I don't believe you." He turned his chair toward mine then too. "You're more distracted than I've ever seen you. You're worrying me."

His long legs now bracketed mine. His frame consumed

so much of my personal space, I found it difficult to breathe. But with his chair moved, he was no longer leaning across the table. No longer right up in my face.

"I ... umm ... well ... I just have a lot going on." I paused to tap my temple with my index finger. Oh God, this was a lot harder than I thought it would be. "In here. You know?"

"I'm getting that much." He smiled easily, and even that small expression warmed me inside. "But this is more than the usual Abstract stuff, isn't it?"

I squirmed. How did he do that? Laser straight into my truth like that? "I—I don't know what to—"

"Just say it, Rio. Release it into the universe, doll. You'll feel better. Lighter. Trust me on this one."

He leaned forward and rested his elbows on his knees, bringing his handsome face that much closer to mine again. I struggled not to inhale but failed. That divine mix of scents— expensive cotton and the cologne he always wore—were a forbidden olfactory heaven. And now, its crisp mystery would be lodged in my senses for the rest of the afternoon.

"Rio."

"Huh?" I blurted, responding as soon as he started snapping his fingers.

"Are you focusing? Even trying to?"

"Yes. Okay." I motioned toward his disregarded food. "But eat while we talk. And don't fucking snap your fingers at me like that. I'm not a dog." I sucked in a deep breath, looking around the office. It wasn't his fault that I was such a mess today. Okay, it partially was, but he didn't know that, and I wasn't about to explain it. "Please. I know how busy you are, and I don't want you to miss your lunch because of me. Not to mention, Hannah and I worked hard on that meal."

"All right. Deal," he said, turning and digging back into the food. "This is really good. I was serious when I said I want you to give me some cooking lessons. I'm so tired of eating out."

"You did great in the kitchen when you were there helping. Or babysitting, rather."

"I can do what I'm told. But when I'm standing there by myself, it's all very intimidating."

"It's hard for me to imagine you being intimidated by anything, Grant Twombley."

"You'd be surprised. But don't try to turn the tables here, lady. You're supposed to be telling me what's got you as scattered as a kitten on the freeway."

As soon as I thought of Robert dodging maniac drivers on the 405, I glared. But damn it, the man had a point.

Ugh. Fine.

It was time to rip off the proverbial Band-Aid.

"I'm—well—I'm having a harder time adjusting to Sean being gone so much. More than I thought I would, I guess."

Grant's reaction was barely a reaction, the exact note of neutrality I really needed. "Gone?" he inquired. "How so?"

A soft subtlety in his tone left me the space to elaborate on more than the obvious, but I stuck to the clearer path. "Well, you probably know he's working late every night. But lately, it's been really late. Last night it was after eleven when he finally came to bed."

Grant nodded, took a drink of his tea, and then asked, "Because of the new job?"

"Yeah, I guess. But last night, I definitely smelled beer when he got into bed. I'd be lying if I said that didn't piss me off a little bit." I held up my hand to interrupt myself. "And I'm not usually that wife, you know?"

"Sometimes the crew gets a beer or two after a long day. I've seen it on a lot of jobsites. It builds morale, and the guys bond that way. It's not unusual, Rio."

"It wasn't really the beer, honestly." I laughed before continuing. "I know what family I married into. If drinking bothered me, I'd be in a world of hurt."

"So what was it?" He leaned in. Not by a lot, but enough. "Really?"

"Perhaps just the straw that broke the camel's back," I confessed, jerking a shrug that felt ridiculous. "I'm probably being tired and melodramatic. But I've literally been sitting at home alone, night after night, for a month. Talking to a stray cat for company. And then he—" Another stupid shrug, this time filled with a lot of the hate I was directing inward. "God. Let's change the subject. I know I sound petty and selfish . . ."

"How's the infertility stuff going?"

I stared at him. Stared some more. "I'm not talking to you about that."

He threw his head back and laughed. Freaking laughed! "Why not? Because it involves sex? Oh, no!" He mock-gasped. "Not that!"

"Stop! Seriously." I shook my head, attempting to laugh too, but sobered much too quickly at the reality of the situation. "Nah, there's nothing to talk about." I paused, running my fingertip along the woodgrain of the fancy table. "Literally . . . nothing."

Grant grew serious too. "So him working late every night is tough for a lot of reasons. I got you. Well, let me see what I can do, okay?"

I snapped my head up to stare even harder at the man— enduring a flood of panic through my body. "Wait. What?" I shot to my feet, stabbing my chipped black nail at him. "What are you talking about? Don't you dare say anything to anyone, Grant Twombley!"

Grant, however, remained as cool as could be. "What's the big deal? One quick call, and I can make sure he's getting out of work at the regular time." He shrugged his muscular shoulders, and I was momentarily distracted, watching the way the cotton of his dress shirt pulled tighter against his form. "Problem solved. Why won't you let me fix this for you?" the handsome bastard had the nerve to ask.

But his frustration was seeping through the cracks— the little tells that I'd gotten to know in the time we'd spent together rarely surfaced. But at that moment, when he thrust his hand back through his artfully messy blond hair, I knew I was making him a little crazy now too.

I flopped back down into the chair and buried my head in my folded arms. "Oh my God. How stupid are you?"

I could hear his weight shift in his chair. "Beg your pardon? I'm trying to help you. How is that stupid?"

I raised my head. "You can't just go busting in and fix everything wrong in the world like that, Grant." I smacked my forehead with my palm. As the crack echoed around the room, I invested in a moment of feeling like crap about it. He was staring at me so earnestly. Holy God, he was truly confused about all this. "I was just venting to you, like a friend would. Like you encouraged me to do. Don't go embarrassing both of us and make things really worse and awkward with my husband by telling his boss to send him home early to his needy wife!"

"Okay, okay." He held his hands up, flat palms facing me. "I get it. I get it."

"Do you?" I demanded. "Really?"

"Yes, damn it. Of course. When you say it like that, I can see your point. I'm just a problem solver, Blaze. It's my nature. Hell, it's my job around here. I fix things for Shark minute by minute. I'm programmed for it." He looked apologetic then. "Sometimes it's hard to shut it off."

"Fair enough. But please, Grant. I'm beeegggggging you." As I drew out the word, his eyebrows jumped. By a lot. At the same time, a sly grin spread across his sinful lips. "What?" I gritted, still feeling pissed off and fired up. "What is that look right now?"

He was the one to give his head a solid shake this time. "Never mind. Sorry. You were saying?"

"To just drop it. Okay?"

"Okay." He straightened in the chair, parking his elbows farther back on the rests. "I give you my word. This stays between you and me."

A breath rushed out of me. "Thank you."

"And thank you for trusting me and talking to me. You know you can call me anytime, right? I'll always pick up when I see your number."

"That's very kind of you. But I'm a big girl, Grant." I stood and started gathering my things to leave. "I have to handle my own shit."

"That doesn't mean you can't lean on a friend once in a while." While he helped me clean up the dishes and trash, he said with soft sincerity, "Thank you for lunch."

"That's why they pay me the big bucks." I added a wry smile to the quip. Suddenly the air between us felt way too serious.

"Rio." He waited until I stopped shuffling around and looked back at him. "It'll even out. The job. The hours. And it'll be worth it then. The job is stable and long-term. And I know Bas made sure Sean was taken care of, salary-wise. Try to hang in there."

His explanation was thick with more of that addicting sincerity, leading me back to more of my default defenses. I went with an extra-light clip. "All good here." My cheer almost sounded fake, but it was a necessity. Otherwise I'd go to pieces. His kindness was bringing emotion up from the pit of my stomach, and I didn't like it one bit. "I appreciate you letting me vent. Or... release into the universe or whatever happy Buddha horseshit you were spewing." I narrowed my eyes at him, looking way up across the ridiculous height difference between us. "I don't even know you sometimes."

"Yeah? That makes two of us. Now get out of here," he said, pulling me in for a sweet hug.

Damn it, why does he smell so good?

"See you later," I called to his assistant as I nearly sprinted past her desk with the cart. I needed to escape his presence before I lost my shit altogether.

Even though I felt much lighter in the elevator going down than I had felt coming up, I was confused on so many new levels. I had an emotional buoyancy that I hadn't felt in quite some time. But I suspected Grant Twombley could give a woman the sort of release that would cure all kinds of woes.

CHAPTER FOUR

GRANT

"Do you have plans for the weekend?" I asked my two best friends on Friday afternoon when our last meeting wrapped up. It felt like one of the longest weeks in my adult life, and I just wanted to go home, maybe open a beer—or better yet, a bottle of Scotch—and forget about the world for a couple of days.

Bas was as good as married at this point. He was also seated firmly in the seventh circle of secondhand pregnancy hell, judging by the stories he'd been entertaining us with about Abbigail's mood swings, food cravings, and random-body-part-swelling episodes. Yet as he shared the anecdotes, the man glowed as brightly as the Hollywood sign on a clear summer night.

Confused didn't begin to cover my position on the whole situation with him. When I thought back to the man Sebastian was just one year ago compared to the man across the room from me now, it was easy to believe anything was possible. I felt a genuine warmth in my chest. It radiated upward and forced a smile to take over my entire face. I probably looked like an absolute loon to my two buddies—not that either of them noticed. They were both so engrossed in their damn phones, I could've been doing the naked tango and they wouldn't have lifted a brow.

Surprisingly, Elijah caught my demeanor change out of the corner of his eye, and he shifted his attention from his nonstop phone scrolling. "What's up?" he asked. "You good?"

"Yeah. Yeah," I said, though my voice was husky with emotion. That had Elijah quickly stuffing his phone into his pocket, which caused Sebastian to look up as well.

"Okay, what's going on with you, man?" Bas narrowed his eyes skeptically before warning, "If this is going to turn into a group hug, you know I'm out."

Elijah and I chuckled, knowing damn well Bas would never willingly engage in PDA—especially an all-male showing.

I tried to wave them off. "It's really nothing. I was just having a moment watching you." I motioned to Bas. "I was thinking about the difference in you from now and a year ago. The gift you were given when that woman came into your life. You know, I think Abbigail may have actually saved you."

My friend's smile began the moment he clued in to what I was saying. By the time I finished explaining my theory, he was grinning wider than the Amazon. "There isn't a day that goes by that I don't think the same thing, my friend. I was on a collision course with my own pride and ego, and it wasn't going to end well."

Three nods matched in agreement.

Elijah wiped a mock tear from his cheek. "This is a very touchy-feely conclusion for you to have come to, Shark. I'm beyond impressed. There are days I feel like I don't even know you anymore."

"Shut up." Sebastian punched his bicep so hard, they both winced from the impact.

"Asshole! That's probably going to leave a mark!"

"Poor pretty boy." Bas pouted toward Elijah with sarcastic drama. "Good thing you've never been in a real fight, Banks. You'd probably cry more about getting your clothes wrinkled."

"You know damn well I've seen my fair share of fights," Elijah answered. "Jesus, when I was with Hensley, I swore she used to start trouble just to see me defend her honor."

"Honor," I echoed on a wry laugh. "Which she had none of, remember?"

"Haven't forgotten," Elijah muttered. "Not for a damn second."

I let that one lie right where it was. The guy's dignity didn't need any more direct hits. He had been the good guy in that scenario and hadn't deserved any of what he was handed. It had been nothing like the way he behaved with women now, and Hensley Pritchett was responsible for it all.

"That woman was a troublemaker from day one," Bas said. "You were the only one blinded by her tits. The rest of us saw right through her con act."

"And her blouse," I mumbled, knowing they both heard me.

Bas nodded in agreement and said, "Every single one."

"Truth." We fist-bumped while Elijah scowled at us.

His frown turned to a full-fledged glare toward Bas. "You wouldn't appreciate if I said things like that about the mother of your child, would you?"

"You're smarter than that. If you were that stupid, you'd be flat on your back because I'd level your ass."

It took a few moments before Elijah spoke again—but when he did, it was to set loose a massive can of worms. "I've been thinking about finding her."

Bas startled with new intensity. "You can't be serious."

"Dude, why?" I asked nearly at the same time.

Elijah shook his head, clearly not to be dissuaded. "I'm sure with the resources I have now, it would take me about two minutes. Maybe three if she actually didn't want to be found."

"Are you sure that's the best idea? Bringing all that up again? Talk about going into the belly of the beast." I was genuinely concerned now. "And maybe if she doesn't want to be found, you should just leave well enough alone."

I really didn't want to see Elijah drag himself through that pigsty of emotional mud again. It was a hard enough time for us all the first time around. But that was how true friends rolled. If one man's ship was sinking, the entire battle group went down with him, until collectively we got the weakest man sailing at his strongest again. Then we pulled the damn boat to shore with ropes tied to our backs, made the necessary repairs to the damaged hull, and lived to set sail another day on the calm waters of life, like the solid crew we were.

Elijah considered my question for a long moment before thumping on his temple with his index finger. "Every day, I live with the fucked-up mess that woman created. Except now, it's even worse."

"Why?" I asked.

"Ever since I was in Twentynine Palms with Abbi and I told her about the history between Hensley and me . . . I don't know. I haven't been able to stop thinking about her."

"You know what?" I decided to flip-flop on the subject for a second. Maybe coming at it from his side would make a difference. "Maybe . . . you're on to something. I mean, you never really got closure with the woman. She made the decision to leave, told you that child wasn't yours, then just up and left. It might be just what you need to finally put it all to bed in your mind so you can get on with a healthy relationship with a woman again."

And shit if that wasn't the pot calling the kettle black. What the hell did a healthy relationship with a woman even look like? I didn't have the emotional scars Elijah did, but I still couldn't paint that Norman Rockwell in my mind.

Elijah shook me from my brood with his next comment. "Well, I only said I was thinking about the whole thing right now." He pushed up from where he had been leaning on the edge of Bas's desk. "Let's go to Lulu's, Twombley. I need to blow off some serious steam."

"Sorry, man." I shook my head while stuffing my laptop into my bag. "Not tonight."

His double take was nearly a blur. "Say what?"

"I'm just not in the mood for that place tonight. I phoned a friend a couple nights ago. I'm solid."

"Why didn't you call me?" He put his hand on the center of his chest, pretending to be hurt.

"It was Cybil. You said you didn't like her last time you were over and she stopped by."

"Oh, yeah. Not my scene, that one. Way too loud. I don't know how you can stand all the dramatics." He made a sour face, causing me to laugh. The man had a point. Cybil did become vocal when her clothes came off.

"What if I set it up on my own?" Elijah persisted, still looking hopeful. He pulled out his phone and swiped through his contacts. "You want to come over to my place? We don't have to go to the club."

I shook my head. "I think I'm just going to kick back at home."

Shit. Why won't he just take the hint?

While Elijah and I bantered, Sebastian walked over to the bank of windows lining the far wall of his office. He gazed out over the city while making a call home to Abbigail. We could tell because the man turned from shark to teddy bear in approximately three-point-five seconds.

Elijah didn't waste a second to capitalize on Shark's distraction. He swiftly stepped in front of me, blocking my view and meeting my stare straight on. But I was grateful because the guy could read me better than anyone. Even better than Bas. Elijah took the time to notice the little things about people.

"All right, level with me," he demanded in a tone for my ears alone. "Do you really want to be alone tonight? Or do you just not want to be with another woman other than Rio Gibson?"

"No," I said with finality. "Just drop that bullshit right now." I looked around him to our other friend still busy on the phone and then swung my bag over my shoulder. "The last thing I want to do is get into this with him. If he overhears you, it will be a reenactment of the Inquisition. Hard pass, thank you very much." Then I raised my voice loud enough for Bas to hear. "Call if you need anything over the weekend."

Sebastian gave a wave, but he was engrossed in his conversation with Abbi—pretty much since she had first stumbled through his office door.

Strangely, and really unsettlingly, I was starting to envy the bastard for it.

"Where are you staying tonight?"

To anyone else, Elijah's question would have been as bizarre as my train of thought. But the man did know me through and through, down to my unusual habitation habits.

While I reveled in having as many homes as possible, roots were a different thing. Roots meant danger. They were the kind of things that came loose and blew away during storms. Nowhere did that truth apply better than in the path of real life.

"I haven't given it much thought," I finally confessed. "I was serious about Lulu's, though. Please don't start with that bullshit again."

Banks held up his hands. "I know, I know. I was going to say I could just come over and we could hang out. No women. Just kick back. Find a game on satellite or something."

"You don't have to do that, man. I'm not in a bad place or anything. You don't have to babysit me. I'm solid."

I offered my fist for him to bump. After knocking his knuckles with mine, Elijah stopped abruptly and stared at me.

"What?" I asked.

"Is it such a big deal that I just want to hang out?"

"No." Shit. I sounded defensive, even to my own ears. I frantically added, "I mean, it shouldn't be."

"I didn't think so either, but for some reason, you're making me jump through hoops to make it happen."

"Dude, I'm sorry." I rubbed the tired muscles at the back of my neck. "I'm just tired. It's been a long week."

"Come on, I'll give you a ride to whichever one of your seventy-two houses you want to go to. And while we sit in traffic, you can tell me what's going on."

"Thanks. That'd be great." I gave my watch a quick glance. "The tangle shouldn't be too bad. It's the tail end of rush hour, and if we go to Long Beach, we can avoid Hollywood and the Westside. Let's go to my place in Naples. I stayed there last night, and that shower is definitely my favorite."

Elijah looked at me sideways and laughed. "Whatever you say, man."

Once we were established on the freeway and traffic was moving along at a nice pace, Elijah exhaled slowly. "So you're actually going to make me ask you?"

I fought against shifting uncomfortably in the passenger's seat. "Ask me what?"

"You really don't know?"

Of course I knew. Didn't mean I was going to just cut open a vein and bleed for the man.

"I thought if I waited long enough, you'd start talking," Elijah finally murmured. "But she really has you this twisted up?"

"Or maybe it's just not your business," I snapped. "Have you ever considered that?"

He let out something between a huff and a groan.

"You sound like an injured farm animal," I said, grinning at his dismay.

"Look, dumbass. I'm just trying to be a friend here. Maybe if you get the shit out of your head, you can plug back into what actually matters." He pretended to give his next comment some thought before saying it out loud. Finally, with his finger still positioned at his chin, he quipped, "Like your job?"

I watched the Southern California night pass outside the window as we sped down the freeway. Goddammit. Of course he had a point. But I just couldn't see anything good coming from talking about all the things whirling around in my head.

A few more minutes of silence stretched between us before my friend tried prodding again. "Okay, at least tell me this. Am I right to assume this concerns Rio Gibson?"

"Eliiijjaaaahhh." I drew his name out, a deliberate chide. "You know what they say about assuming."

"Would you grow up for a minute, Twombley? I'm serious

about this shit. Right now, only I'm still noticing it, but that won't be the case for long." He dared to flash me an annoyed glance. "You're so damn distracted all the time, man. Totally off your game. Not just at work. It's happening everywhere. Tonight's a perfect example. You didn't want to go to the club. Then you even turned down a chance to have someone over to the house. I don't think I've ever—and seriously, I mean ever— witnessed you turn down a chance to get your dick wet."

"Well, there's a first time for everything," I volleyed. "And I'd hardly say that's a reason to deem me 'preoccupied' or 'off my game' or whatever."

"Bullshit."

"What's bullshit?"

Elijah laughed. "Says the same man who had his appendix removed and then had a nurse riding his cock in his hospital bed where he lay recovering just twelve hours later. Dude, I don't think you know how to turn down pussy."

"Pffft. We both know that nurse was hot. You can't say she wasn't."

"Beside the point, man."

"Then what is your point? Just get to it already."

"My point is you're not yourself! And it's because of this Gibson woman!"

"So what if it is?" Screw it. I finally snapped. He'd worn me down with his badgering. "What do you want from me on this?" I yelled, my deep voice bouncing off the glass and metal and then thundering back twice as loud.

Elijah flopped back against the headrest of the driver's seat and threw his hands up, momentarily letting go of the steering wheel. "Shit! Thank you! Why was that so hard?" As the air settled, he grabbed the steering wheel again. "I'm not here to judge you, man. I'm your fucking best friend. We've been through"—he thrust a hand back through his sandy-colored hair—"we've been through everything together. Why would you think Rio Gibson, and whatever you're dealing with here because of her, would be any different?" He shook his head and stared out the windshield with the focus of a Le Mans driver.

After another few moments of painful silence, I finally sighed deeply and said, "You're right." I shifted in my seat to face him, ensuring he felt the gravity of this next part. "I'm sorry. I don't know why I've been acting like such a dumbshit. I should've known you'd have my back."

Elijah nodded along while I spoke. "Yeah. You should've. Just like you'd have mine."

"It's just—" I looked out the window again, trying to get my thoughts organized. "I'm so confused. I know what I'm feeling is wrong, man. Really goddamned wrong. But no matter what I tell myself, I can't make it go away. I can't get her out of my fucking head." I looked back over to my friend, and he was nodding again. "Why are you just nodding? You look like a fucking bobblehead."

"Because I feel you on this shit. I get it. I get where you're coming from."

Did he, though? Really?

"She's married, Banks. You remember that part, right? A one hundred percent no-fly zone. And believe me, zero Grant Twombley planes have put wheels down on that runway. Not even a practice touch-and-go. I might be a lot of things, but I'm not a poacher. That's a hard and fast rule."

"I already know that about you, my friend. We've spent most of our lives landing on airstrips together, remember?

God save me for beating up this metaphor with you, though."

"Yeah, yeah." Now I caught a case of the nods. "So maybe I'm just saying all this for my own benefit," I muttered under my breath but carelessly loud enough to be heard.

"So what are you going to do? You can't keep this shit up, walking around like a love-sick zombie puppy."

"What? That's not what I'm doing," I insisted, despite how he tilted his head to the side, wordlessly calling bullshit on me. "Elijah, she and I are just friends. Rio really needs someone to lean on right now, and it can't be Abbigail. She's too wrapped up with the baby and Sebastian. God fucking knows dealing with him can be a full-time job."

"So call me crazy here, but what about her husband? Where is he during her time of need? Or whatever this is being called?"

"He's never home. As you know, Bas gave him the foreman job at the Edge, so he works all the time. With her mental health"—I paused, treading carefully when labeling the situation at hand—"issues, she's a ticking time bomb."

I was saved from having to go into that sticky subject when we pulled onto my street along the water in Naples.

After he parked along the curb in front of my place, Elijah emitted a low whistle. "Dude, nice location." He got out from behind the wheel, stretched his arms above his head, and stared out across the sand.

While we watched the waves crash against the shore, I said, "Thanks. I like it too. I've been spending a lot of time down here lately."

He swung his gaze back over his shoulder. "Doesn't Rio live around here somewhere?"

"They're in Seal Beach," I said with a pointed frown. "So

no, not really." Wanting to change the subject, I asked, "Can you pop the trunk so I can grab my bag?"

Elijah didn't budge. For a few more beats, he just stared out toward the horizon. Finally but without a word, he turned and opened the back of the car. He handed me my bag, grabbed his own, and then locked the vehicle.

"Want a beer?" I asked when we were inside the house.

While his sudden quiet wasn't disconcerting, since the guy had a tendency to turn on the radio silence when diving into his deepest thoughts, I was getting curious about what those musings exactly were. "Or something with a little more kick?"

As we walked through the great room and into the kitchen, Elijah checked the place out.

"Beer sounds great," he answered at last.

"Coming right up." As I strode over to the fridge and reached inside, I added, "Then maybe in exchange you'll tell me what's buzzing your control tower."

The guy narrowed his eyes, not missing my shameless ping at the airport theme again, but accepted the bottle of German brew with a smile. "I was trying to remember if I'd seen anything about Rio's family in any of my investigations. At least someone beyond her husband. Maybe a relative who lives close by who she could call to talk to."

"Investigations?" I cocked my head while popping the cap off my own brew. "You mean back when Bas was suspicious of everyone from his secretary to Abbigail's dry cleaners?"

"Well, sometimes the secretary really is the crazy one."

I laughed my way through a shudder. "And let's not go there."

"Agreed," he stated. "But yeah, my digging included

thorough looks at everyone remotely close to Abbi. I can't seem to recall anything out of place with Rio, though."

"She doesn't talk much about her family," I confirmed. "Definitely no brothers or sisters who she's mentioned. Parents are still married. They live back east. Maryland, I think?"

"That sounds familiar. Yeah, Baltimore. That's where she had the priors. Did you get to the bottom of all that?" He tipped the beer bottle to his lips and took a long pull.

"I guess it was a post-breakup, first-love kind of thing." I shrugged, expecting he was about to make a big deal over something that really wasn't. "I mean, we've all done stupid things when we were young and brokenhearted, right?" I threw in a chuckle, hoping the mood would stick.

"Grant."

I looked up from where I was spinning the bottle opener on the countertop. "What?"

"Cut the shit, man. She's got a serious problem. I never lit so much as a match over pussy, and I'm damn sure you never have either. This isn't some teenage prank we're talking about here."

"You don't think I realize how fucked up this is?" I said quietly. "But what do you want me to do, Elijah? Walk away from her? I care about her. I'm fucking laying my throat under your boot right now and admitting it to you. I care. About. Her. She's a married woman, and like a dumbshit, I've let myself develop feelings for her."

My friend's stare darkened with obvious pity. I wanted to throat-punch him.

Fucking pity.

Shaking my head in disgust, I said, "Don't look at me like that. I don't want your pity."

"Then what do you want here, dude?" He set down his beer, threw his arms up, and began pacing back and forth. "If I tell you to cut and run, you'll say no. If I tell you to throw your hat in the ring, you'll say no. If I tell you to go fuck her out of your system with someone from your contacts list, you'll say no." He stopped pacing and faced me. "What do you want from me right now? Just tell me. Seeing you like this is getting on my nerves. And honestly? It's starting to get to me here, too." He thumped his chest with his fist, and the gesture made me feel like I was suffocating.

I chugged my entire beer and slammed the bottle down onto the counter. "Jesus Christ, what a mess I've gotten myself into."

"Won't argue that one," Banks muttered.

"What do I do, man? I'm asking sincerely here."

Elijah took more steps—this time to circle the kitchen island and grab a second beer for himself. "Maybe . . . you've just got to slowly distance yourself from her."

"Slowly." I nodded while echoing it. Then again. Shit, it was like I'd never heard of the word before. Granted, when one was helping Sebastian Shark run a worldwide empire, "slow" wasn't a concept that got indulged very often.

"Exactly," Banks reiterated. "So it doesn't seem like you're abandoning her, and she has time to adjust to either being by herself more or Sean will start being home at a regular quitting time by then."

The plan didn't seem that far out of line. It could seriously work if, like Elijah suggested, I backed off over time.

"Another idea? Tell Bas to start sending her husband home on time. Damn, now that one's good. Why haven't you thought of that?"

"I have," I protested. "But when I mentioned it to her, she lost her shit. Made me swear I wouldn't say anything that would make Sean look bad at his new job. And dude, when I say lost her shit, you don't know a meltdown until you see this woman melt down."

"Why would you tell her first? Why not just go and do it? That was your mistake, dumbass."

"Yeah, I know that now. But at the time, when she was going to pieces in my office, looking like a zoo animal in desperate need of a tranquilizer, I was trying to calm her down with any idea I could come up with. It seemed like a logical idea."

"It is a logical idea . . . to a sane person. But that's where you went wrong, see?"

"Don't be a jackass, Banks."

"Okay, okay. Seriously, though. Call human resources. Tell them to call down to the job site and tell Sean Gibson he's reached his max on overtime for this pay period. At least the problem will be temporarily solved."

I dipped my head, agreeing with him—until my mind hit another roadblock. "It would sound viable coming from HR, but I'd still have to make sure my name stays totally out of the exchange."

"Easy solution to that. I can make the call. I'll tell them I was reviewing payroll, and we're over budget. They won't question me—not that they'd question you either, but if you don't want to risk having your name attached to the bulletin, then I'll handle it. You won't be anywhere near the whole matter."

I nodded with steadier intent. "It's a solid idea."

"Of course it is. It's mine."

"Now I don't know whether to hit you or hug you."

He grimaced. "How about neither?"

I chuckled. "Fair enough. But seriously, I think this could totally work."

"Of course it will," Elijah assured.

I still didn't hit him. Or hug him. But I did raise my bottle and extend the neck, bestowing a wide grin on my friend when he knocked his bottle against it. "I really owe you one, man."

"Dude." He tilted his head back to take a long swig of his beer. "You owe me about a million and one at this point."

CHAPTER FIVE

RIO

"Are you sure you don't need me to stay?" Hannah asked while folding her apron into a perfect square. "I don't mind."

"I'm absolutely positive. That's the fifth time you've offered, and this is the fifth time I'm saying you've already been so much help. Go on home and enjoy the rest of the day. It's beautiful outside! When I took out the trash, I couldn't believe how warm it was. Not bad for February."

"And people across the country wonder why we're willing to put up with earthquakes," she laughed out.

I motioned toward the back door, which was open wide to the breathtakingly sunny day. "Exhibit A, ladies and gentlemen."

"Preach on, sister. Preach on."

I raised my hands above my head and gave my hips a little shimmy. After Hannah whooped and clapped, I ordered, "Now get the hell out of here, or I'll hand you a mop."

Her big, apologetic eyes searched mine. "I said I would stay..."

"Go!" I pointed sternly toward the exit. A necessary move. She'd stay if I didn't. Hannah was one of the kindest people I'd ever met. Abbi and I had already vowed to find the girl a suitable man as soon as I had my own personal life squared away and little Kaisan made his debut. How Hannah Farsey was unattached was one of life's biggest mysteries.

After she left, I let out a contented sigh. The day was beautiful, and life was good. Things were even looking up at home. The day after I had my bout of crazy in Grant's office, Sean had gotten a call from the Shark Enterprises human resources department. He was way over the limit on overtime hours—imagine that—and had to start leaving work at the designated quitting time each day.

Without focusing on the impetus and more on the result, we were now enjoying dinner together every night, followed by television, reading, household projects, or running local errands. For me, it didn't really matter what we did. We were able to spend time together again, and it was absolute heaven.

I started washing the lunch menu marinara dishes, normally one of the shit shifts of our kitchen, but today I was grinning like a total dork through the whole task, recalling the conversation from last night that my husband had initiated. He had come into the kitchen with a stack of mail in his calloused hand and a goofy grin plastered on his face . . .

"I think you're going to be very happy to see what came in the mail, Mrs. Gibson."

One look at his beautiful smirk, worthy of a kid on Christmas morning who'd just unwrapped a deluxe erector set, and I knew he couldn't have been that excited about the lower gas rates headed our way.

"What's going on?" I asked, wiping my hands on the dishtowel slung over my shoulder.

He separated one envelope from the rest of the stack and held it between us. "Do you know what this is?"

"You have a gazillionaire uncle I don't know about, and that's your inheritance?"

Sean cracked such a wide grin, the top of his suntanned cheeks crinkled. "Hmmm. Fun idea, but no . . . "

I took advantage of his momentary distraction and snatched the envelope from his grip, giggling at my own mischief—until my gaze fell on the logo occupying the top left corner of the thing.

"Holy crap," I squealed. "Are these our new insurance cards? Already?"

His radiant smile was all the assurance I needed. I threw my entire body into him, nearly knocking him to the ground with my exuberant celebration. He dipped his head and kissed my ear before whispering the best words in the world into it.

"We can finally start the fertility treatments, baby."

I kissed him back before rasping, "My hero."

And he truly was. After that, he'd become so much more. He'd turned into my favorite caveman, throwing me over his shoulder and hauling me off to our bedroom. We'd spent the rest of the night practicing—as he'd taken to calling it—for when the drugs were entirely on board and we would need to be fucking like rabbits. I'd assured him I didn't foresee a problem, that his skills were in peak form, but he insisted that a job worth doing was a job worth doing right, and who was I to argue?

I continued milling around the Inglewood prep kitchen, getting as many of the day's chores done as possible. Abbi and I had agreed to hire a cleaning company to do the quarterly deep cleaning, but I knew we could save some money if I pitched in. Plus, I found scrubbing and mopping therapeutic.

With some music blasting in the background, I set to work on the stovetop. The work surface was the spot that took the biggest beating every day. If this appliance could talk, it would tell quite a story. It had seen our little business grow over the past several years into the thriving partnership it was today. Those burners knew all the arguments we'd had and heard all the silly stories we'd laughed about. It had listened to all the quiet secrets we'd whispered when we were alone here in the early morning hours.

My phone, vibrating on the stainless-steel worktop, shook me from my musings. I jumped a little but smiled when I saw Grant's name on the display. It had been days since I'd heard from him, and I'd vowed not to be the one to message first. I needed to prove to myself I could go without contacting him. But I couldn't deny how happy I was to see his text message.

I'd been missing my friend. It was really just that simple.

Hey. Where are you? The kitchen?

Yep. Why? What's up?

Stay there. I'm on my way.
We need to talk.

Uhhh … OK … you good?

Be there in ten or less.

The messages were odd and cryptic, even for Grant Twombley. No—especially for Grant Twombley. Normally, his straight-shooter mien was one of his best features.

I dumped the dirty water from the mop bucket, rinsed out the sink, and put the cleaning supplies away to stay busy while I waited for Grant to arrive. I scooted into the small bathroom and finger-combed the hair that peeked out from the bandana I had tied around most of my head, "Rosie the Riveter" style.

A quick whiff of my pits confirmed my deodorant was still holding up after all the manual labor.

It was just a few minutes later when I heard the handle on the side door jiggle. I realized it was still locked from when Hannah had ensured I was safely inside when she departed. I rushed over. "Who is it?"

Grant's distinctive baritone vibrated through the barrier. "It's me, Blaze. Open up."

Was that a cracking croak that actually entered his voice? But I didn't waste time to process that analysis.

"Whoa . . . hey," I said quietly as he stepped inside, walking past me a few feet before he turned back to look at me. His healthy glowing smile was gone. In its place, his ghost-white and tear-streaked cheeks and jaw ticked with anxiety.

"Grant?" I choked with concern. "What's wrong?"

I would bet my entire paycheck, and my husband's too, that I had never seen the man look so somber in the whole time I'd known him.

"Rio. Let's sit down for a minute. We need to talk."

I followed him like a puppy, panic chilling my blood. "You're freaking me out," I said, quickening my steps to keep up with his long stride. "Grant." I repeated his name again, but he was on a mission. He was going to sit down, and I was going to join him apparently.

"What's going on?" My voice pitched higher at the end of the question.

"Sit down, Blaze." He pulled out the chair at my desk and waited for me to sit before he took the chair by Abbi's. He rolled right up to mine, nearly knocking his knees into mine. When he reached for my hands, I willingly . . . trustingly . . . placed mine in his.

Grant wrapped his long, warm fingers around my entire hands. He was so much bigger than I was, and I realized he had never touched me this way. Never just freely taken the liberty to show me open affection.

"Tell me what's going on. Please," I begged, finally pulling my stare from our joined hands to his face and then almost wishing I hadn't. The emotion I saw there was so raw, so agonized, I knew that whatever he was about to say was going to hurt us both deeply. So deeply, we would forever be changed. Elementally scarred and damaged. Possibly never be whole again.

"Fuck." He let his chin drop to his chest and rested there for a moment. Finally, when he lifted his face again, a tear ran from the corner of his eye and tracked down his cheek. "Fuck, this is harder than I ever imagined," he rasped and then wiped the drop away with the back of his fist.

"Do you not want to be my friend anymore? Is that what this is about?" It sprang out of me so naturally, welling from a lifetime of insecurity. I was battling my own tears then. They were threatening to break loose and tumble down my cheeks, but I had years of practice at holding them back. I was an expert at not showing weakness.

So, I gulped.

Once. Then again.

"Just tell me, Grant. Get it out. Get it over with."

I tried to pull my hands from his, but he gripped them tighter.

"No. No, baby. That's not it. I will be here for you." He shook his head and then whispered, "Always."

I was even more confused. *Baby?* He never said things like that to me. He called me Blaze. That was the furthest he'd strayed from Rio. Ever.

He sucked in a huge gulp of air, steeling himself to finally say what he needed to. The man sat up taller and straightened his spine, appearing stronger by doing so.

"Look at me, Rio." His voice was back to the velvet command I was used to. Seconds passed while he waited for me to meet his dark-blue gaze. When I finally did, he said with quiet clarity, "There's been an accident. A terrible accident."

"What? Where?" I shot to my feet. "What do you mean? Who's been hurt? Is it . . . Abbi?" Oh, God. If it was Abbi . . . But why else would Grant be here to tell me this news personally? "Is it Abbigail? Oh no, oh God, no. The baby? Are they okay?" I started grabbing things off my desk . . .

"My keys. Where are my damn keys?" I muttered, searching frantically through the papers beside the computer.

"Rio, stop. Stop." His voice was firm. Tone assertive. "It wasn't Abbigail. She and the baby are fine."

But why was he still sitting there as if an emergency wasn't underway?

"What? Who? Who, then?" I continued to plead. "Tell me, Grant! Fuck! Tell me!"

"Please. Sit down." He waited for a beat before repeating the request. "Please sit down. So I can tell you what happened."

"Grant!" I yelled his name then, my shrill voice bouncing off the stainless counters and the pots and pans that hung overhead. "Fucking tell me what's going on!" Madness crept up my spine and neck, stretching its boney fingers around to the front of my throat and pressing in so that I couldn't breathe.

When I finally looked at his face—I mean really looked at his face—I knew. I already knew. The pity in his magical eyes and the way he held my hands. The gentle tone he had taken while talking to me.

I shook my head.

Harder. Harder still.

"No. No. You're lying! Liar!" I swung my head so frantically from side to side, the whole room started to sway, and still, I kept denying what he was trying to tell me, even though he hadn't said a word. "No. No, I don't believe you. How could you be so cruel? This isn't funny, Grant Twombley!" I insisted. "Please, no," I whispered as I watched him stand and approach me cautiously.

"Rio." He held his arms open to me, and I batted at them.

"No. No! Get out! You get out of here! I'll call him right now, and you'll see! There's been a mistake! There's been a terrible mistake." I tried to make a beeline for my phone.

Shit! Where the hell is my phone?

"I'll call him. You'll see. But he may not answer. Sometimes, if he's busy, he can't answer right away," I babbled on with excuses, and Grant continued staring with that fucking look of pity that I wanted to shove down his throat. So I just kept insisting, "He's very busy. Sean's very busy now. But he'll call back as soon as he has a break when he's not busy. Where's my phone? I just had it before." I looked frantically from side to side, not really seeing anything at all. I had it right before Grant arrived because he had sent me the text that started all this nonsense.

As if being jolted with electricity, I raced toward the stove. Or tried to . . .

Grant snaked out a strong arm as I darted past and wrapped himself around me, even though I tried to push him away. He held me to his chest, and still, I tried to push him away. "No! Let me go!"

"Rio. Stop this. Listen to me so I can tell you what

happened. I can take you down to the hospital if you'd like."

I froze. Something about those words caught my attention. I pulled back to look at him before asking, "Why?"

Grant took in a suffering breath and let it out with an equally painful sigh. "Rio—"

"Answer me. Why would you take me to the hospital?" Suddenly, everything was so confusing. "Grant? Who's at the hospital? Is it Abbi? Is she in labor?"

He closed his eyes for a few long seconds and just breathed. "There are things..." He cast his eyes toward the ground, struggling to find the words he wanted to say, his strong arms still belted around my waist, holding me against him. His light-brown eyelashes, resting on the sharp blades of his cheekbones, were stuck together from the tears he had shed earlier.

"Grant?" I worked an arm free from his embrace so I could reach up and touch his face. "Say what you need to say. It's okay. I'm okay."

His voice broke when he gently said, "As Sean's next of kin...his wife...you'll need to handle some things. I'll stay with you if you'd like some help or just some company. Come on. Grab your stuff. I'll drive. I don't want you behind the wheel."

"Okay." I could barely utter anything else, and the anxiety from the last few minutes ebbed away. I watched Grant scurry around the kitchen, checking the major appliances to ensure nothing was left on. He flipped the overhead lights off and turned on the one light we used to deter theft. He knew the kitchen's shutdown routine from the month he'd watched over me.

"Tell me the code for the security system, Blaze." He

nudged me out to the front stoop while he stood inside the door and waited to punch in the code.

"Zero five one nine." My voice sounded like an automaton as I recited the digits that Abbi and I agreed to. Something we knew we could both remember.

Sean's birthday.

My husband. Her brother.

"Abbigail." I searched the doorway for Grant, but he hadn't come out yet. When he appeared, all I could manage was to repeat her name. "Abbigail." Tears threatened to obliterate my vision.

"Sebastian's on his way home to talk to her. Come on, baby. It's going to be okay. Give me your keys. I'll drive." He held me against his body once we stepped out of the protection of the building's vestibule until we got to my car, shielding me from the fierce late-afternoon wind that liked to whip through the industrial park.

I looked at him, confused. "You don't have a car."

As if he were talking to a child, he explained very carefully, "We're going to take yours. I'm going to drive your car, Rio. Give me the keys." He reached over the roof of my Fiat with his palm open, waiting for me to hand over the keys.

"You don't need them. Just get in, and it will work with the key in my bag." The automatic doors opened on the passenger side first, since I had the key fob, and I unlocked his door from there while continuing to babble. My mind was all over the place, and trying to organize a useful thought wouldn't be happening. "It's like magic. I don't know how it works. Not really. Maybe it's like Bluetooth or something? Do you know?"

I looked over to Grant because he hadn't said a word in response, but then I saw why. At six and a half feet, the man had to bend his frame at the strangest angle to fit into the car with the seat adjusted for me. He was frantically reaching alongside the chair to find the control to reposition himself. When he could sit upright completely and inhale a full breath, he engaged his seat belt and adjusted the mirrors.

"Can you drive a manual transmission?" I asked. "I'm fine to drive. I really should be staying here, though. I wasn't finished with the cleaning, and I don't want to sit at home alone all night. Who knows how late Sean will be working." I stared out the window, noticing how many cars were still in the lot at the business park, and then checked my watch to see it was only four in the afternoon. When I realized we hadn't moved from the parking spot, I looked over at Grant, only to find him staring back at me.

"What?" I asked.

"Rio." Grant sighed. "Did you understand what I said? In there?" He pointed back to the kitchen, concern twisting his ordinarily handsome face.

I thought for a long moment and then pressed a palm to either side of my head. "Yeah. Sorry," I said softly. "My brain is so scattered. This can't be happening." I began rocking back and forth in the passenger seat as we pulled out of the parking lot. "This can't be real. This can't be real. This can't be real." My voice trailed off, repeating the words over and over in hopes that if I said it enough times, I could will the nightmare out of existence.

When we pulled up in front of Cedars-Sinai Medical Center, I knew, once again, my wishing powers had failed me.

"Grant!" I looked over to him as panic gripped me all over again. "Please! Please call this off now. You've made whatever point you're trying to make. Joke's over. It's not funny anymore.

Stop this right now! I'm not going to be paraded in there and made an ass of in front of God knows how many people." I lowered my voice, begging with all I had, "Please. Please just take me home."

"Blaze." He tilted his head, that damn pity darkening his face again. "Do you really think I would do something like that to you?"

He searched for my hand, but I yanked it from his reach. In a desperate need for fresh air and space between us, I threw my door open and bolted from the car, hightailing it across the parking lot toward the hospital. I didn't even know where I was going or what I was looking for at that point. I just couldn't be in a confined space with Grant Twombley for one more second.

"Rio!" he shouted from about fifty yards behind me. "Lock your fucking car."

I still had the key fob in my bag, which was slung diagonally across my body. I wasn't about to double back and have him trap me again, though. I'd have to risk the safety of my car and its contents over my own.

"Just press the button on the door!" I shouted over my shoulder, not slowing my stride. If he went back to do his usual Boy Scout do-gooder bit, there would be that much more of a gap between us.

Excellent.

While pausing for the automatic doors of the hospital's lobby to *whoosh* open, I heard feet pounding on the sidewalk behind me. But I barreled through the doors as soon as they were open and strode up to the grandly polished-wood information desk. Orange oil and carnauba wax scents hit me first, followed quickly by the overpowering sweetness of the stargazer lily arrangement waiting to be taken to a patient's room.

"Rio." Grant said my name firmly, sounding a little frustrated and a lot out of breath. "They wanted us to come in through the Emergency Room."

When I turned to look at him, he actually looked a little pissed, too.

"And how was I supposed to know that?" I griped.

"If you had waited instead of running off in a huff ... "

"Don't start with me, Tree," I growled. "Not now, okay?"

"Come on. I think we can just go through here. The signs point in that direction." Grant signaled with his outstretched arm, but I ignored him. Instead, I walked up to the clean-cut volunteer who'd been listening to our exchange.

"Hi." I smiled brightly. "Can you point me in the direction of the Emergency Department, please?"

"Your friend has a good head on his shoulders. It's that way. Just follow the red signs overhead. Through that set of double doors and across the courtyard. You can't miss the ambulances lined up out front." The man actually winked in Grant's direction before meeting my fuming gape.

"Thanks," I said, much less cordially.

We checked in at the desk in the Emergency Department and were promptly ushered into an all-purpose waiting room. About a dozen inconsistent chairs lined the perimeter, leaving the center of the room wide open. Two mystery stains claimed portions of the carpet at the opposite end of the room, repeatedly drawing my eye in that direction. I became preoccupied with solving their origin and wondering if the rug would ever be restored to its low pile/no pile glory.

When the stains lost my interest, I got to my feet. Nervous energy propelled me around the room to examine the low-budget mismatched artwork that adorned the walls.

Undersized and sun-damaged, two of the motivational prints had come loose from their mass-produced nondescript mattings and hung precariously beneath the plexiglass.

This wasn't a waiting room. It was an office decor graveyard. A lonely place where neglected, discarded furniture and wall hangings went to die. All that was missing was a dead ficus tree dropping leaves in the corner. An empty water cooler would really set the mood.

The door opened. I jumped, shaken from my dark humor, and instantly felt guilty about it. People were lying in beds all around me. Some were very sick and probably lonely. Some were even dying, right in this very building.

Wait. Why am I even here?

"Let's have a seat, shall we?" the shorter man said, pushing the surgical cap back, revealing a balding head.

A goofy grin spread across my face. The thought of mentally describing the man as "shorter" amused me. Next to Grant, wouldn't everyone be described as shorter?

Speak of the devil.

My friend took my hand and squeezed it a little harder than he usually did. He kept his eyes pinned on the doctor. I followed Grant's lead and gave the man my undivided attention. We could discuss this new hand-holding habit when we were in private and wouldn't cause a scene.

"Hello, Doctor. I'm Grant Twombley, and this is Rio Gibson." Grant let go of my hand to shake the doctor's after offering his name with complete authority. He even introduced himself like he belonged in the room, as though he were totally in control of the situation. "Rio is Sean Gibson's wife."

I offered a limp handshake when my turn came, feeling like a shell of my usual self. I still couldn't piece together why we were even here.

"Nice to meet you. I'm Dr. Swift. Mrs. Gibson, my deepest sympathy. The trauma team and I did everything we could for your husband when he arrived this afternoon. I'm not sure what you've been told so far?"

The man volleyed his gaze back and forth between Grant and me. When both of us just stared blankly, he continued with what seemed like a well-rehearsed speech.

"Unfortunately, after the injuries he sustained at the construction site where the incident occurred, there were no signs of life when he arrived here." He flipped to the second page in the file on his lap, then looked up to us again. "We attempted advanced life support for several minutes, but there were no positive results. The paramedics held off on the pronunciation en route, but shortly after arrival in the Emergency Department, your husband's life was determined to have ended." He scanned the chart in his hand a second time. "At three seventeen this afternoon." Dr. Swift looked up from the chart and added, "Again, my deepest condolences."

I stared at the man.

Deepest condolences? Three seventeen?

I shot a look at Grant, but his expression hadn't changed. "What is he saying?" I asked and then shot to my feet. "What are you saying?" The volume of my voice rose, along with a *whooshing* sound in my ears. "Three seventeen? What happened at three seventeen?"

I swiveled my hips to look back to Grant again but kept my feet planted firmly in place. The odd movement nearly caused me to topple over, so I twisted my body back toward the doctor. No one moved except me, and I had to look like I was doing some odd version of the Hokey Pokey.

And still no one else moved . . . did not dare breathe. They looked . . . concerned.

"Mrs. Gibson," the doctor said gently, "please, calm down. Why don't you sit down? I can have one of our grief counselors come in and speak to you. We have excellent resources here at the hosp—"

I ripped the chart from his hands. Slammed the thing down to the table and frantically flipped through the pages, one after the other, not able to focus on words. Was he making it all up? Full-scale panic clutched my throat, making it impossible to breathe.

"Three seventeen. Three seventeen. Three seventeen. Three seven—"

Strong hands seized me by the shoulders and shook me slightly.

"Rio! Look at me. Look at me now!" Grant nearly shouted.

I could hear him, but I couldn't make my body comply. I had to find the time. There was no way my husband was—

No. Possible. Way.

"Does she have underlying psychological issues? Do you know?" I thought I heard the doctor asking Grant.

"I'm not sure. Maybe? I don't know. I've never seen her check out this badly. Normally she comes right back." My friend gave the answer in a hushed voice, sounding a million miles away instead of the two feet he actually was.

I'm standing right here, motherfuckers.

And my husband is dead.

Dead? No. No. This can't be happening. This can't be . . .

I couldn't breathe. I had to go. I had to leave. Now.

I threw the chart at the doctor, hitting him in the middle of the chest, causing the papers to flutter to the ground like a two-dimensional snowstorm. Then I bolted for the door, making sure to topple two of the miserable chairs behind me to deter

Grant from closing in on me too quickly.

I ran. I ran as fast as my shaky legs would carry me—toward the door we came in—but barreled right into the one and only Sebastian Shark on the way. I reared back and glared when I realized who was gripping my arms to steady me.

"You!" I seethed and then spit in his face. "I hate you!" I screamed the words as loud as my voice could manage and wrenched from his grip. Air sawed in and out of my burning lungs while my chest heaved up and down. "You . . . you greedy, selfish bastard! I hate you!"

Calmly, Sebastian wiped his face with a handkerchief he'd conveniently pulled from his breast pocket. Of course he did. Because everything always came up roses for this guy. He was Sebastian fucking Shark.

"Rio!" Grant yelled my name from the corridor behind us, and whatever few sets of eyes weren't already watching now focused on seeing the scene unfold. Camera phones were being pulled out of bags as quickly as they could be found by searching hands alone. No one dared to take their eyes off the action.

"Hold on to her, Bas. She's freaking out!" Grant shouted, jogging toward us.

Sebastian eyed me cautiously, really considering his next move. "You don't say," he said dryly to his best friend.

"Don't. Touch. Me," I growled. "And if you want to keep your balls intact, step out of my way."

Wisely, the man held his hands up in surrender and stepped to the side, clearing my path to the front door. I didn't stop running until I reached my car and was behind the wheel, frantically readjusting the seat so I could reach the gas pedal and clutch.

In my rearview mirror, as I took a sharp turn out of the lot—nearly on two wheels—I saw Grant standing there, hands grabbing fitfully at his hair, his blue eyes filled with storms of torment and fear.

And maybe rightfully so. Things were about to get messy.

Hot and messy.

CHAPTER SIX

GRANT

From the moment her little car had disappeared from sight, I'd felt like a hysterical parent who'd lost their child in a crowded shopping mall. Panicked thoughts ping-ponged in my brain about her safety. Nervous fear extinguished sparks of hope each time my cell phone rang or vibrated with an incoming message, only to see or hear a memo from a concerned friend instead of Rio.

Calls to her phone went straight to her voicemail. The thing wasn't even ringing at that point. Now, just her pixie-bright voice delivered the ridiculous greeting I always teased her about. My heart ached when I thought of the difference between her anguished voice from earlier this afternoon and the melodic one I heard when I dialed her number.

I stabbed the End Call button and tossed my phone onto the brand-new downtown condo's kitchen counter. It was the only address I could recall when sliding into the back of the Uber at Cedars, and I'd been pacing laps around the modern kitchen ever since.

When my phone vibrated, I answered it without looking at the screen. "Rio?"

"Hey there. No, it's Abbi," Sebastian's woman said from the other end of the call. "You . . . you still haven't heard from her?"

"No." I sighed. "I'm guessing you haven't either, then?"

She cut into the call with a sharp, painful sob. "Grant, you need to find her!"

"I know." I stabbed a hand through my hair—for the hundredth time in the last couple of hours. "Goddammit, I know."

"She really shouldn't be alone, and Sebastian won't let me go out to look for her."

"He's right," I said. "You need to take care of yourself and the baby. We don't need a second tragedy tonight. I've just been trying to come up with a plan. Places to go look so I'm not backtracking my steps when I do head out. Do you have any ideas about where she might go?"

"I don't know." Her voice swelled with despair. "Maybe the kitchen in Inglewood?"

"I'm going to start there. That's where we were when I told her about the accident this afternoon. As we left, she was rambling about needing to finish cleaning, so it's the first place I thought of too." Another drag of my hand through my hair later, I prompted, "What else? What about places that were special to Sean and her? Where they met, maybe? Where he proposed? I don't know. I feel like I'm grasping at straws . . . "

"No . . . no!" she protested. "Those are good ideas! I'll text you a few addresses of those places and if I think of any other special spots."

The woman's voice crumbled at the end of her sentence. My chest squeezed and my heart ached. Though I knew Bas was probably nearby, I felt bonded to Abbigail right now in a way he might not understand. It was strange but reassuring to be talking to someone who cared as deeply about Rio as I did.

"We'll find her, Abs," I declared. "I promise."

She sniffed. "I believe you, Grant. I do."

"Maybe she will just head home. Is anyone watching her house?"

"Wait. You're not there?" A surprised tone usurped her grief.

"No. Why would I be there?"

"I don't know. I . . . I just assumed you would be. I have no idea why, though. I mean, why would you be there?"

There was a long, extremely awkward pause as we both digested what had just been said. How many other people just assumed, or just knew, how close Rio and I had become?

"I need to go lie down," she said, suddenly sounding very tired. "I'll text you those addresses."

"Thank you, Abbigail. I'll do my best to find her."

"I know you will, Grant. Thank you."

As we disconnected, I expected my gut to unwind by at least a fraction. When it didn't, I grimaced. Shit. Maybe I needed to take a giant step back and check myself here. What the hell was I doing, running around after a newly dead man's widow like I had every right to be doing so?

I could tell myself, along with everyone else, that I was just worried about my friend, a woman I'd grown fond of over the past several months. I could validate it further with the excuse that we'd worked together and that I'd helped keep her safe—as part of a job and nothing more.

And if I could keep selling that load of horseshit to everyone, I could probably unload that rusty heap of metal spanning the East River from Manhattan to Brooklyn.

Thank God I bought this place furnished, so I at least had a place to flop down while I waited for my car to arrive—and berate myself some more. As I sank into the plush sofa and stared out across the city lights of Los Angeles, the horrible details of this afternoon's accident played over and over in my mind. I almost wished Elijah had never filled me in on exactly what had transpired at the Edge's construction site . . . the tragic mishap that had claimed Sean Gibson's life. But I knew that once Rio settled down, she'd insist on knowing the specifics for herself.

I just prayed I wasn't the one she turned to for the explanation.

But if she did, I wouldn't refuse her.

I was incapable of telling that woman no, no matter what she asked me for. Those big, whiskey-colored eyes. The long, sable lashes that outlined them more expertly than any cosmetics brand could dream of. Mother Nature had gifted the woman with the most unique, stunning beauty.

But her genetics had also played a bizarre joke on her.

That gorgeousness danced with a brilliant and bright but confounding and curiously confused mind. A brain that worked like no one else I'd ever met. The woman could enchant me in one moment and enrage me in the next. There was never a boring moment around her.

God help me.

Because her whole package called to me like no other woman had ever done before, and even now—God strike me where I sat, even this soon after her husband's tragic death, I couldn't stop thinking about her.

And my thoughts weren't completely pure ones.

But the guilt that was mounting because of those thoughts was starting to overwhelm and unsettle me.

Did the universe really punish people for wanting things they shouldn't? Was this accident some sort of cosmic retribution for my misguided attempt at "friendship" with Rio—the woman I secretly desired? Had I brought on this whole mess with my impure thoughts and fantasies?

I'd never been a religious or spiritual man, and even allowing such ridiculous ideas to run around in my mind seemed like maybe I was the one who was losing it. Or perhaps she was rubbing off on me a little. That thought made me chuckle out loud into the stillness of my empty home, reminding me I needed to get up off my ass and get out into the city's nighttime streets and search for the woman like I'd promised her loved ones I would do.

Because no matter what fate's reason was for all this upheaval, one fact blared as a surety here.

Things were going to get worse before they got better.

I knew that woman. As warped of a playground as Rio's mind was, I had a relatively easy time following the path that wove through it. She already blamed Sebastian for Sean's death and would continue doing so. Subsequently, a giant chasm would form between her and Abbigail. That would lead to her being all alone in the upcoming weeks. Rio's anger with the Sharks would affect my relationship with them, as well. But I wasn't willing to give up either party, so I'd be caught right in the middle of their feud.

Great.

But my dread brought forth a new epiphany—and then sparked a new plan. As soon as the car pulled up in front of my building, I directed the driver deeper into downtown, toward the financial district. I was hoping my theory was a long shot, but while I was this close, I needed to check it out.

There was a side to Rio Gibson that had a flair for the dramatic. It lent fire to her humor and dazzling flair to her culinary creations, but it also made her an impossible whirlwind to be around at times. Right now, it was the nexus of the clue I followed. It would be just like her to zero in on the scene where her husband was killed. She'd want to open the proverbial wound at its most visceral level—to emotionally bleed where he had bled. Let her heart break where his heart had stopped beating.

From the information Elijah had shared with me earlier about the accident, I had a general idea where on the job site the incident had occurred. The entire property was usually lit up like an international airport twenty-four hours a day, but with a death happening on the scene, OSHA had shut down all activity until they could thoroughly investigate. Security lighting was still in place, but it was much dimmer than what I had seen when making other nighttime visits. Trying to stay on the well-worn walkways, I made my way to the taped-off place Elijah described. Sure enough, as I approached, I could hear her.

She was on the ground, sitting back on her heels, looking like a little girl instead of a grown woman. She was wearing the same clothes as when I found her at the kitchen this afternoon—an old T-shirt with some band logo I didn't recognize and a pair of jeans—but now the knees were torn out of the denim, and muddy patches stained her ass and hip.

Protective fire rose within me at the thought that she'd probably fallen at some point. I instantly wanted to rush over to her, but I stayed in the shadows and simply watched, trying to give her some privacy. But no way in hell was I leaving altogether. I'd keep her safe, whether she liked it or not. The promise was ingrained in my soul and would never change.

Her face was dirty too. I moved closer, trying to make out

what she was saying in a low and sultry tone. When I got closer, I realized her voice was rough from crying. Probably yelling, too. Tear streaks had dried tracks into the dust on her cheeks. The bandana she had in her hair earlier was bunched in her fist. Her hair stuck out in twenty-two different directions, as if she'd been pulling on it in frustration. I knew that move really well by now.

"I'm going to fix this. I'm going to fix it all for you," she muttered. "This won't happen again, I promise you." She kept busy while she talked, but I couldn't make out what she was doing. "That bastard's greed . . . his controlling bullshit . . . it all stops tonight. I'm going to make sure no one else pays the price you did. No, I know. I know. But I won't get caught. There's no one here. I made sure of it."

With that promise, a sly grin spread across her lips. She sat back again, seeming to admire whatever was in front of her.

Moving under the protective covering of one of the overhanging beams, I was able to get in a little closer. The steel skeletal structure of the building was almost complete, and the ground floors' support posts were wider than my entire body. I stepped behind the next one to my right, bringing me that much closer to where she knelt.

I could likely move over by one more pillar, but that one had a large fire extinguisher mounted to the girder, so I wouldn't have the same protection. But even from this position, I had a clear view of what she was working on.

She had dug a shallow pit in the dirt—and judging by the filth that coated her fingers and palms, she'd used her own hands to do so. There was a lot of loosened dirt, gravel, and pebbles next to her earthen bowl. In the pit, she was piling construction debris. Stakes, paper, fistfuls of dried grass, and weeds that sprouted up along the orange safety fencing were also in the pit.

Jesus. Christ.

No.

The next fifteen seconds were like every bad thriller or action movie sequence I'd ever watched on cable television—slow-motion special effects and all.

Rio pulled a box of wooden kitchen matches from her bag. With fluid efficiency, she struck the two-inch stick along the side of the box. With anticipation that took visible hold of her posture, she held the mini-torch close to her face and watched the flame dance in the light breeze.

I sprang into motion.

I didn't even consider the reaction I'd instigate from her.

Which, of course, was the first thing I should've done.

"Don't do it!" I shouted as I lunged and tried to bat the flame from her fingers. But my little Blaze was too goddamned quick. Without hesitating, she tossed the match onto her carefully built pile. In seconds, the small nest lit up like a dried-out Charlie Brown Christmas tree. Within seconds after that, I knew why. While wrapping my arms around her and yanking her back, I caught a potent whiff of accelerant—gasoline, probably.

Shit, shit, shit.

No, no, no.

"Fuck! Rio! What are you doing?"

She looked up at me—no, she looked through me—before scrambling upright and then focusing back to the makeshift fire pit and grinning.

Fucking grinned.

"It's done now," she whispered.

"It's not done, damn it! Help me put this out!" I lurched up and kicked dirt over the fire. But she'd apparently spilled gas across the surrounding ground, too, because my actions made the flames shoot higher.

I spun back around as Rio stood too. I was prepared to grab her again, but she was as still as a statue in a church fire. The only thing not eerily frozen about her mien was her face, twisting tighter and tighter with utter confusion.

"Grant?" Her query was soft and stammering. She peered around with more wonder until the growing fire distracted her again. She halted in place, openly appreciating the blaze.

"Fuck," I growled. "Fuck, fuck—" But then I dropped my hands out of my hair. "Hold up. The fire extinguishers!"

I raced back into the empty building and yanked the nearest canister from its mount. On my way back to Rio and the fire, I yanked the pin from the handle and pulled the nozzle free. "Get back!" I bellowed while aiming the foam at the base of the fire. Rio didn't move. She shot me a defiant glare before stepping around to position her body in the direct path of the canister stream and the fire itself.

"Rio! What the—"

"No!" she shouted over the dull roar of the growing flames. "Just get out of here, Grant. Stop trying to save the world!" She swiped the tears from her cheeks with angry sweeps of her fists. "Stop trying to save me!"

"This has nothing to do with you! Get out of the way or I'll knock you down, Blaze—so help me God!"

"Seriously?" Planting her little hands on her hips, she looked up at me with a fiercer glower. "I'd like to see you try!"

"Goddammit."

She was forcing my fucking hand. I really didn't want to

physically move her, but the fire was getting bigger while we argued. A few more feet and it would be precariously close to the base of the skyscraper.

"Last warning, girl!"

"Fuck off, Twombley."

"Not a chance, honey." To my shock, and clearly to hers, my snarls suddenly turned into soughs. My fury was now a collection of heartfelt pleas. "I won't let others pay the price for your maniacal show of grief. There are other ways to do this, Rio. Don't you understand that?"

She blinked hard. Stared at me with even more fervent force. "Understand?" she stammered. "Understand...my what?" Her big brown eyes widened, revealing a new slew of emotions. Disbelief? Fury? Fear? Heartbreak? "My...what?"

Her repetition made things clearer. She was enraged. At me. Probably for what I'd just said, but maybe for other reasons. But there was no time for figuring out that morass. Not right now.

I squeezed the trigger of the fire extinguisher and snaked the hose and nozzle right around Rio, hitting the fire wherever I could. I no longer had the luxury of time. With a sob, Rio lunged and grabbed, battling to stop my progress. At the last second, I dodged out of the way. She landed on the ground with a thud, bracing her fall on her palms.

Quickly, I hit the base of the fire again, making good progress at putting out the flames. By the time Rio was back on her feet and rushing me again, most of the fire was out. Because her body weight was no match for mine, I barely swayed as she clung to me. I steeled my jaw, getting in a few more finishing shots to the fire before dropping the red cylinder and wrapping the hysterical woman in my arms instead. I gripped her so tightly, I made her flailing arms immobile.

"Okay. Okay," I crooned. "That's enough now."

I lowered us to the ground and held her in my lap while she wailed. This time, she didn't put up a fight. With a low moan of abject misery, she twined her arms around my neck and held on for dear life.

"I know, baby. Ssshhh. I've got you. Sssshhh. All right." I gently rocked back and forth with Rio in my embrace. I felt just as torn as her. Part of me was trying to calm her hysterics, but part of me thought she needed to really just let it all out. Get it all out of her system so she could grieve and eventually heal.

We sat until the fire completely stopped crackling in the shallow hole and the light wind turned too cold to stand. Rio shivered in my arms, and even the protection of my large frame wasn't enough to keep her warm.

I leaned back and brushed her hair away from her face. My heart broke a little more when I saw the expression there.

Haunted, hollow eyes looked back at me. Lifeless and dull, lost in deep circled pits that made her face look thinner and more frail than just an hour before, when her features were alight with insanity as she watched the flames dance in the fire pit.

"Let's get out of here," I said. "I'll take you home."

She stiffened instantly. "No. No, Grant, please. I can't go back there. Not tonight."

I nodded, understanding at once. The place was filled with too many memories of Sean. "All right. I get it. But first, let me call Abbigail. She's been worried sick. Everyone has been. I can take you to their place in Calabas—"

"No!" She jerked out of my arms. "Not there! I don't want to be anywhere near . . . him," she spat.

Oh, here we go again.

Maybe I shouldn't have mentioned Abbi, but for Christ's sake, the woman was Rio's sister-in-law. Her family. The only family she had in the local area, as far as I knew.

"Fine," I murmured. "So not Calabasas. Where else, then? Do you have any other relatives nearby?"

She got back to her feet but shifted her weight uneasily. "Why can't I stay with you? I won't be in the way. And you love my cooking."

I got to my feet while dusting off my suit pants. When I finally got the courage to meet her gaze, she looked so hopeful—so desperate—that I couldn't say no.

"Fine. You can stay at my place. Do you want to stay local, around here? Or would you rather head back to Naples? Somewhere else? Hollywood Hills? Brentwood? What do you feel like?"

"Grant, I don't care. Please."

"Where is your car? I'm assuming you drove here?"

She thought about it for a moment and then looked at me, her eyes brimming with tears. "I don't know," she croaked, and her voice cracked with emotion. Rio cradled her face in her palms and started crying again, so I pulled her against my body and took out my cell phone. I was going to have to call in some backup.

Elijah picked up after the first ring. "Twombley. Shit, I was hoping it was you."

"Yeah," I replied. "I've got her. But listen, man. I need your help."

"Say the word. Where are you?"

"At the Edge's construction site."

My friend heaved out a tense sigh. "That's what I was

afraid of. How can I help you, though?"

"She was going to burn the place down. I stopped her, but some cleanup needs to happen. Probably a little camera work too, if you know what I mean?"

"Yeah," he muttered. "Yeah, I do."

"Cool."

There were security cameras all over this property. Every move Rio had made, from the moment she stepped onto the job site until the time we'd leave, was likely caught on tape. We would both be charged if the authorities saw the footage—unless Elijah covered our tracks.

"I'm all over it, my brother," he assured me, before adding with his cockiest best, "and yes, you do owe me. Big-time."

"Thanks, man. I think the mess is pretty close to where the accident happened. You won't be able to miss it, though, because I had to discharge a fire extinguisher."

"Oh, fucking joy," he deadpanned.

"Thanks again. I'll touch base with you later."

I stabbed the End Call button and shoved my phone back into my pocket. Rio was watching with wide eyes when I turned to get her attention.

"What?" I asked.

"I'm so sorry, Grant," she said quietly, not able to hold my gaze.

"For what?"

"That you're in the middle of all this."

I wanted to laugh. Long and hard. Couldn't she see? Didn't she know by now that I'd be in the middle, on the top, on the bottom, or anywhere in between if it meant being by her side?

The pledge was so strong in my heart and so hot in my blood, I almost went ahead and spoke it. But then I looked deep into her eyes again and felt every shred of the sorrow and loss that ached in her soul.

"Come on. Let's get out of here."

I held out my arm to tuck her into my body. The night temperature had really dropped, and she shivered against me. I rubbed her shoulders, grateful for the chance to warm her in that small way. To protect her.

I'd always protect her.

Always.

CHAPTER SEVEN

RIO

I spent the next few days being shuffled from one pitying embrace to another. Friends and family did their best to make sure I ate, slept, and took care of myself in the most basic ways. Other than that, they gave me a pretty wide berth to grieve as I saw fit.

Abbigail was doing only marginally better. The rest of the Gibson clan had flown to California from the East Coast and was camped out at Casa Shark. This was the second loss their family had endured, and they gathered together to weep, share, and grieve like a group of mental health professionals. It was all neat and orderly, very much by the textbook standards.

I'd never felt more like an outsider.

After an hour of the group hug-it-out ordeal, my skin felt like I had live bugs crawling under it. I bolted from Abbi and Sebastian's Calabasas home, obsessed with thoughts of starting a fire. As fast as I could, I asked Grant to take me back to his place. Once we were there, I made every excuse I could think of for Grant to leave me alone, but the damn man wouldn't leave my side.

After finding me at the construction site the night of Sean's accident, the bastard was on to me and my unhealthy way of coping with the tough stuff. Although he hadn't brought it up yet, I knew he eventually would. Grant Twombley wasn't the kind of man who left stones unturned, and this was a damn boulder. It sat, big and bulky, in the middle of every conversation we had.

Today, we were on our way to the Central Area Police Station to hear about the official accident investigation findings.

Oh, goodie.

But that wasn't exactly fair. These men were just doing their jobs, and what had happened to my husband—whose name I still couldn't bring myself to vocalize—was truly just an accident. But while all that logic sounded good on paper, it made no sense in the depths of my heart.

When I woke up that morning, I had to fight with myself just to get out of bed. I promised myself I'd have a better attitude when I did. And I was really trying.

"Did that really just say get off on the 101? Why would you choose a route that involves the 101?" I bitched at Grant, who was hunched over in the passenger side of Kendall. He squinted at my phone's screen, shielding the image from the bright sunlight blasting in from the moonroof. "Have you really lived in Los Angeles your entire life?"

He crudely pointed up toward the roof and asked, "Can you close this? I can't see the screen for shit. And listening for the instructions is impossible over this…this…miserable excuse for music."

The man was in a foul mood today—matching where I'd already been for the past few days. Neither of us was sleeping well. I knew part of it had to do with me insisting on sleeping in his bed with him—but I wasn't about to feel sorry for that. I was feeling very alone in the world, and I was scared—evidenced by the awful night terror I'd had on night one. That, of course, triggered Grant's paranoid fear that he'd accidentally come into contact with my body in some way, spurring a fresh episode. I was pretty certain he was petrified of even breathing the wrong way. As a result, we were both exhausted and cranky.

"Linkin Park is an extremely talented band," I protested, but I turned down the volume after hitting the switch to make the roof shade close.

"Uh-huh," he mumbled.

"I think I should go to my own house tonight," I blurted. "I don't think this is healthy for either of us."

"Are you sure?" Grant finally said. "I mean, are you ready to be alone? I don't want you to ... "

"Just say it. Say what you're afraid of, Grant."

"I'm not afraid of anything, Blaze," he retorted quietly.

"Bullshit. You think I'm going to torch something again. Admit it."

"Well ... " He looked out the window, glowering at a wall graffitied with *Be Happy* in bubble letters, and sighed. "The thought crossed my mind."

I tapped my fingers on the wheel in a nervous rhythm while waiting for his next comment. I was sure one was percolating in that busy mind of his.

"So ... how often do you do it?"

"You really want to know?"

"We just never really talked about it. I mean, I saw you that one day in the kitchen, but never again after. I just don't know much about it."

As he spoke, his posture seemed to wilt into the seat—leaving me beyond confused. What was going on here? Did he feel like he'd failed me somehow? Like my hobby was somehow his responsibility?

"Grant," I said calmly. "You can't fix me. I've tried explaining this to you before."

He pushed his hair back off his forehead and clasped his hands on top of his head afterward. "If you won't tell me how often, will you tell me how long you've been doing it? When did you start coping with your problems this way?"

"Wait. Is that what you think I'm doing?" A wide grin spread across my lips. Why did this amuse me so much? Hearing his take on the situation?

"Isn't it?"

"No," I snapped. "I mean, it's not like that. That's not how I see it, at least." I thought about it a little longer. Really considered the thrill from lighting things on fire. The rush I got from it. "Yeah, no. It's not like that. Not at all, actually."

"Then what is it like? I'd really like to understand."

I looked at him for a few seconds, trying to gauge what was really going on here. Was this judgmental crap, or was he really trying to understand the things that went on in my mind? What was his angle?

Luckily, traffic inched forward and I could refocus my attention on the road instead of the uncomfortable elephant in the car with us.

"Don't shut me out. Please," Grant said in a weirdly quiet voice. With the same odd expectancy, he watched me navigate through the streets toward the police station. Once we'd gotten off the freeway, I was familiar enough with the area that I didn't need the assistance from the navigation app.

"I don't want to get into it, Grant—especially right now. This meeting is going to be hard enough."

"Yeah. Okay." He said it like a solemn promise. "I understand. Later."

"Thanks." I glanced over at him quickly, then back to the road so I wouldn't rear-end the car in front of me. "Will Sebastian be here? Do you know?"

"I'm not sure. I haven't talked to him since the day we were at the house with your relatives. It would make sense if he were, though. This shit happened at his building, to his employee."

"Yeah. You're right." I issued it without a shred of joy, grimacing while stretching my neck to see past the building beyond his side of the car. "I think there's parking attached to the station, if I remember correctly." I flipped on my turn signal and waited for a few cars to pass to turn into the garage.

Once we were parked, I held out my hand for my phone, but Grant just stared long and hard at my open palm. "What?" he finally asked.

"I need my phone, please. I need to check the email from the investigator to see where the meeting is. My brain is so foggy right now, I don't remember the floor or room number. Not sure if it's the lack of sleep or what the problem is. But that brings us back to my original comment about going home today. I can take you home when we're done here, but I'm going to grab the stuff I have at your place and then head back to Seal Beach. I can't run away from this shit forever."

"Let's just see how this goes, okay? No hasty decisions. I don't want you to feel like you have to leave. If you're not ready, you can stay with me as long as you'd like." He grinned. "Plus, I've gotten used to your snoring. I think I'd miss it." Wisely, he predicted and dodged my smack the moment the comment was made.

Once inside the station, we checked in with a deputy behind a large bank of windows. From there, we were directed to the room for the meeting. The investigators were already waiting for us, and Sebastian Shark strode in just a few minutes later.

"Gentlemen," he said, shaking everyone's hand as if he were the one who'd called the meeting—until he came to my place in line. After one look at the expression on my face, he stopped short.

"Rio. How are you doing?" The man studied my expression while asking, and at least five different replies flashed through my mind in rapid succession. Before I could organize my thoughts enough to vocalize one of them, he continued. "Abbigail wanted me to tell you that she would really like to see you. Also, to ask you to please come over and see her at the house. She says she misses you."

"Yeah," I rasped. "I miss her too."

"Lastly, she would like to talk to you about helping you plan the service."

The addendum had me narrowing my eyes. His cordial tone, as if he were suggesting Abbi and I plan a crafting night instead of how we'd bury the man to whom I'd promised "till death do us part" grated on my nerves.

This wasn't a fucking social hour. We were here to talk about how and why my husband died. I had barely given anything else a moment's thought, and now Sebastian Shark brought it up like an action item he had to cross off his list?

How dare he.

How dare they all, looking like this was just another day at their damn office!

My head was spinning with questions. With frustrations.

With anger. So much anger.

Just as I pulled in a sharp lungful of air to launch into a tirade, telling Shark where he could stuff his invitations, a firm hand landed on my shoulder. I snapped my glower around as Grant squeezed in and tugged me back. Though I fought to look away, he made it impossible to ignore his presence, pressing his warm, huge body right behind me.

"Hey, Bas," he said, stepping off to my right to give his best friend a brotherly hug-handshake combination.

"Twombley," the bastard murmured back, adding a surreptitious dart of his watchful gaze between me and his best friend.

"Let's sit down, shall we?"

At the officer's suggestion, we all took seats around the long conference room table. The two investigators gravitated toward the end of the table, closest to the room's built-in podium and whiteboard that hung across the front wall. Grant and I sat right in the center, and Sebastian positioned himself across the table from us.

I steeled my shoulders. Pulled in another lengthy breath. Neither action helped my racing pulse.

Is it hot in here? Why am I having such a hard time breathing all of a sudden?

Grant leaned over and whispered, "You okay? You're very pale."

"Fine," I said through gritted teeth. "I'm. Fine."

But I was the furthest thing from that. Grant, seeming to know that with the same certainty I did, rested his long arm on the back of my chair. He rubbed my upper back every few seconds, reminding me that he was still there with me.

I wasn't alone.

"To start the debriefing, there are some legal disclaimers that need to be read and recorded," the officer began. "All in attendance must respond accordingly, also on record. So, when I signal to you, as a group, you say 'I do.' All right?"

We all agreed and then moved forward. The investigator turned on a recording device in the overhead sound system and read from a laminated card. He signaled to us with a hand gesture, and we did our part like the law-abiders we were and agreed for the recording.

He sat down at the head of the table and looked at me first and frowned. "Mrs. Gibson, on behalf of the City of Los Angeles and the entire police department, please let me start by saying how deeply sorry we are for your loss. Especially from the men and women on the force who have had to walk in the shoes you are currently, our hearts are heavy as we wish you peace in your time of grief, and we sincerely hope this investigation can bring you some closure so you can begin to heal."

"Thank you" was all I could manage in response. What other alternative was there, after his kind and seemingly heartfelt message?

"According to eyewitness accounts, security footage from the job site, and forensic evidence collected at the scene, we can piece together the following chain of events. Sean Gibson and the crew he oversaw reported on-site on the morning of February fifth. Routine safety checks had been conducted by the off-going team, and pass-downs were given to the foreman as per standard operating procedures that are set forth by the company policy of Shark Enterprises. Mr. Gibson signed into the operations log as the shift foreman, and the shift commenced. Regular work breaks were given from nine forty-five to ten o'clock that morning, and all personnel were accounted for."

The second investigator stood up and took over with the report recitation. "Normal workday routine from there, really. Two men checked out at lunch and were gone for the rest of the day at doctor's appointments, leaving Mr. Gibson slightly shorthanded. A delivery was made at"—he scanned the report, clearly more open to summarizing than the first officer—"three in the afternoon. Mr. Gibson assisted with the storage of the materials, and while he was directing an equipment operator from the ground via handheld radio, a load of steel beams broke free from the cable tie-downs on the forks of a large-capacity material handler. Footage shows Mr. Gibson was instantly crushed under the weight of one of the free-falling beams."

At once, my whole body clenched as if I'd been punched in the gut. No. As if I'd been crushed under a steel construction beam. My vision swam. I dropped my head and wrapped my arms around my middle, keeping all the bile down only by supreme force of will.

Don't throw up.

"Rio? You okay?"

I nodded. I think.

"You need a second?"

I shook my head with violent force. Why was I being such a frail wimp? This was what I'd come all the way here for, right? To hear all this at last? To know the total truth?

So what the hell had I expected, then?

I guess I hadn't given it much thought. That I would have to sit here and listen to the gruesome details of the accident. Already, I wasn't sure how much more I could bear. Regardless of how brave I was trying to be or which mental trick I employed to detach from the words being spoken, I couldn't come out on top.

The city buildings usually kept the air conditioning running on full blast, but suddenly the room was way too warm. Beneath the table, I ran my sweaty palms along my denim-covered thighs a few times. Not helpful. Not at all. Even though I was way too hot, I was also freezing.

Goose bumps popped up along my exposed forearms. In my peripheral, I caught the sideways shift of Grant's body and the way he narrowed his gaze at my skin. He was dressed in his usual suit and tie and looked quite comfortable, so apparently I was a one-person climate control problem. That knowledge didn't make me feel better, but I tried to refocus on the investigator's droning voice.

"The other workers attempted to free Mr. Gibson to no avail. Paramedics arrived on the scene shortly after. We want to note here the impressive response time of the city's first responders..."

Almost as if I were separated from my own body, I felt myself stiffen at his words. The man literally flowed from one thought to the next with no transition. *Hey, yeah! We know your husband, your reason for existing, is lying there squashed like a beetle—but hot damn, did you see how fast those firemen showed up to do nothing at all to help him?*

"Round of applause for the fucking firemen, y'all!" My outburst was loud and obnoxiously bright. Everyone gaped in my direction as I clapped my hands. I smacked Grant's arm, encouraging him to join me by exaggerating my example of how it was done.

Grant didn't spare a second in speaking up now. "I think we need a minute, gentlemen. Why don't we take a short break?" He sat forward and turned his tall frame toward me, effectively blocking my antics from everyone's view. "Let's get some air in the hall," he offered, every word calm despite the tension defining his jaw. "Move around a little."

"I'm fine," I growled. I didn't need his protection all the damn time. It was high-handed and out of line that he treated me like a child in front of all these men.

But the man wasn't getting that, no matter how hard I glowered or fiercely I fumed. He leaned in closer, ensuring only I could hear him, and said from between clenched teeth, "Please don't fight me on every fucking thing, Rio. I'm trying to help you right now."

I rose to my feet, standing so abruptly my chair teetered on its back two legs before settling back to the floor. My brain bobbed inside my skull with matching energy, trying to find level ground in my mental muck. Just when I was sure I'd wobble all the way back over, Grant flattened a huge hand across my back, steadying me.

"We're going to get some air." He directed his repetition at everyone else in the room this time. "Just give us a few minutes."

"Twombley." Sebastian sighed. "Is this really necessary? I have a mee—"

Grant whirled on him. "I said give us a few minutes, you heartless, arrogant son of a bitch!"

His voice thundered so loudly through the small room, the fluorescent light fixtures in the ceiling shook. I dug my short nails into the material of his suit jacket sleeve and tugged a little.

We were out in the hall before he spoke again. "I'm sorry. I'm so sorry about that." He rubbed the back of his neck, then his temples and forehead. When he finally looked down at me, his blue eyes were lined with stress and full of agony. "I should have told you those details before now."

I stopped our slow-paced walk to turn a confused look up at him. "Why are you apologizing? None of this is your problem, Grant."

"You shouldn't have heard all that"—he thumbed over his shoulder toward the meeting room—"for the first time in a setting like that. It was heartless."

"It doesn't matter," I answered flatly.

"Doesn't matter?" he croaked. "How can you say that?"

"There's no heart left in here." I thumped on the center of my chest and finally looked away. "How don't you get that by now?"

"Don't say that." The emotion in his voice compelled me to focus on his face again, but I couldn't remain that way for long. There were so many feelings vying for dominance of his features, though I couldn't figure out which ones exactly. I wasn't sure I was in any condition to know anyway.

"Truth too much to handle?" I said instead. Bitter and sassy always served me well when the heartstrings were pulled too tightly. At the moment, mine were stretched tighter than a violinist's bow—though the concerto they played was probably some avant-garde thing, since I immediately swung from the heights of anger to the valley of tenderness inside two seconds. The result of that swoop was my soft, trembling murmur. "Thank you for putting Shark in his place. I'm not sure I can be responsible for my actions around him today."

"I figured as much," Grant muttered. "And for what it's worth, I'm sorry about all that ugliness with him too."

"Why?" I folded my arms. "You're not the bastard's keeper."

"Yeah, but I saw the minute things were going south in

there. But that man just doesn't know when to stop sometimes. I'm not sure how much longer to expect this to go," he said with a sigh. "Do you want me to tell them I have to take you home? I think you being here is really just a courtesy. Bas is the one who has to sign the report since he owns the company. Sean was acting as a legal representative of Shark Enterprises at the time of his death. That's why they keep citing the logs and shit."

"Thank you, but no. Let's go back in and finish this up. The sooner it's over, the sooner I can go home."

We took a few steps in the direction of the meeting room, but I stopped again. "Grant?" I put my hand on his forearm. Even that part of him was a strong rope beneath my touch, my personal lifeline at a moment when I needed it the most. I kept my grip there while waiting for him to turn back and give me his full attention. Once he locked his intense sapphire stare down on me, I murmured, "Thank you."

His forehead creased. "For what?"

"For knowing me so well. There are times you know what I need before I do. Or at least before I'm ready to admit what I need." I pulled in a long breath, and this time it felt calming. Cleansing. "You're an excellent friend. This whole mess has made me realize how few of those I actually have."

"You're welcome, Blaze. And thank you ... for letting me be here for you. I consider it an honor. Honestly."

He opened his arms, and I stepped in closer, letting myself cherish the strength of his solid, warm embrace. But just as quickly, I pulled back. "Let's get this over with," I said, pivoting and tugging open the door to the conference room.

Once we were settled back inside and everyone had taken their seats, I cleared my throat, making it evident that I needed to say something. "I'm very sorry for all of that, everyone.

Unfortunately, that was the first time I had heard most of those details, and it affected me adversely, as I'm sure you can imagine." I looked around to each attendee and tried to keep a pleasant smile on my face. "Please, do continue."

One of the officers, a third man who hadn't yet spoken much, pursed his already-thin lips. "Mrs. Gibson, on behalf of the City of Los Angeles, I truly apologize. We were not aware that you were not privy to the incident details. We would've been happy to provide some type of support for you, had we known. If you'd like to postpone this meeting until those arrangements can be made . . . "

"No," I protested, waving my hand. "I'm fine now. I'd really like to just finish up here if you don't mind."

"Of course," he replied. "I understand. We're almost done, actually." The officer scanned the report for a few moments and then began reading again. "Our investigation is limited to only what happened at the construction site itself. Once the paramedics arrived and began assessment, treatment, and transportation, the resultant events were recorded by those respective teams. Meaning, of course, the ambulance company and the hospital."

The officer moved over the document line by line with his index finger until he came to the information he needed.

"Ah, yes. Here it is. I believe Mr. Gibson was transported to Cedars-Sinai Medical Center?"

"Yes." Somehow, even through the chaotic memories bombarding me, I managed to nod. "That's correct."

"I can give you the contact information of the case manager there, if you need that. I realize it's a huge facility, and it can be like finding a needle in a haystack when you are trying to find one particular person."

He finished with a kind smile, but I couldn't force myself to return the gesture this time. My mind was too consumed with a nagging thought. A dogged hunch that swiftly intensified into a possibility—and then into gut-wrenching logic . . .

And before I knew it, I was actually spurting out that troubling theory.

"You know, Officer . . . I was just thinking of something you said that doesn't quite make sense." I tilted my head. "Do you know if the equipment on the job site goes through routine maintenance checks? And, if it does, when was the last time the machine involved in this particular accident had maintenance performed on it? Additionally, who did that inspection and maintenance? Do you keep records of those things?"

Sebastian's sigh was one of annoyance. I wanted to wheel around and call him out for his asshole behavior, but the man himself took care of quashing any interjections I could possibly issue. "Yes, all the machinery, vehicles, and equipment are inspected per OSHA standards. Logs are kept accordingly, as well. Where is this line of questioning going?"

As he shot a glance at Grant, it occurred to me that maybe to him, I was asking dumb questions. But Grant kept his eyes trained on me, lending the fortitude I needed to stand firm and connect the dots.

"What do you think may have happened?" Grant asked me at last.

I felt my cheeks coloring. "Nothing specifically." And wasn't this doing wonders for Sebastian's perception about my comprehension of the whole thing? But Grant's encouragement had bolstered me. I was determined to be heard, even if I looked like an idiot while doing so. "I just didn't hear any of that specific information included in this investigation's report. Why would the tie-downs, or cables, or chains, or whatever, on that machine just snap? That seems pretty unsafe, right? If inspections are done routinely and repairs are made when necessary, I would think accidents would rarely happen. Not accidents like this. Not complete fluke things." I looked around from one man to the next, trying to get a sense if I was on the right train of thought. "Not flukes that have the power to kill a man."

Grant stiffened with quiet steadiness, his demeanor reminding me of a modern John Wayne. "And you don't think that's what this was?" he pressed with matching somberness.

"I'm not saying that, either. I just want to be sure every angle is looked at. My husband is gone, Grant. Dead."

Finally, I raised my head high enough to look him in the eyes, an action I'd been avoiding as much as possible lately. I couldn't stand the pity I'd been seeing in his intense gaze ever since the night he found me at the Edge's construction site.

Since he'd caught me indulging my . . . hobby.

Just the memory of it made my heart ache harder. The pain was nearly intolerable and demanded immediate attention. Was it possible to split in half from misery and emptiness?

With a tight, soft choke, I crossed my hands over the center of my chest, praying no one could see the gaping hole where my heart used to be. But I forged ahead, despite my shaking voice giving me up for the fraud I was. "If I have to live the rest of my life with this emptiness and heartache, I refuse to let it be in vain."

Then, I swung my stare across the table—back toward the individual in the room who'd been all too silent during my exchange with his second-in-command.

Refocusing my attention on Sebastian was an energizer

for my rage. I pointed my index finger at him. "Are you really telling me it hasn't crossed your mind that someone may have done this deliberately? That my husband didn't pay the ultimate price in your stead? Because another one of your enemies came collecting for some shit stunt you pulled?"

Sebastian crossed his arms. "And are you actually listening to yourself right now?"

Throughout my new clash with Sebastian, the police investigators had been very quiet. They'd just listened to me ramble, looking increasingly unnerved. Perhaps they already knew that my point deserved a follow-through. Whether it was Shark Enterprises' faulty equipment or some maniac trying to cause another headache in the press, the preventability of this tragedy was viable. So potentially, this could be a new lawsuit in the making. An ugly legal snag from the family of a deceased employee who also happened to be an extended family member. The mess would tie up progress on Sebastian's precious Edge for months, maybe years.

Holy hell, how I would love to watch that. How satisfying it would be to gloat as the bastard struggled through his courtroom drama. It wouldn't be complete retribution, but it would help. Maybe it would ease a little of the hurt, agitation, and grief that were my new besties.

But I had to consider Abbigail.

And Grant.

I wouldn't—I couldn't—see my sister-in-law suffer alongside him. And damn it, the jackass's best friend had been the one person by my side through every minute of every hour of every day since that girder stole my husband's final breath.

Grant.

And that was just one of the problems with this twice-

baked relationship I had going with the billionaire asshole.
One of so many.

CHAPTER EIGHT

GRANT

Being on the sun-drenched, bohemian-meets-trendy-chic streets of Seal Beach in April was like stepping into a tourism board advertisement. Within one weekend, there was an antique car show, a professional sand volleyball tournament, and a street fair for local artists to show and sell their work.

Then there was the celebration to end all celebrations. Baby Shark's "welcome to the world" shower. Even though I wasn't convinced she was up to the task, Rio insisted on going through with the hostess duties of holding the soiree at the home she'd once shared with Abbigail's brother.

The guest of honor was on scene earlier than expected, using the excuses of unpredictable traffic and wanting to lend a hand with last-minute party preparations. I watched Rio's spine stiffen as soon as the woman entered. One look at her face told me what she was thinking. Abbi's arrival was an unspoken suggestion that she didn't have things under control herself.

My protectiveness over Rio was getting more intense by the day. I rarely made it through one cycle of sunrise to sunset without wanting to cause bodily harm in her honor. All right, I'd make an exception for Abbigail today, but only because the woman looked hot and tired in her very pregnant state—

and because Rio was now dragging me across the living room, explaining the how-tos of helping her construct a diaper cake.

"A diaper...what?" I blurted, once my brain actually linked the two words.

"No, no. C'mon, think outside the box." Rio gestured as she spoke, explaining the final goal regarding the diaper stack in the nearby laundry basket. "It's supposed to look like a wedding cake when it's done. You know, with several tiers?"

"Okaaay." I glanced back down at the basket, which was filled with the smallest diapers I'd ever seen. "So how many tiers do you think all of these will make? So I know how big to make the base."

"Huh?"

"I'm serious. I have to calculate all this all out if you want it to look right."

"Oh my God. You're being such a guy right now."

"And you're being fucking adorable."

"What?"

Time for a topic redirect. Now. "All right, a wedding cake," I stated, bracing hands to my hips. "But I thought this was a baby thing, not a wedding thing?"

She scrunched up her nose and wiggled it back and forth, reminding me at once of a little bunny. It had to be one of the cutest faces I'd ever seen her make, and I couldn't help but grin. Then wider.

Which led to the next action I couldn't control myself from making. I pulled her body tight and close to mine. I held her there while she wrapped her arms around my waist, hugging me back freely. The moment was...nice. Over the last couple of months, we'd gotten very comfortable holding one another like this, in friendship and comfort. "Yep. Adorable,"

I said and dipped in to give her an affectionate peck on the forehead. "It's nice to see the brightness back in your eyes."

For another long moment, Rio didn't answer. I wasn't surprised, but I was forced to acknowledge the new wave of tension through my system. It wasn't like I hadn't been through this before. Every once in a while—but seemingly more often lately—these moments of comforting intimacy ended with one of us becoming unusually quiet and then pulling away. I couldn't vouch for why Rio did it, but I knew damn well what was happening when I did. All the pressure, potent and powerful, that the woman brought to my body in those moments.

In the deepest recesses of my mind, I imagined she did it for the very same reasons.

I'd forgotten Abbigail was standing in the room with us. As soon as the woman cleared her throat and awkwardly shifted her weight, it was obvious that Rio had too. When we turned and beheld the uncomfortable look on the mother-to-be's face, we both dropped our arms. Rio jolted farther from me, blushing like Abbi had caught us doing something wrong.

Instantly, I was annoyed by that. Neither one of us should be guilted about hugging a friend. While Abbigail was one of the sweetest humans I knew—she had to be if she'd agreed to put up with Bas for the rest of her days—her demeanor seemed judgmental.

"Look at all the diapers I have." Rio quickly got back to cracking the whip to break through the brick of discomfort in the air. "Just use them up, okay?"

She tilted her head up to ensure I was on the same page with her goal, and I was able to give her a quick, mischievous wink. "Yes, my queen."

I bowed with a gallant sweep, enjoying her soft giggle as my reward. I turned and got busy with the diaper tower while the girls worked just beyond the kitchen island. They set out tray after tray of snacks and little sandwiches around the living and dining rooms for the party guests to enjoy. While they worked, they caught up on every topic under the sun. I was warmed from the inside out, listening to them chat away about everything from family gossip to what equipment was showing its age at the Abstract Catering kitchen.

Then Abbi grew unusually quiet. Rio noticed it about half a minute after I had. I kept my attention trained on my diaper creation, but my ears were sharply tuned to their conversation. Even the air in the room had gotten heavier. Yeah, beyond what it had been after Rio's and my quick clinch. Based on that alone, I tried not to tense up too tightly, preparing for whatever verbal torpedo she was about to drop.

"Hey." Abbi reached for Rio's hands. "There's something I've been wanting to ask you, and there just hasn't been a good time."

I could see Rio stiffen at the contact, but she quickly recovered. She wasn't naturally comfortable with unsolicited physical contact, and the ability to hide it from outsiders had gotten much worse since Sean's death. Truth be told, many of her standard coping mechanisms had slipped since the accident. I'd definitely noticed—a fact she was very aware of, as well. Though I tried suggesting she find a grief counselor or even a support group, that conversation had ended with the woman kicking me out and telling me to never come back.

Needless to say, she'd been much more dramatic lately, too.

But Abbigail knew her better than I did, meaning she

also knew to hold on tightly, not letting Rio pull away. She ducked her head, re-engaging her sister-in-law's stare before speaking. "If it makes you unhappy or uncomfortable, you have to promise you will be honest and tell me, okay?"

"With this kind of lead-in, girlfriend, you're already freaking me out. Not going to lie," Rio answered back pertly. Her go-to way of handling uneasy moments was to distract with sass and disarm with wit.

"Well..." The woman took a long breath. "Sebastian and I were talking. With your blessing, of course, we'd like to name the baby Kaisan Sean instead of Kaisan Albert." Abbi studied Rio's reaction with her enormous green eyes, trying to interpret every twitch and tic. "How do you feel about that?"

"I think that's a beautiful idea, Abbi. It's a lovely way to honor your brother's legacy. Your son will be proud to share his uncle's name one day when you share your memories with him."

"And when *you* share them too."

Rio only answered that by pulling her sister-in-law in for a tight hug. But the intensity of the embrace didn't match the rest of her mien. Her face was impassive and her eyes were completely dry. Abbi was spilling over with rivers of tears and torrents of emotion. I couldn't help but wonder if Abbigail discerned the way Rio only referred to Sean concerning his relationship to Abbi.

"Are...are you sure?" The pregnant woman dabbed her cheeks with the back of her fist.

Again, Rio responded with evasive action instead of direct communication. As if bolting from a burning bush, she broke away from their embrace and came over to where I was building the diaper tower. On a small end table nearby, there was a box of tissues. I grabbed the cube and thrust it toward her, not about to throw away the chance to make eye contact with her. But all I received for my trouble was another huge dose of deflection. She tossed me a quick eye roll, plastered on a ridiculously fake smile, and turned back toward Abbi.

"You little lawn sprinkler, you. Here. Fix all that before you ruin your makeup. You don't want to look like a raccoon in all the pictures today."

Her singsong voice cut through my eardrums like an ice pick.

After grabbing a tissue and dabbing her tears away, Abbi got serious again. "Why are you pretending this is all okay when clearly it's not? I really thought this would be a good thing. That you'd be happy..."

Rio sighed heavily and flopped down on the oversize ottoman in the living room area. The one-story bungalow had been opened up to flow freely from one space to the next. My realtor, Char, would call it "open concept." It was a perfect way to get the most out of a small amount of square footage.

"Honey, listen," Rio finally said, sounding frustrated and weary... such a smaller version of her normal bold brilliance. "I'm fine with you naming your child whatever you want. It's your baby, Abbigail. Let's not make a big deal out of it, okay? I want this day to have only good memories attached to it." She finished by rounding her slim shoulders forward.

Even from where I stood, her exhaustion wasn't just on her face anymore. It settled over her entire body.

Abbigail sat on the upholstered rectangle with her. The woman was clearly not about to let the subject rest. "Okay. What is this really about? I want to help you grieve Sean's death, but how can I do that? You don't return my calls, and you're so distant while we're at work. Do you think I haven't noticed you talk to everyone there but me? Even Sal, the delivery guy, gets a bigger hello."

"That's not—"

"It is true, damn it." At last, through the sheer magic of persistence, she landed a hand on Rio's shoulder. "If you're not going to talk to any of us about this, then maybe you should talk to someone. You know, a professional?"

I winced at her words. The mere mention of mental health professionals usually sent Rio running for the hills, a fact Abbi should've known by now, but for some ass-backward reason, she had chosen to pursue it today.

Today.

Of all the damn days . . .

But then she went and made the whole confrontation even worse.

"Sebastian was telling me that Shark Enterprise's health plan—"

Now Rio was the one doing the interrupting. "You know what, Abbigail? Do you know the last person I want to hear suggestions from right now? Sebastian Shark. Especially where grieving the loss of my husband is concerned."

Abbi's mouth fell open. Then stayed there. "Rio," she stammered. "Please. I—I didn't mean to—"

"You didn't mean to what, Abs? Offend me? Upset me? Hurt me with insensitive suggestions on how to pick up the pieces of my life after your fiancé destroyed the thing I loved more than my life itself?"

A long moment went by.

Another.

I ping-ponged a terse look between the two women. I

considered interrupting the train wreck, but one fast glare from Rio, and I knew to back off. Good Christ. And I thought Bas and Elijah were the clear trophy winners for throwing down with the glares.

And still, the women were gridlocked. Rio, in a fuming and furious stare. Abbigail, in silent and immobilized shock.

Until, as if some hidden gong was suddenly struck, Rio lifted her shoulders in a careless shrug. The gesture was cavalier, though she looked anything but.

"Abbi." Just like that, my firestorm's flame settled from a four-alarm blaze to the comforting lick of heat along a ski lodge fireplace. "I love you with all my heart. You are, and always have been, the closest thing to a sister I have ever known. All I can hope—and pray—is that when I finally wake up from this nightmare, our friendship is still intact." Rio joined Abbi in pulling in a bunch of restorative breaths before continuing. "But do not ask me to consider anything—*Any. Thing.*—that comes out of your man's selfish, greedy, twisted, heartless mind or mouth concerning my husband's death. Okay?"

Before Abbi could process the rant, Rio hauled her into a tight hug before quickly pecking her on each cheek. While this was certainly better than the bitter yelling, Abbi's composure was good and wrecked. For a long moment, she just kept staring in speechless wonder.

Then Rio abruptly stood and headed back to the kitchen. On her way, she briskly clapped her hands, motivational-coach style. She might as well have been psyching us up for the championship game—with hors d'oeuvres and tea sandwiches instead of electrolyte drinks and butt smacks. Though right at this moment, Gatorades and spankings were sounding damn good to me . . .

"Now let's have a party, yeah?" the woman finally bellowed. "Who's with me here?"

She had to add the addendum because Abbi and I weren't exactly at the high-five phase of this thing yet. We were locked in a long, silent look. I was certain my expression mirrored hers—bewildered and baffled—but what choice did either of us really have? In a very short time, this home would be filled with well-wishers, all excited to shower love and attention on baby Kaisan and his mama. So together, we buried our dumbfoundedness and went to join Rio in the kitchen. She was busy at the sink, whistling a happy tune.

Yeah. Whistling.

"I . . . uuhhh . . . think I need a minute." Abbigail spun and hurried down the hallway toward the guest bathroom. Couldn't say I blamed her. At the same time, I was grateful to have a few minutes alone with the she-devil hostess.

Without a word, she thrust a bottle of champagne into my chest. In the same sweep, she looked up at me but halted her traveling gaze at my throat instead of my eyes. The attention coaxed an involuntary swallow from me. Shit, even the muscles in my damn neck jumped at the woman's command.

"Can you open this?" She pushed the bottle more firmly into my chest. "Three of them?"

She shoved two more bottles in my direction, sliding them across the countertop.

"Do you want to talk about what just happened?" I spoke quietly while setting to the task.

With a decisive yank, she opened the refrigerator door. She nearly dove inside the thing to avoid my question. "Nope." Her voice echoed back from within the all but bare icebox. Everything was already out and waiting for the guests to arrive.

I worked the cork free from the first bottle but was too distracted by the sight of the woman's ass so stunningly angled out of the fridge that the cork popped loudly. The bubbly bang startled Rio, who abruptly stood. I grimaced as the back of her skull smacked into the fiberglass encasing of the cooler. The crack was nearly as loud as the cork I'd just popped.

"Shit!" we groaned at the same time.

Rio slammed the fridge shut with a pained wince and a string of profanity. As she rubbed the back of her head, I quickly set down the magnum I was working on. I pulled her into me, yearning to comfort her—but also to personally inspect the back of her head.

"Let me see," I whispered, trying to soothe her with my voice as well. I could feel her little body jackhammering from head to toe from being so agitated.

"I'm fine," she gritted and tried to pull away.

"Blaze, please. Let me care for you. For one second. Just let me make sure you're not bleeding."

She pushed on my chest again but only with half the effort. "Damn it, Grant. I'm fine."

"I'll feel better after I get a look. Then you can go back to buzzing around here like a gerbil on crack."

Finally, she sagged into me with the soft, sweet weight of her entire body. "Don't be mean." She sighed the words more than spoke them. The feeling of her warm, trusting breath on the exposed skin at my collar . . . it was stunning. Breath-robbing.

I let my eyes fall closed and just savored the heaven of holding her. Just a few precious beats of time. That was all I wanted. Needed. A few moments where we were both completely still in a morning that had already been a mixture of magic and madness.

Inwardly, I allowed myself a quick chuckle—because that basically summed up life with Ms. Rio Gibson. It was torture but rapture. Perfect peace within complete chaos.

Why was that so enticing . . . so addicting?

I just didn't understand.

★ ★ ★

Hours later, the little house was calm again. The guests were gone, the dishes were done, and the last few decorations were put away. Rio, who'd put away more than her fair share of champagne throughout the party, was now snuggling against me on the sofa.

That was right . . . snuggling. And right now, I was kind of enjoying it.

It was rare to see Rio relax. The woman rarely settled down under normal circumstances. There was always a part of her in motion. She always had a toe tapping, a leg bouncing, or several fingers drumming. Even now, she idly toyed with the buttons on the cuff of my shirt.

I never wanted her to stop.

And if she went on for another fifty years, I'd still be here watching her. Still as wrapped up in the expressive glory of her beauty.

"Well, what do you think, Madame Hostess? Are you happy with the way the party turned out?"

"Hmmm."

I wasn't sure how to interpret that, especially because she drew the hum out while pushing more of her soft curves against me. I swallowed hard, wordlessly conveying that she was sneaking into a risky physical zone for my self-composure, but—shock of shocks—she just accepted my reaction with a pliant sigh.

I dipped my face, burying my nose into her hair. And got away with it.

I rolled out a low hum of my own, inhaling the lush scent of her herbal shampoo. And got away with that, too.

Okay... I liked all of this. Especially this affectionate, submissive version of the woman.

"Yeah." She grinned up at me. "I think it went really well. All the food is gone. That's always a good sign. Okay, scoot down."

"Huh?" I blurted as she pushed at my thigh. I wasn't really sure what she wanted or intended but complied by moving farther down until I was sitting against the high cushioned arm on my right. She had the kind of sofa that swallowed a person up. The deep cushions and loose pillows made the thing more like a giant cloud rather than a couch.

Once I was settled, the woman hit me with yet another surprise by tossing a pillow onto my thighs and then plopping her head atop it. For a long second, my voice was stuck in mute mode. Did the gorgeous little imp know what kind of fire she was playing with this time? But did I even want her to?

She gazed up at me, and I wondered if she knew how dangerously high she was ratcheting the heat.

Big and expressive, her eyes seemed to promise so many clues to unraveling her. Did I dare take her up on it? Did I dare peel back a few more layers of this mysterious tangle of a woman? My rising desire said yes. But the hard-core sense of my brain?

Well, damn it. That part was saying yes too.

The intrigue and complexity of Rio's personality was just as sexy and alluring to me as her tight, smooth skin and glossy, raven-colored hair.

"Grant?"

I gave my head a mild shake to yank my mind out of its musing and back to her. So fully on her. The task wasn't hard, especially with the new husk in her voice. Damn it, so sexy. I wondered what had inspired it. Was she reacting to the champagne...or to our physical proximity?

"Yeah?" Mine matched hers then in seeming commiseration.

Which meant I was probably well and truly fucked.

"Will you...can you... I mean..." She squeezed her eyes—and her thighs—closed.

"What is it, Blaze? Just say what you need. You don't have to feel self-conscious around me." Did she hear my sincerity, even through my lust? "You should know that by now."

She jerked her head quickly. "I do."

"Good." I reached in and threaded my fingertips through her cute bangs.

"Touch me," she whispered.

I stopped breathing. "What?"

"Please, just touch me."

When I finally allowed myself to breathe again, I sharply sucked air through my nose.

Rio jolted off my lap and sat forward. "Is it that repulsive of an idea?"

"Rio, shit," I grated. Turning to face her, I grasped her hands, much tighter this time. "Touching you—fuck, even the thought of touching you—is the furthest thing from repulsive. Christ. I just—"

"What?" she demanded, gripping me tighter. "You just what?"

"I've just been waiting to hear those words for so long. Damn. My cock is so stiff at the moment, it might split my jeans."

"Oh." She blinked several times. Her lips parted, forming an entrancing blossom of temptation for my gaze. She repeated the word, officially taking care of the few cells in my body that hadn't combusted by now. "All right, then. Well . . . "

I cut her short by sliding to my knees in front of the sofa—and her. At first, all I did was stare. My first priority was to gauge just how tipsy she was. There was no way I'd take advantage of a drunk woman, especially in light of the day—hell, the month—she'd already been through. I was relieved when my closer inspection revealed only her slightly glassy gaze. Otherwise, she was clear and focused.

And, if I wasn't mistaken, getting as aroused as me.

I braced my hands on her knees and nudged at her legs. "Open," I said, keeping my stare fixed on hers.

Her nostrils flared at my command, but she did what she was told. I moved forward until bumping into the sofa. "Shit, yes," I groaned, grateful for the friction of the cushion against my agonizing hardness.

"What is it?" she asked with raised brows.

"Nothing," I said in a strained voice. "No. Everything. Already feels so good, just being closer to you."

"Oh." An impish energy tugged at the corners of her plush mouth. "Well, in that case . . . "

She trailed off with a defined air of sensual invitation. I didn't need any more coaxing than that. After leaning over her, I nuzzled at the sensitive spot behind her ear with the tip of my nose. But just as decisively, I pulled back. Fuck me, she smelled so good. As soon as my senses filled with the luscious spices of her skin, mixing with the heady musk of her arousal, I wanted to tear our clothes off and mount her—claim her—in one motion. My body kept screaming at me to just do it, that I had to take advantage of the dream-come-true before fate decided to take back the blessing.

"Tell me what you want, baby." I pushed back in and teased right beside her ear again, just before nipping at her earlobe. She tasted as good as she smelled, an incredible mix of exotic scents and rare flowers. So singular. So special. So her. So beyond what I'd ever fantasized she'd be like.

But now, it was happening.

I had her permission—her pleas—to touch her. Really touch her.

Rio pressed her face against mine, and we stayed there, man and woman, cheek to cheek. I contemplated saying something, but why? If things only went this far tonight, I'd go home a happy camper. The perfection of this short taste . . . the bliss of feeling her heart beating so close to mine . . . If this was where it all stopped, it was enough. More than enough.

"Grant, please," she finally whispered. "Kiss me."

So maybe it wasn't enough.

With a slight turn of my head, our lips finally met. The paradise I'd longed for. The place I'd dreamed about and thought I'd never have.

An inch of motion became an infinity of pleasure.

One kiss. Then after that, I would stop. Give her the space to still change her mind. To understand it was the alcohol making her brave and not real desire. To recognize she probably wasn't ready to cross this bridge, because it was a bridge made of crazy decisions. We had something good here already. It was insanity to mess it up with a moment of unthinking lust.

But shit—this moment.

I changed the angle of my chin until my lips explored nirvana even deeper. The soft, silky skin of her cheek burned hotter beneath my mouth.

"Blaze," I murmured, not wanting to move away. The nickname never seemed more appropriate than at this moment, as I reveled in the pulsing heat of her silky curves.

"More."

Even if she issued that exact plea.

"Mmmm. I don't know, baby. I think we should stop."

"Huh?" she blurted. "Why?"

"Because it'll be easier to put on the brakes now. Before we do something we'll both regret."

"No." She reached forward and gripped the front of my shirt. "No, Grant. Please. I need more. I'm not above begging for it right now." She dropped her head, but not fast enough to hide her wobbling chin. "Please," she repeated, this time in a shuddering whisper. "Grant . . . do you have any idea how lonely I've been?"

I leaned back. I didn't want to, but I had to. With brutal focus, I studied her expression—and almost wished I hadn't. I couldn't assign just one word to what I saw on her face, especially in her eyes. Loneliness? Yes, she'd just admitted that. But there was much more beyond that. Need? Possibly. But that still wasn't enough.

In the end, desperation seemed to be the most accurate descriptor for what I observed . . . and felt. Her desolate pain gutted me. Carved out a new place of pain inside me. I could not endure looking at her like this for much longer—not when

I had the power to take it away for her. Maybe not all of it. But at this point, some was better than none.

"Oh, baby. My beautiful baby."

I pressed my forehead to hers, needing another moment to check everything out. My eagerness. Her readiness. Synching up the two in tandem. Holy God, I was never more concerned about fucking something up so completely—which led to me pulling back again and looking directly into her captivating eyes.

Finally I felt steady enough to speak again. "Rio . . ."

"Hmmm? What is it?" She looked up, watching me get back to my feet with a stare that could only be interpreted as panic. "Grant? Talk to me. Are you changing your mind again?"

"No. Really. Shit."

"Then what is it? Where are you going?"

Surprisingly, I was able to shoot her a little laugh. "If we're going any further, baby, then it damn well won't be on your sofa."

"Oh." She grinned too, and the beautiful look remained as she put her hand into my outstretched one.

As I tugged her up next to me, I added, "And baby, I'll need you to steer this ship. At least for now."

My own words ensured the continuation of my grin. If things between us ever progressed further than this experience, she would understand how rare it was that I handed over control this way.

"Well, I definitely think this is going to make our lives more complicated. But I also know I don't give a single fuck about that right now."

I laughed—or tried to—but the noise sounded more like an injured animal than anything else.

"Listen to me," she ordered in a sultry rasp I hadn't heard from her before. If I had, I seriously would've remembered the occasion. "I've been walking around here like a zombie for months. Most mornings, I don't even want to get out of bed."

A few beats passed. The woman just kept staring at me. My reaction wasn't much more refined. In the space of a few simple minutes, everything had changed between us. Now, it was like we saw each other for the first time. Or perhaps we'd finally allowed ourselves to see. And holy hell, it was amazing. Goddammit, she was so stunning.

"So . . . what do you need now, baby?" I issued the question from the depths of my gut . . . the core of my soul. "What can I do for you?"

Anything. Everything. Just name it.

"My husband died, Grant. I didn't. And I'm tired of feeling like I have. I'm sick of feeling like I'm dead inside. I want to feel like I'm still alive. I need to feel again." She met my stare with a hopeful one of her own. "Do you understand that? I mean, does that make sense at all?"

"It makes perfect sense."

But it was all I could get out before taking action again. I couldn't stand another second of not being closer to her. I crowded into her personal space until our bodies were flush again, pressing her against the wall nearest to the bungalow's three bedrooms.

Our height difference made kissing nearly impossible without ducking way down, so I simply bent over and fitted my mouth to the shell of her ear once more. "If you don't show me to a bedroom right now, Rio, I'm going to be very tempted to demonstrate firsthand some of the fantasies I've conjured while I've had nothing but my hand and thoughts of you to keep me busy." I leaned back to get a good look at her flushed skin as her breathing accelerated. "Believe me, Blaze, I have a very active—and dirty—imagination."

I pivoted on one foot, turning out so she could escape my bodily trap. My breath seized in my chest while watching her process everything I just said, and we both considered her options. Finally, she indulged a long, slow visual stroll up my body before meeting my stare with a hooded one of her own. She held my gaze for another perfect beat and then quietly turned and power walked down the hall toward the bedrooms.

Thank. Fuck. Because if she had gone back toward the living room, I would have had to excuse myself to go beat off in the bathroom. Hell, screw the excusing myself. I'd probably do it right in front of her as punishment for blue-balling me so badly with that sexy, saucy eye fuck she'd just given me.

Trying to follow behind casually but failing miserably, I was inside the guest bedroom door right behind her. Even though she had about twenty-five-foot head start, my long strides and eager anticipation had closed the gap within a few steps.

Rio paused in the doorway to fumble with the light switch. With a feral growl, I pressed in against the curve of her ass with the crux of my body. She sighed, so throaty and sexy, and rolled back into mine. The movement consumed her, starting with her shoulders and neck and then rising through all of her head, until there wasn't a sliver of space between us.

Heaven. She was glorious heaven in my arms, against my cock... in my soul.

Thank God I couldn't physically bear the latter, though the rest was definitely doable. I wanted all of this inconvenient clothing gone. Right fucking now. I followed that purpose at once, feeling for the hem of her T-shirt where it skimmed the waistband of her low-slung jeans. With a brutal swoop, I lifted the little cotton memento up and over her head.

"Exactly how many band T-shirts do you own?" I asked while tossing the black shirt off to the side. "And turn the lights back on."

"Do you mind if we don't?"

"Actually, I do." I breathed it along the back of her neck, smiling at the subtle shiver I sent down her spine. It took every ounce of my fortitude to step away again, but patience was going to be my best friend if I wanted to make this good—no, spectacular—for us both. "I want to see you. I've been dreaming about touching you, exactly like this, for so long."

"You have? Oh!" Her outcry was delightful, even perfect, as I spun her to face me with an effortless grip of her small, soft shoulders. Enough light spilled into the room from the hallway to allow me to move about the unfamiliar space without bumping into furniture.

I wasted no time in stepping backward until I was able to sit on the side of the bed. Just as quickly, I pulled Rio to stand between my legs. The result was a grander dose of paradise. Her petite, pert breasts were now perfectly aligned with my mouth. As soon as I took in a full gaze of their glory, my erection seemed to defy biology—or at least the bonds of my expectancies. I'd been certain the damn thing couldn't throb more painfully. I'd been wrong. So wrong. As soon as my head got the notion I'd be finally sampling her, at least a pint of new blood crashed between my thighs.

I struggled to readjust myself. "Still with me, Blaze?" I asked, taking her breasts in my hands and squeezing, loving the velvety soft flesh against the rougher feel of my own skin.

"Yes, of course."

"Put your hands on me while I taste you."

She tugged her lower lip beneath her teeth and watched as I tried to decide where my feast should begin. "Rio." With my face buried between her tits, I breathed her name with reverence. "Rio. You're so beautiful, baby."

She moaned out her thanks as I formed my arms around her hips. The fit was so natural, as though they were made specifically to hold this one woman. I already knew how empty they would be without her.

Thoughts for another time, asshole.

I skated my hands up her sides, over her ribs, and around to the delicate wings of her shoulder blades. I spanned my large hands over the surface of each smooth side of her back before pressing her even closer. The whole time, I teased between her breasts with slow, sensual circles of my nose. The black bra she wore was a dangerous satin temptation, so much like the woman herself. Though the lingerie's construction was sensible, the material itself was a luxurious touch of self-love. The color was the easiest to figure out. It was naughty but melancholy, a tribute to the badass warrior woman who wore it.

But for all that contemplation about her bra, I was still dying to get the damn thing off her. By the time I skimmed my fingers up and worked at the black fastener of the thing, the woman was panting in a series of quick, urgent gasps.

Rio moaned and let her head drop back on her shoulders. The few longer layers of her hair skimmed my hands where I had been working the fastener of her bra. A new idea sparked to life. After quickly unclasping the three little hook and eye fasteners, I grabbed a fistful of her black hair and held close at her scalp.

"Mmm, I like this." I hummed against where the pulse thrummed in her neck. "You have nowhere to go now. Still good, Blaze?" I asked, trailing my lips down to the spot where her neck and shoulder met and filling my mouth with her soft flesh. The more skin I sampled, the more lust pounded through my body.

"I'm still good." Her smoky husk centered me a little. "Grant...please?"

"On the bed." My voice sounded so rough, as though the words were being strangled by my emotions. Inwardly, I cringed. I wanted to be gentle with her for the first time, but the dominant male part of me had no idea what that even meant. "First, undress. I'm so goddamned hard for you, Rio."

Luckily, she seemed to accept that as a high compliment. Her eyes were hazy but heated as she moved to comply with my dictate, working the button and zipper open on her jeans.

At the same time, I made quick work of my own clothes. I stalked around to the other side of the bed to leave a few condoms on the nightstand and then pulled the covers back. With a low groan, I watched her crawl like a sexy kitten onto the mattress. As soon as I joined her, I rolled her over and positioned her against the mountain of cushiony pillows.

"Lie back, baby. Get comfortable. I want to spend as much time as I can ... " I looked up and saw her with my whole mind and spirit—and dare I say it? I looked at her with my whole heart.

I gave myself those few magical moments I had been denied all these months. Judging on how right everything felt now, I knew how bad it would feel when it went all wrong.

And it absolutely would go wrong.

This, us—whatever Rio and I had between us—was

marked for doom. I was deluding myself to think otherwise. Was it because it was so soon after her husband passed? Or had I damned us by being so crazy for the woman for such a long time, despite the ring on her finger that should've been my No Trespassing sign?

And what did any of this mean to her? Was I just a scratch for her itch of loneliness?

Maybe. Probably.

I knew it all, and I didn't care. I knew every damn part of the truth, and I yearned to fuck her anyway. I would bury myself deep within her luscious body for as long as she'd let me. And when we were done, I'd beg her to let me do it again. We hadn't even started, and I already knew that was how it would end. I was in a battle for her time and attention, and my most worthy opponent was a damn ghost.

Again, thoughts for another time.

Rio perused my body with open appreciation. She'd been timid about touching me unless I specifically asked her to, and I'd been letting her set the pace. I just wanted amazing memories of the night when it was over. Nothing bad to get in the way, if this was the one time we had together.

I positioned myself between her parted legs before hovering above her to kiss her lips. Finally, savoring the moment with slow care, I pressed my mouth to hers. At once, she slid out her velvety tongue, seeking mine. She licked my lower lip first, following by nibbling at the top one.

I groaned from deep in my chest, not even trying to stifle her effect on me. I didn't bother trying to hide my erection anymore, either. She should know what she did to me, the way my body responded to hers. She should definitely know what she was in for, too.

I worshiped her body for most of the night. I did everything in my power to make her feel so damn good. I lavished my adoration on her from the inside and then along the shivering, dewy inches of her outside. And I touched her everywhere in between too. Every corner and crevice, every enticing curve and secret spot of arousal. With my lips, tongue, and teeth, I brought all her nerves to life. I imprinted myself on every inch of her flesh.

Not long after the midnight chimes of the church up the street, I was certain I had to be existing on a borrowed chunk of heaven. With my head between her thighs and the woman's hands digging at my scalp, her honey soaked my tongue as her screams filled my ears.

"Grant. My God!"

I smiled against the lust-plumped cushions of her beautiful pink core. "Hmmm, that works. You can always just say 'Almighty Lord' or 'Ruler of my pussy.'"

"How about just 'stop'?" she snapped. "Oh...please, Grant...just stop!"

"Now where would be the fun in that?"

"Oh, Jesus Christ!"

"Not that one either."

"What are you doing to me? I can't take more! Please, Grant!"

I just chuckled—and continued my eager ravishment of her delectable pussy. I was so hungry for her. It was like I hadn't had a meal in weeks. I'd watched this woman come twice already tonight but would never grow tired of the sight. Her explosions had quickly become the most fascinating thing I'd ever seen. She orgasmed with a unique and curious gusto that made other women's performances pale in comparison.

Her third trip to O-town, courtesy of my mouth and fingers, was the most stunning show. She thrashed her way to the edge of the bed in a messy collection of sighs and screams, which led to me kneeling on the floor between her thighs. Rio was draped off the mattress from the hips down, so before setting her off this time, I anchored her with my hand splayed wide across her lower abdomen—or she'd have ended up on the floor with me.

When I was sure she had calmed down a bit, I stood to my full height and stretched across the bed for a condom. It couldn't be put off another moment. As long as she was still agreeable, I needed to be inside her.

"You're incredible, Rio. So fucking delicious and sexy."

I licked her taste from my lips and looked down at her flushed body beneath me. She grinned lazily, like a cat stretching out in the afternoon sun.

"I need to be inside you. So badly." I stroked my hard length, and she followed the movement with hungry eyes. "You good? Are we still good?"

She gave a tight nod, but I needed to hear her say the word. I needed to hear her say she wanted this too.

"Blaze?"

"Yes. God, please. I want to feel you too."

She moved back to the center of the bed and then held her arms out for me to join her. I went to her, settling my weight between her parted thighs, a forearm outside either shoulder. My erection rubbed against her stomach while I kissed every inch of her face.

"You are so beautiful." I brushed her unruly hair back from her face.

"I bet I look freshly fucked, hmmm?" She grinned up at me.

"Not yet, but you're about to." I smiled back while stroking her flushed cheek with the backs of my fingers. "Ready?"

"More than. You've got quite a reputation to live up to, you know."

Still studying her, I moved to align my cock with her sex. "Is that right?" I asked, distracting myself from anticipating that first heavenly feeling of her cunt welcoming my cock. Still, my eyes nearly rolled back in my skull.

"Absolutely." A sly little smile played at the corner of her kiss-swollen lips until I circled my hips and nailed the most sensitive part of her clit with my pelvis. Her eyes widened at the pleasure and then fluttered shut while the sizzling sensations crept across her body. "I've thought about this moment so many times, there's no way you can live up to the hype." Rio chuckled, then tilted her head back when I lined my cock up at her entrance.

"Open your eyes and watch me. I want you to know exactly who's filling you so perfectly, Blaze."

I thanked myself for issuing the order. Her eyes were the texture of butterscotch, soft and sensual and warm. I enforced the commanding tease by slicking the taut head of my cock through her wetness a few times. I went deeper this time, attempting to ease the intrusion, before pushing even deeper. I went as slowly as possible, but even with the condom on, her body's heat coated every inch of my clamoring dick. It created a particular type of madness in my groin. My body began moving on instinct, seeking pleasure by way of natural impulse and drive. I worked my hips at a pace that was good for us both. Quickly, Rio fell into rhythm with me, and our bodies began moving as one.

"Shit. Shit, slow down, girl, or this is going to end sooner than we want." I closed my eyes and pressed my forehead to hers. We both had a fine mist of sweat coating our skin, and I impulsively wanted to taste her again. "Goddamn, you feel so good," I snarled against her lips. "You're gripping me so tight. Every…inch…of me…"

There wasn't any part of her I didn't want to know about. Then, next time I saw a little bead of sweat on her brow at the kitchen or a backyard barbeque, I would remember what that dew felt like. Smelled like. Tasted like. I'd have her essence imprinted on my brain.

Jesus Christ. Stop it, man.

I really just needed to come. Sooner rather than later. The quicker I climaxed, the faster I could disconnect. That would be the best thing right now. I was already getting too sloppy and emotional, and both of those meant stupid was coming next. And if stupid was next, that meant potential damage I couldn't fix. Like telling her I loved her or something equally irreparable.

Pushing up off Rio's body, I sat back on my heels and stared down at her. She watched me with curiosity, and her hungry, greedy eyes went right to my engorged cock, still thick and full, testing the confines of the condom.

"Hands and knees or sit here and ride me. Pick one."

The sassy girl sat up and licked her lips once more. "Ohhh, lady's choice, is it? Well, who says you're not a generous lay?"

"I don't think anyone would say that, as a matter of fact. And for the smart mouth, I'll go ahead and pick for you."

I pinched the inside of her thigh, and she squealed with playful passion and then tried to scoot out of my grasp. But I had speed and longer arms, so I easily caught her ankle as she scurried up the mattress. I dragged her with me to the edge of the bed, where I planned on starting all our fun. With little effort, I scooped one forearm under her hips and lifted her ass in the air. She was still able to support herself on her hands and knees, which was a damn good thing. With my other hand, I lined up and rammed back into her.

"Fuck! Jesus, Grant. Ooohhh." She let her head hang down between her braced arms as I stroked my hand up and down her spine.

"Can you come again?"

"I don't . . . I don't know. God, it feels so good, though. Jesus. I'm so full."

"Mmm, yeah. Yeah you are, baby. My cock fills you so good."

"This is . . . so much better . . . than all my fantasies."

"Mine too." I pumped with thorough strokes, letting everything from my cockhead to my balls be squeezed and gripped by her sexy pussy. "It's so good."

"Yes," she said. "So, so good!"

"Play with your pussy, Rio. Get yourself there so we can come together."

"Okay. Okay," she panted.

A couple minutes of unadulterated flesh slapping, panting, and moaning, and Rio was chanting my name, telling me she was going to come. Not a moment too soon, thank God.

"Good girl. Yes, so good. I feel you squeezing me. I'm going to come with you, baby."

"Oh, God. Oh, God, yes! Yes!" Her shoulders shuddered. Her skin broke out in goose flesh. Her ass cheeks clenched. Her thighs trembled—before spasming with the stress of her fourth orgasm of the night.

Watching her body come apart again sent me into the

stratosphere, and I stilled behind her. My own release bolted through my dick and into the condom in hot, jerky bursts that seemed to go on and on. Yet somehow—not long enough.

Rio collapsed beneath me, and after a few minutes, I got up to dispose the condom and wash up. I was back beside her soon, pulling the covers over us both. I could already hear soft, snuffly snores coming from her side of the pillow and chuckled. I knew I'd gone at her pretty hard, but I'd also hoped she'd fall asleep on her own for a change. Hopefully we could make it through till sunup without a night terror, and we could both get a solid block of rest.

Robert, the cat, came and settled between us on the bed and started purring. The soothing tone lent a calming soundtrack to my rioting thoughts. Before I knew it, I was waking up to nature's morning light streaming in through the curtains.

Robert was stretched out where the sun's beams crossed the bed near the footboard, and I quickly realized the damn black-and-white cat was the only pussy I'd be touching this morning. Rio was already awake and absent from the room.

CHAPTER NINE

RIO

"Ugh," I moaned while pressing my thumbs into my eye sockets, trying to alleviate the pain. The ibuprofen I took when I first sneaked out from under Grant's warm, gloriously naked body still wasn't doing the trick on my pounding headache. I was getting too damn old for this kind of punishment after overindulging even just the slightest bit.

But my real indulgence had come after the shower guests left. Then the champagne I had carelessly tossed back, glass after glass, gave me the tenacity to finally reach for the brass ring—aka Grant Twombley.

Reach? Ha! The experience was more like cliff diving into a red Solo cup. The man and I had been flirting with sexual danger for far too long to have any semblance of control once a little alcohol untethered the albatross of guilt and loyalty to my deceased husband. After I said goodbye to those shackles, all bets were off on acting like a lady.

Oh, but the familiar burden was back now. It felt like an anvil around my neck. If I weren't pulled down by the weight of guilt now, the repeated stings from the shame I was lashing myself with would be my undoing.

And still, the desire to crawl back into bed with him and do it all over again—right now—was strong enough to say fuck it all and just do it. Live in the moment and just feel good.

How could that be wrong?

Friends and family had been encouraging me to start living again. They wished I would find healthy ways to reclaim my life and move forward. Well, sex was a natural, healthy form of expression, right? After the night of revelation I'd just had with Grant, I could come up with a list of things I'd like to express to the man.

My ridiculous train of thought made me laugh out loud, breaking the silence of the empty kitchen.

"What's so funny?"

I spun around like the gorgeous hunk had brought a string of lit firecrackers with him. After taking him in, my heart sped as if he really had. The man, standing half-naked and beautifully disheveled, had never looked more godlike. His scratchy, morning-after voice was just as perfect. The rough sound raced up my spine, filled my ears, and then sent its sultry impact down through my whole body.

"You're awake!" I stated the obvious and turned to face him. It would've been impossible to miss the erection tucked behind his unbuttoned jeans. My eyes seemed to have their own agenda this morning, widening as I stared at his crotch and then licked my lips.

"Careful, girl," Grant rumbled as he took a menacing step closer.

I could actually feel my heart rate quicken. When he took the second step in my direction and I smelled his familiar scent, I swayed toward him.

"What cologne do you wear?" I blurted out. "I love it." I closed my eyes and took another deep sniff. As a woman who spent so much time focusing on culinary art, I was acutely aware of smells. So often they went hand in hand. There was an incredible combination of different trees and citrus in his cologne and something distinct I just couldn't put my finger on. I closed my eyes and concentrated harder, really taking the challenge to heart.

When Grant spoke, he was inches from my ear. "What are you doing?"

"Smelling you."

He chuckled silently. It was that sexy thing he did when his body laughed but no sound came out. I looked up to find his gorgeous ocean-blue eyes staring back down at me. Without warning, he lifted me by the waist and set me on the kitchen counter, aligning our faces closer. He tried to nudge his way between my legs, but I wasn't cooperative with his mission.

A predatory sound came from the back of his throat before he said, "Let me get closer to you, Blaze."

"I don't know if that's a good idea."

"We both know it's a terrible idea." He thought for a second and grinned. "But it's too late for all that. Now do as I say and spread your legs."

The second time he pushed at my knees, I allowed him to arrange my thighs to accommodate his frame. Something about his deliberate movements and the quiet confidence in his tone had heat and desire instantly throbbing at my core.

A tight, needy moan escaped from my lips before I could slap my hand over them. Grant kept his stare fixed on me while he easily pulled my palm away from my mouth. He slid it down, resting it beside my hip on the countertop.

"Don't hide from me. I love the sounds you make when you're getting hot."

"You ... you do?" I croaked.

"Mmmm, I do." He ran his nose along my jaw to my ear and then kissed me just under the lobe. God, it all felt so good. In a wild rush of thought, I imagined it wouldn't take much coercing to have me right back in the guest bedroom, out of my clothes, and waiting for him to enter me any damn way he pleased.

But without the champagne preamble, I had no excuse for recklessness today. All my inner warning sirens were ringing, loud and clear. Still, I paused and savored the moment. All of it. How good this man felt. How good it felt for me, clutching his bulging muscles and stunning body. Being back among the living felt so good.

So damn good.

"Grant," I whispered but couldn't even discern if the entreaty was for him to stop or to go faster. Or harder?

"God, yes, like that," I moaned while he kissed up and down my neck. Somewhere, lost in the lust haze in my mind, was the version of me that was telling him to stop. But sitting here on the kitchen counter? Well, that was the wanton woman who was tilting her head farther to the side to give him better access to my sensitive flesh.

"You taste so good," he groaned into my neck as he sucked. "I could do this all day. Kiss you . . . " He moved across my jaw to my lips and nibbled until I opened for his seeking tongue. "Taste you . . . "

Before I could comprehend what was happening, I watched the man drop to his knees in front of me. Yes, right here on the tile floor of my little eat-in kitchen. The leggings I had pulled on when I first woke up were a quick casualty of his quest, as he yanked at the waistband with his long fingers and then dragged my hips to the edge of the counter to pull them off.

"Grant," I protested weakly, gripping the edge of the flat surface so I didn't end up on the floor with him. Watching his gaze scan up and down my body shut down the ability to say more. He looked at me like he'd never seen a woman before, although he'd seen more than his fair share. His skill set in the bedroom was proof enough of that.

"Your pussy is so sexy, Rio. I can't get enough of it. And now that I've seen it..." He crudely spread my labia to examine things closer. "And touched it, and tasted it..." He sucked in a fierce breath while sliding his middle finger into me. "And Christ Almighty, been inside here..." He pushed in his finger until his knuckles were against my ass. "Yeah, baby. You feel how tight you are around me? God, I'm so hard for you again."

A low moan of pleasure was my only response before he leaned forward and licked at my intimate folds, but he didn't pull his finger out. Nor did he move it. He just kept his hand there, filling me. Possessing me. And goddammit, it felt so good being invaded in that way while he licked and sucked my clit. I was surely going to come within seconds. He added another long finger beside the first, and I could feel my arousal dripping from my entrance and running down to my ass.

"I wish you could see this," Grant growled. His voice had an edge of need that bordered on pain. "You're so wet, it's dripping from you. Do you need my cock again, Blaze?" he taunted and then sucked the little bud of my clit roughly.

"Fuck!" I wailed and bucked at the intense sensation when he made contact that time. I was so ramped up, the response was uncontrollable. "Grant! Yes!"

"Ask me for it, baby. I'm feeling pretty generous this morning." He took long, lazy swipes around my entire pussy then, his tongue creating utter madness through my whole body.

"Whaaa? What?" It was hard enough to process my own thoughts while the sensations pummeled my body. Now I had to organize some sort of question for him too?

"Beg me to fuck you, Rio." He pulled his hand from my pussy, and I whimpered at the loss. While he stood up, I watched him pull down his jeans, just far enough around his hips to free his cock. My mouth hung open in awe while he gave himself a few casual strokes before expertly rolling on a condom.

He looked at me with a brow raised expectantly. "Waiting, Rio. Let me hear you."

I glared at him, instinctively reaching down between my legs to rub myself, not wanting to lose the buildup that was hovering low in my belly. He grabbed my wrist and held it a few inches above my body, slowly shaking his head.

"Goddammit, Grant. Stop fucking around and give it to me!"

"Mmmm, no. That's not how you get what you want, is it?" Mischief danced in his eyes.

I threw my head back and felt like I was pleading with the ceiling fan. "Please! For Christ's sake! You're an asshole when you want to be."

"Please, what?"

"Please fuck me." I leveled my stare back to him and said in my most lethal tone, "Now."

"Better. Could use some work, but it's a good start." He lined the head of his cock up at my slick entrance and thrust in. With one efficient stroke, he was buried deep inside me. My cry of intense pleasure filled the entire house.

"Fuck! Yes, so good!" I chanted over and over.

"Won't. Last. Long." Each of Grant's gritted words coincided with a powerful thrust. He reached between us to rub my clit while he fucked me. When he pinched the swollen nub between his thumb and forefinger, I might as well have stared into the sun. My vision went completely white. Fantastic tingles shot through my body, from the tips of my fingers all the way down to my toes.

"Coming ... I'm ... coming!" I gasped, trying to let him know he was good to let loose with his own orgasm. I could barely breathe amid the sensations racing around my body, though.

"Fuck! Yes! Rio! So good, girl!" He thrust one more time and held himself deep within my channel. He froze there, his thighs trembling and his eyes rolling back in his head. I couldn't be sure, but it looked as though he had as epic of a release as I did.

Christ. How were we ever going to stop doing this?

I wasn't sure I could.

Or that I even wanted to.

★ ★ ★

By Thursday that week, I had used every excuse I could think of to keep Grant away. I knew if I were in the same room with him again, we'd just end up in a similar position as the night of and the morning after Abbigail's baby shower. Our chemistry was too potent ... and too undeniable.

And so damn good.

I'd spent a lot of time partaking in self-love since that morning, and while the new fantasy material was fantastic, nothing would ever compare to the real thing.

Grant Twombley had officially ruined me for all others. Probably for all time.

Between his persistent phone calls and text messages and Abbi's side-eye looks and under-her-breath comments, my fake good nature was wearing thin. Someone was going to have a verbal dressing down or the knuckle sandwich lunch special if they didn't watch themselves. When did my business become everyone else's business?

"Hey, what's all that stuff in your car?" Abbi asked nonchalantly while we were cleaning up after making lunches. Hannah had set off with the deliveries, and we were the only two left in the kitchen. Dori was running an errand for her boss lady and was expected back in a few minutes.

"Huh?" I replied. I knew exactly what she was referring to but thought if she had to explain her beyond-nosy question, she might hear how invasive she was with the inquiry and back off. Moments like this, it made sense why a lot of people felt that working with your family members was just too much time spent with the same people. It gave your relatives a sense of comfort that wouldn't typically be felt among regular coworkers.

She shrugged, maybe finally feeling a bit self-conscious for prying. "Oh." But she forged ahead anyway, dashing my hope of her discovering some clarity. "When we pulled in earlier, Dori parked beside your car. Since my truck sits up so much higher, I could see directly into your windows and that giant sunroof you have. It looked like you have a bunch of trash bags in your car. I was just wondering what all that stuff is."

My sister-in-law wasn't going to like this conversation. I also assumed now wouldn't be the best time to point out that maybe she should mind her own damn business. "I've been packing up Sean's stuff. Those bags are for Goodwill."

"Oh," she repeated.

We were both quiet, working at various jobs around the kitchen, but I could feel the air growing more and more tense with every minute that passed. I was putting dishes away when she started in on me again.

"Rio, did you think maybe Bram, Flynn, Zander, or I would like to go through Sean's things to see if we wanted any of it?"

I let out a heavy sigh because I'd had a feeling we would end up here. From the moment she brought up the bags in my car—no, from the moment I decided it was time to start packing the stuff up at the house—I knew I'd be judged for it. Maybe I really had made a mistake here. Perhaps I didn't. I had nothing to go on. But ultimately, wasn't that my call to make?

"Abbigail, listen. I'm trying to do everything right. Or at least by the impossibly perfect Gibson family standards. But I've never dealt with this sort of thing before, and I'm doing the best I can. Does that make sense?"

I waited for her to answer, but she just stared at me.

Judging.

Judging and staring.

"Sean's will was very specific. That was something he did after you lost your mother. He explained it to me. I thought you were all satisfied without additionally picking through his belongings. If you want to go through his old underwear, then have at it. I'll hold on to the stuff for a few more weeks, and you can come over when it's convenient for you. Just let me know when you can fit that into your schedule. Okay?"

I knew I had just gone overboard with my comments, but

her judgmental tone and disapproving glare had sent me over the edge.

"You don't have to get so nasty about this. I don't think I'm asking that much. He was my big brother."

In typical Abbigail fashion, she started up with the waterworks. At once, I wanted to turn on my heel and walk away. I'd already had all I could take. Add in the crocodile tears, and I couldn't endure another second of the conversation.

But no...she continued in an even more accusatory tone. "It hasn't been three months since he's gone. I just don't understand why you're in such a big hurry to pack it all up and get rid of his memory?"

My mouth hung open while I tried to form my outraged thoughts into a coherent sentence. "I'm not getting rid of his memory. How dare you say something like that to me? You have no idea what I'm going through, Abbigail. So don't stand there and judge me." I started to walk away from her just to get some physical distance between us but whirled back after only a few steps. Clutching at my chest, I said, "My memories are in here, in my heart, not in a bag full of old clothes." I shook my head. Why did I have to stand there and defend myself and my actions? It was so unfair. There wasn't a manual on grieving. There wasn't a right way and a wrong way to do this sort of thing.

In an angry huff, I grabbed my purse and jacket from the hook on the wall and turned on Abbi one last time. "See, Abbi, looking at his stuff—day in and day out—is painful. But you wouldn't understand that." I shook my head as one hot, fat tear finally escaped and trailed down my cheek. "Because your man is still alive."

When I went out the door, I slammed the thing so hard,

it bounced off the frame and flew back open. I didn't bother going back to close it.

★ ★ ★

By the time Grant called, I was speeding home and desperately fighting the urge to burn something. The dry hillsides that lined the freeway taunted me as I picked up the call and tried to sound cool. "Hey" was all I could choke out because I was still seething from Abbigail's bullshit and battling so many internal demons.

"You okay?" he answered. His calming voice filled the small cabin of Kendall and felt like soaking in a Jacuzzi. Comforting and warm, relaxing and exhilarating, all at the same time. How could he do that with one question?

I let out a heavy sigh before answering. "Yeah, fine. I got into it with Abbigail at the kitchen before I left. Nothing I can't handle."

"Do you want to talk about it?" he offered, his tone rich with tender thoughtfulness. "Maybe it's hormones?"

"No." I let him hear my eye roll. Sometimes I thought "hormones" had to be the conversational catch-all. It was easier than trying for substance. "I don't think it's something you'd want to get into anyway."

"Well, if you change your mind, I'm here. I'd be happy to lend an ear."

"I appreciate that." Changing the subject seemed like the best plan. "Anyway, how was your day? Or your week, rather. We ... uuhh ... haven't really talked."

"Yes, because someone has been dodging my calls." He chuckled but stopped pretty quickly, imparting the instant impression he wasn't really amused by my behavior.

"Who? *Moi?*"

A low, tight growl from his end. And then, "Coy doesn't really suit you, Blaze."

My stomach flipped over a few times, and so did body parts south of my lap belt. "No? That voice you're rocking certainly suits you, though." I squeezed my eyes and legs shut quickly. I opened my eyes again right away, though, since I was driving, but I wanted to smack my palm to my forehead. I could not believe I just said that out loud.

"Well, you're the one who's kept me at arm's length all week. Think of all the fun, sexy times we could've been having. Now you have to wait for the weekend again."

"Oh? Do your weekday girls get jealous if you step out on them?" I teased.

"See? That's where you're wrong." Somehow his voice was even deeper then.

"Explain it to me."

"There are no weekday girls. Or weekend ones, for that matter. I only have eyes for one girl at the moment."

Now his voice was seductive and promising. Or at least that was what my ears heard.

"Is that right?" I egged him on, wanting to hear more of this subject for sure.

Without a moment's hesitation, Grant answered, "Yes. One sassy, sexy, bratty, crazy, smart, beautiful, tiny little number. Seriously, I just can't seem to stop thinking about her."

"Hmmm. Is that so, Twombley?"

"It is."

Boldly, I pressed on. I had so much pent-up energy, I

needed to do something to release it, and taunting the sexy devil on the other end of the phone was working wonders for my frazzled nerves. "Do you beat off thinking about her?"

"Every day. Twice already today, as a matter of fact."

I couldn't help but laugh. Poor guy. "Impressive stamina, man." I pulled into my driveway, picturing Grant stroking his hard cock and how amazing he felt when he pushed into me. Once my garage was open, I parked inside and turned off the engine. I grabbed my phone and made sure Grant was still on the line before continuing, "Dude, you've got it bad. Does this girl know? I mean, about your masturbating problem?"

"No. But I'm about to show her." His voice came at me in double time. Once over the phone and again in real-time because he was standing beside me in my garage. I nearly jumped out of my skin. I had not expected to see him here— especially with that sexy, mischievous grin firmly in place.

"Christ. I can't wait to see th—"

He cut off my smart remark by covering my mouth with his in a demanding, hungry kiss that had me breathless by the time he finished. Thankfully, he held me steady for a few moments while I regained my balance, or I would have tumbled over my own two feet.

"Let's go inside. Unlock your house door, Blaze."

I stared up at him, helpless to do anything but follow his dictate. Well, attempt to. No way could I form a coherent thought, let alone a sassy comeback. I closed the garage door first and then searched for the house key on my key ring while he crowded behind me, greedily groping my ass and the backs of my thighs, making it very difficult to accomplish the simple task.

"Sometime today, or I'm going to fuck you on your garage

floor," he growled directly into my ear, causing me to drop the key ring with a metallic clatter. "Put your hands above your head, Rio. Palms flat on the door."

"Wha—what?" I looked back over my shoulder while complying once again.

"Now let me show you what happens when you leave me with too much time alone. I've told you before, my imagination is a dark, dangerous place, Blaze."

With one skilled hand, he reached around my front, flipped up my T-shirt, and worked the button and zipper open on my jeans.

"Grant—" I tried to protest, but he cut me off.

"Shhh, baby." Then in that sexy rasp right beside my ear again, "Is this pussy wet right now?"

"Graannnttt." That time, his name was much more of a plea than a protest.

"Just yes or no, Blaze," he said with husky calm while he finally found the right key and unlocked the damn door. But he didn't open the thing. Then he turned and looked at me expectantly.

Finally, I started to move my hands down to open it myself, but a censuring arch of his brow made me stop in my tracks.

"Yes! You know it is! It always is when you're around." I looked down at my wild cherry Converse before adding in a mutter, "Asshole."

His dark chuckle worried me at first, but I closed my eyes and relaxed into him when he pressed in behind me once again. His body heat was comforting. So strong.

"I heard that." His tone flowed over me, as dark and silky as melted chocolate, as he slid his hands down into the front of my open jeans and into the thin band of my panties. There, he found the wetness he was so interested in.

"Oh, baby. Feel this cunt." He made a strangled sound low in his throat. "Christ. How can it be better than I remembered?"

"That feels so good," I moaned in response as his fingers teased my slick folds.

"Yeah, it does." He skated a finger over my clit, and I bucked my hips into his hand. "Do you want to come?"

"Standing here? Like this?"

"Mmmm." He growled and kissed along the side of my neck. "Of course."

"I don't think that would happen. I mean . . . "

"Oh, Rio," he clucked. "You poor girl."

I couldn't begin to imagine what that meant, and I didn't dare ask. "Let's go inside. Plus, my neighbors will hear us. The houses are too close together."

Grant looked from side to side, scanning around my orderly garage, and then abruptly pulled his hands from my pants. Despite how I'd been the one suggesting we get into the house, I whimpered at the loss.

Actually whimpered.

I hung my head between my extended arms. What was I doing here? This whole scene was ridiculous—and hot. So fucking hot, I couldn't organize enough brainpower to object. I watched him stalk across the small space to the supply shelves and grab something from one of the open storage bins. He worked quickly with his back to me and then turned back to face me, his mischievous grin firmly in place.

"Eyes straight ahead or closed. You pick."

"Always so generous," I retorted with an eye roll for good measure.

His long stride brought him back to my side quickly. "I

knew this was the right call. I have just the thing for that sassy mouth."

I fell right into his verbal trap, because when I turned to question him, he swiftly placed a wide swatch of blue painters' tape over my mouth. He had a second piece stuck to his hip that he quickly smoothed diagonally over the first, ensuring no sound could escape. I glared at him, using my eyes to scream every obscenity I could think of. Some freshly created ones, as well.

"Your dirty looks are making my dick harder, baby. Was that what you were going for?" He ground his crotch against my hip, and I let my eyes flutter closed. The man was impossible.

"Now," he said, stepping back a few inches, "I think there was a challenge—of sorts—issued?"

I cocked my head to the side, basically asking, "What are you talking about?"

"You didn't think I could get you off while you stood here." He shrugged. "I can." He cradled my face in his large hands and then kissed my temple, maneuvering my head however he wanted with his strong fingers. "And I will." Grant continued the trail of kisses down to my ear, where he said, "In less than one minute."

I rolled my eyes, overwhelmed with pleasure but also with a shred of disbelief.

"Hold on tight. This is going to be hard and dirty, Blaze. Never said I played fair. Scream if you need to."

He gave me one of those sexy, infuriating winks and moved in to kiss below my ear, already not playing on even ground because that was one of the most sensitive spots on my body. After a few more lazy kisses and nibbles there, Grant moved back around to stand in front of me. He yanked my jeans and panties down to my knees in one forceful tug.

The bastard held my gaze while seductively sucking his middle finger into his mouth until I moaned behind my muzzle. When it was slick with saliva, he lowered it directly from his mouth to between my legs.

"Spread your legs, baby," he growled. "Let me in that hot pussy."

He rammed his finger into me so fast and so deep, I almost came from that single thrust. It was the intense way he stared at me while he made every move. Like he was crawling into my soul while he felt my body with his hands. He flicked and rubbed my clit with his thumb and index finger, fucking me with his middle finger at first and then adding his ring finger as well.

"Feel good, baby? Your gorgeous cunt is so tight. I feel you squeezing me like you're going to come." He leaned closer and started saying filthy things in my ear between biting and licking the skin nearby. Grant whispered dirty words about licking my come from my pussy after I orgasmed, fucking my ass, my mouth, owning every inch of me . . .

Until, just moments later, I exploded. I moaned and cried behind that damn blue tape, sucking air through my nose in deep, gasping pants until I felt actual tears running down my cheeks. Grant stood back a bit and watched me with fascination, as though he'd never seen a woman climax before.

He took me in from head to toe, seeming to catalog every nuance of the experience, and whispered, "My God, you are a revelation. Thank you for that, Blaze. Such a firestorm inside this little body." He stroked my short hair behind my ear with one hand and held me steady with the other arm wrapped around my waist, while I concentrated on just staying upright.

Finally, I let my arms slide down the wood panel that led inside, and that movement seemed to shake him from his trance.

"Here we go, baby." He picked at the corner of the blue tape and ripped it off in one quick jerk, freeing up my esthetician's three p.m. slot next Tuesday.

"Fuck!" I shouted, touching my upper lip gingerly. If he hadn't just sent me to the moon in coital bliss, I would have given him a smack.

"Hey, I passed on the duct tape. You should be thanking me," he teased. "Get your ass inside. I don't think I'm done with you yet."

I finished closing my jeans and whipped my hands to my hips. "You're awfully bossy today. What's gotten into you? And . . . are you forgetting this is my house? And that maybe I should be the one giving the orders?"

"Hell no. I don't roll that way. Ever. And I'm not bossy today; I'm bossy every day."

"You weren't like this the last time." I checked over my shoulder as I walked inside to ensure he followed.

"I wanted to be careful with you the first time." He paused for a second, his jaw ticking as he seemed to weigh his words carefully. "I wasn't sure where your head was at."

"I see. And today? My head is . . . where?" I finally asked, leaning against the kitchen counter.

Grant made direct eye contact again. Holy shit, he was alluring when he was so sure of what he was saying. "Needing a firmer hand," he asserted. "You still do. You always do. That's what makes all of this so—"

But then he stopped midsentence. And I knew why. He wasn't faltering because he couldn't find the right words.

He'd hesitated because what he was about to say was wrong. Wholly, utterly wrong. No matter how right everything had felt the other night, or even how right they still felt, we were on the brink of crossing a really rickety bridge. A point of no return. A mistake we wouldn't be able to fix.

And we both knew it.

"Grant." I heaved out a lungful of air, all the weight of my shitty argument with Abbigail coming back to rest on my chest and the aching heart inside it. "What are we doing here?"

Better yet, what the hell was I doing here?

I had no business fooling around with another man so soon after losing my husband. Maybe my sister-in-law was right. Maybe I was an awful person. An awful wife. An awful human, all around.

"I...I really think you should go. We can't keep doing this, Grant. We—we just can't."

"Hey, hey. What's going on? Talk to me." His voice shifted from the dominant sexy man to the cautious caretaker.

I, on the other hand, grew more resolute with every passing second. "No, Grant, I'm serious. I want you to leave. Abbi's right. I'm bad at all of this." I waved my hand around the kitchen randomly while Grant continued to stare. He had no idea what was going on in my confused mind. Again. It was so often the case these days. So he gave me a few feet of space and let me riot with my thoughts.

Finally, he tried to calmly reach me again. "Babe," he started, but I quickly shut him down.

"No!" I shook my head violently from side to side, figuring if I did it aggressively enough, the sound wouldn't be able to penetrate my ears. "No. No 'babe.' No 'baby.' Maybe we shouldn't even be friends anymore, you know? It's just going to keep leading to this. Or that!" I pointed frantically back toward the garage. "Don't you get it?" I yelled hysterically.

"No, actually, I don't. What we're doing doesn't make us bad people, Rio."

"It does! How don't you see that? People are already talking about me! That I'm a bad wife. My husband's body isn't even cold in the ground yet, and I already have another man in my bed. What do you think that makes me, Grant?"

"It makes you human, Rio. It makes you want to be alive. It means you are healing and trying to be healthy."

"No." I stabbed my finger toward him. "That's where you're wrong. It makes me a whore." I sighed as hot tears burned in angry streaks down my cheeks. "It makes me a heartless whore, Grant."

He shook his head and took a few tentative steps toward me. "You're wrong. So wrong. And whoever put that bullshit in your head..." He held his arms out to embrace me, and I wanted it so badly. I wanted to bury myself in his chest and inhale that smell that had come to mean comfort. Breathe in the citrus and cedar and lose myself in the peace I could only find within him these days.

But then, with impeccable timing, Grant's cell phone rang. The ringtone sliced through the moment like a dirty, rusty blade, eviscerating the ties that bound us to one another. Because I already recognized that ringtone after spending so much time with this man.

It belonged to Sebastian Shark. And the call would be a four-alarm, Shark-style emergency.

"For fuck's sake!" Grant hissed.

Yep. He knew it too.

"Just go," I said quietly, wiping my face with the hem of my

T-shirt. The phone rang again, and I physically winced from the stabbing reminder of which people really pulled the strings in both our lives. "Grant," I gritted. "Just leave. I'll be fine."

Grant whipped the phone to his ear and growled, "I'll call you right back." A quick pause, surely while Sebastian demanded his full attention. "I said I'll call you right back." He gripped the back of his neck and looked heavenward. "Yes, I understand that. Three minutes. Asshole." He stabbed at the screen to end the call and then shoved the thing into his pocket and looked at me. The anguish in his eyes nearly knocked me off my feet.

"I'll come back when I get this handled."

"No. Don't," I said with resignation. "I wasn't joking. This has to stop." I motioned back and forth between us.

"No."

He stalked toward me. And then kept coming. He yanked me against him so quickly and so fiercely, I made an *umph* sound when my body thumped against his.

"This isn't over, Blaze. Not by a long shot." He bent and kissed me so tenderly, so completely at odds with the fiery look in his eyes, it left me dazed when he stepped away.

And then he walked out the door without looking back.

He was off to save the world in the name of Sebastian Shark.

Again.

CHAPTER TEN

GRANT

My phone was a constant vibrating distraction until I reached the downtown offices of Shark Enterprises. The only factor in my favor about the return drive into the city during rush hour was getting to go against the majority of the rush hour crush. All the people who weren't so beholden to their boss that they'd leave the woman they loved while she was still trembling and emotional after they broke down her defenses...

Wait.

"Goddammit." I muttered the curse under my breath as the driver pulled up in front of Shark Enterprises.

I definitely was not in love with Rio Gibson.

Rio was still broken over the tragic loss of her husband, and our agreement about it all was very implicit. We were just scratching an itch together. Because we both knew—all too well—what a bitch loneliness could be. Not to mention I was not the kind of guy someone fell in love with.

What did I have to offer a woman long-term? Yes, I had money and a stable job. I had plenty of places to sleep at night. Hell, the fucked-up childhood scars I refused to deal with ensured that. But that line on my résumé was reason enough not to saddle a woman with the likes of me.

Fine, so I made decent arm candy. I had plenty of women stroke my ego over the years. Although I wasn't as pretty as Elijah, I did okay in the looks department. Also, I knew I was good in the sack. Again, I didn't have Elijah's Prince Charming reputation or Sebastian's devil's spawn notoriety, but the ladies I slept with always added my name to their contacts for a repeat performance.

But when I was being honest with myself, which I tried to do as a way of living, I'd make a shitty husband. I'd had no mentor to guide me growing up, and I wasn't sure it was something innately inside me like there seemed to be in Bas.

If I really cared about Rio, like I was completely sure I did, I would stay away from her. Her words of insistence ran through my memories from when I was leaving her place less than an hour ago.

So why did they feel like a broadsword being thrust through my sternum? Not a nice, clean impalement like a long sword, but a messy, difficult execution. It was to be expected when you didn't use the right tool for the job.

Which was much like abandoning Rio. No matter how adamantly she'd ordered exactly that. There was a better solution here, something in the middle of the two extremes. The proverbial dagger for this stabbing. I just needed to figure out what that looked like in my painful, emotional reality.

By the time I walked into Sebastian's office, Elijah was already there. Both men were divested of their suit jackets and ties and were huddled behind Sebastian's computer monitors. They were deep in conversation.

"All right. Gang's all here. What's the big emergency that couldn't wait until tomorrow?" I couldn't keep the bitterness from my voice, despite Elijah shooting me a warning look from where he stood behind Bas. But his expression was Hello fucking Kitty compared to the glower on our boss's stubbled, stressed-out features.

"The investigators' reports came back," Bas bit out. "They showed there was definitely foul play with the equipment that led to Sean Gibson's death. At the very least, we're going to have a huge OSHA test to deal with. The timeline is so fucked." He thrust a hand through his hair in frustration. As he scowled down at his blotter, Elijah and I traded terse looks.

"I'll start working with the superintendent and foreman first thing tomorrow to prepare for OSHA," I said, keeping my gaze fixed on Elijah's. "The inspector assigned to our site has been pretty easy to work with up to this point, so hopefully that will continue."

"This has the potential for a spectacular lawsuit if the wrong person hears about it, too. So I think discretion is in our best interest," Elijah added.

"Oh, that's going to be the tip of the iceberg. Rio Gibson is both crazy and unpredictable, and we all know it," Sebastian said in a snarky tone. "We'll be lucky if she isn't calling the daytime talk shows by lunchtime. The grieving widow bullshit gets huge ratings. The networks will be all over this."

Red. I actually saw a red haze over everything after hearing those words come from my best friend's mouth. "Grieving. Widow. Bullshit?" I stared at him in utter disbelief. I knew the man could be heartless, but this was so over the line.

"Bas, what about Abbigail?" Yeah, I just went there. And I'd do it again without hesitation if it meant reining his shit back in.

"What about her?" he clipped carelessly.

"Sean was her brother," I reminded.

"And?"

"And you just said he was basically murdered. You think that's going to sit well with her?"

"No, I don't. Not at all. But she's not a little whackjob like her sister-in-law."

It was taking every bit of inner strength I had to not leap across the furniture separating us and knock him on his ass. Apparently sensing this, Banks rounded Shark's desk and came around to physically restrain me if necessary.

"Listen to me, motherfucker," I seethed. "You know damn well that I care about that woman. She's my friend. It's in your best interest to stop with the comments about her mental health, or you're going to be eating my fist. It's the only warning I'm going to give you, asshole."

I lasered my stare right at him and let the silence that filled the room punctuate just how serious I was. I had a very clear memory of our fistfight over Abbigail in this very office because I did something very similar. I wasn't above turning the tables and going to the mat with the bastard again.

Only this time, I'd be fighting for Rio.

"Is that right?" Sebastian was on his feet by the time Elijah was between us, ready to defend himself if need be.

Elijah held his arms out wide, as if he were Moses parting the Red Sea. "All right, you two. That's enough. Let's use our big boy words. Every time she comes in here, Pia still grumbles about the last fight you two apes had and all the stuff you broke."

Bas flopped back down into his leather desk chair and planted his elbows on the armrests. He rocked back and forth a few times, aggressively testing the limits of the seat's springs.

Walking over to the bar, I asked, "Who needs a drink besides me?"

They both held up a hand, so I poured three glasses of whatever whiskey Sebastian had in the crystal decanter on the counter and came back over to distribute the liquor. "So what were you two looking at when I walked in?"

Elijah, having gone back around to the far side of the desk, slammed back his drink and set the empty glass down on the low bookcase. He made very pointed eye contact with me before saying, "We were looking at video surveillance of the construction site from the night of Gibson's accident."

I froze with my glass halfway to my lips and asked, "You mean of the accident itself?"

"No. After the site was shut down and everyone was sent home for the day," Sebastian said, not taking his eyes from the monitor.

Shit. I already had a bad feeling about where this was headed, but I needed to keep cool and play along. "Uhhh, what am I missing? Are you thinking someone broke into the site and stole something? Did the police find evidence that leads you to believe that happened?"

Finally, Sebastian sat back from his computer and took a sip from his glass. Then he looked at me for a long time before he asked, "Remind me, Grant, where did you find Rio that night? When no one else could find her?" He tilted his head to the side slightly, giving the whole line of questioning an air of condescension. I swore I could feel my heart rate rise in direct proportion with my ire, but I tried desperately to keep it in check as he continued. "I seem to recall you were the one that texted Abbigail and told her Rio was safe."

"She showed up at my condo," I said as nonchalantly as possible through clenched teeth. On the night in question, after Elijah went to the construction site and cleaned up after

Rio and me, we all agreed this would be the most believable story in case we were ever questioned. "What does any of this matter? I'm still not following you, man."

"Well, here's the thing . . . " He got up and strolled over to the windows, sipping leisurely on his whiskey as he went. The sun had long since set, and the downtown skyline was aglow with neon and manmade stars. "Evidence was collected on the scene that is consistent with a fire having burned there."

"I was there the very next day. I didn't see anything that looked damaged. Burned or otherwise. The area was sectioned off with police tape, and that certainly didn't look melted. What is making them think there was a fire?" I was starting to get agitated, and Elijah gave me another stern look. Since Bas had gone over to his usual window "thinking spot," we hung back and sat on the sofas.

Keeping my voice very quiet, I asked him, "Are you one hundred percent positive that surveillance footage was scrubbed?"

"Yep. But if you don't settle the fuck down, you're going to hang yourself. You're acting like a Muppet right now."

I gripped the back of my neck. He was right, and I was trying my best, but I was freaking the fuck out. I'd promised Rio I would take care of everything. I'd told her I wouldn't let anything happen to her for breaking down that night. Anyone would understand why she'd done what she had. Anyone with an ounce of compassion in their soul, at least.

"So Twombley. Tell me this, then." Bas strolled closer to Elijah and me.

Shit, why wouldn't he let up on this?

"What's up, man?" I considered putting my feet up on the table just to piss him off or, better yet, to derail his train of thought. He was acting like a first-responder-trained bloodhound who had scented a lost victim.

"Where did Rio say she had gone in that time between spitting in my face at the hospital and showing up randomly at your house? And now that I'm thinking of that bit of information, didn't you stay at your most recently purchased place downtown? How would she even know where that place was? You would've only been there for what? A few days, at most, when the accident happened?"

"This is crazy. I mean, do you hear yourself? You're firing questions at me like I'm on the witness stand. Like I'm the guilty party here. Of what, I've yet to figure out, but you've got something going on in that head of yours. Maybe I should have a lawyer present?" I looked across to Elijah to see if he agreed. "Is it me, or is he going overboard right now?"

Elijah sat forward, planted his elbows on his knees, and calmly folded his hands out in front. "What are you getting at, Bas? What's with all the questions?"

Sebastian shrugged. "I don't know. I'm just trying to connect the dots."

I sat forward too, almost mirroring Elijah's pose. Although I was much more on edge because Sebastian Shark's hot seat was a very tense place to be sitting. "Let's backtrack for a minute. What dots? Maybe that will help me understand what you're trying to get me to tell you."

"Or just come right out and ask what you want to know," Elijah suggested.

I threw my hands up in the air. "There's a fucking novel idea! See, Banks? This is why we keep you around. It's more than your pretty face. You're actually the sensible one."

Elijah tilted his head in warning. He knew I was trying to

lighten the mood, and this was all part of our normal banter. He gave me the middle finger for good measure.

"I love you too, sunshine."

"Hey, speaking of all that, I still need to get laid. I'm getting desperate enough to deal with Cybil the Banshee. Do you think you can set something up?"

"Hmm, yeah, maybe." I picked my phone up off the coffee table and opened the security screen as if I were about to send a text message but then stopped. "For tonight? Wait...what day is it? She might be working."

"Hey, Tweedledee and Tweedledum, I'm serious with these questions. I need answers. Try to focus. You can worry about getting your dicks wet when we get this figured out."

I wouldn't really call Cybil anyway, and Elijah knew that. It was a deterrent from Bas's dog-with-a-bone obsession with Rio's whereabouts the night of her dead husband's accident.

I shook my head as if clearing from confusion. It wasn't that far of a stretch, really. I had no idea why he wouldn't let this shit go. "Okay, sorry, man. What is it I can help you with?"

"For fuck's sake, Twombley!"

"Hey! Don't fucking yell at me! Just because you're on some wild goose chase and we don't feel like entertaining your ass with it." I stared at him, really trying to convey I'd reached my limit with his bullshit for one day.

"All right, all right. Let's settle down," Elijah verbally stepped in. Always playing peacemaker to our hotheaded exchanges. We all took turns in the role, actually. It just depended on who was arguing with whom at the time.

"Just stop being evasive," Bas said, forcing calm in his voice.

"Evasive? I've told you what you wanted to know."

"You haven't answered a single question I've asked you!"

"You asked me where I found Rio. I didn't find her. She came to my house. I told you that."

"How did she know where that brand-new place was?"

"I told her about it. Why is that such a shocker? We're friends, Bas. Friends talk about what's going on in their lives. I bought a new place. I told her about it. Hell! I may have even shown it to her to get her opinion on the location. I don't remember. We both work downtown. It's not that big of a deal." At least it didn't seem like it should be.

"Did she tell you where she had been in between the hospital and coming to your condo?" Sebastian asked.

"No. Not that I recall. She was fucked up, Bas. Her husband was just crushed to death on a construction site. I had to be the one to tell her about it. Remember all that bullshit?" The room got silent for a few moments as we all remembered the horrible accident scene. The pictures and video footage we'd seen from the incident itself were the kind of images that you just couldn't forget. The kind of things that gave you nightmares.

Then, Sebastian turned to Elijah with a question out of left field. "Banks, didn't you say that Rio Gibson had prior arrests for starting fires?"

Goddammit. Of all the things for Sebastian to remember about Rio's past, this was the tidbit that stuck with him?

"Well, no, not exactly," Elijah answered smoothly.

"What the hell does that mean? Yes or no? Did she or didn't she?" Bas's tempered flared again.

But Elijah stayed calm as a summer breeze. "She did not. No."

"I distinctly remember sitting in this office talking about

that woman and pyromania in the same conversation."

"Arson and pyromania are two different things," I said coolly and with authority. Believe me, I'd done plenty of research—and way past what you found on Wikipedia.

"Look. I don't know what the two of you are covering up for that woman, but so help me God, if I find out she lit a fire on that job site the night her husband died and one or both of you knew about it? You will wish it was you under that falling beam instead of her husband."

"For fuck's sake, Sebastian! Get a grip on yourself," Elijah said. "You're trying to make connections where there aren't any because you're in a panic. You know the shit's about to hit the fan because someone tampered with the equipment that killed Sean Gibson, and you're looking for any way to divert the attention off yourself."

God bless Elijah Banks. Because if that had all come from my mouth, it would've just seemed like I was defending Rio. But when he said it, it finally made Bas take pause.

Then he went on. "I don't think a three-ring circus of naked cheerleaders would be able to get the attention off you in this situation, my friend. In case you haven't noticed all the reporters hanging around that job site, they're waiting to scoop up any scrap or morsel they can about what happened to cause that accident. Hell, someone down at the police station has probably already leaked the investigators' reports to them."

Finally, I found my voice again. "Focusing on Rio's teenage mental health problems won't help anyone right now. I'm going to point out again, she is Abbi's sister, just about. Hurting Rio is just going to hurt Abbigail. I don't think that's something you want to do, man."

"Don't tell me how to handle my woman."

I held my hands up in front of me. "That's the last thing I would try to do. Lord knows I have no experience in the field. I just know the close relationship those two have, and I saw some pretty strained moments at the baby shower. Did Abbi tell you about that?" Yes, finally, a chance to change this damn subject altogether.

Please take the bait. Please take the bait. Please take the bait. I kept up the mental chant while staying busy with nonexistent lint on my slacks.

"Yes and no. I got the overly emotional Abbigail version of the conversation. So you stayed for the whole shower? What's wrong with you, man?" Bas chuckled while asking.

"Rio kept giving me tasks to do. Every time I thought I was home free, she'd have something else she needed help with."

"So you've basically stepped in as the man of the house around there?"

"Don't even joke about that shit. She's in a bad spot emotionally. But the last thing she's looking for is a replacement for the husband she just lost. She's a good friend."

"Well, then. Tell us what the women were arguing about," Elijah said, jumping in on supporting the subject change. There was no way he actually wanted to hear the details, but anything was better than letting Sebastian have control of our camp's spirit stick again.

"Well, apparently Bas and Abbi think it'll be nice to honor Abbi's brother by using his name for the baby Shark's middle name. Rio said she didn't mind but has some... bitterness... currently where Daddy Shark here is concerned." I paused for a moment as bigger puzzle pieces started clicking into place. "Oh shit... dude."

I cradled my face in my hands as the gravity of the

situation, as it pertained to Rio, really sank in.

"What is it, Grant?" Elijah asked.

"It's just hitting me from a different angle." I waved my hand around the office. "All of this."

Sebastian's phone rang with the familiar ring we all knew to be Abbigail's personal number, so he excused himself and moved away from our trio to talk to his baby mama. But I was glad for the time alone with Elijah, who understood what was really going on with me and Rio. Well, more than anyone else, at least.

"Talk to me, brother. What's going on?" he asked once Bas was out of earshot.

"Rio has been off and unstable. That's probably being generous, in a matter of terminology." I winced at my own word choice, instantly consumed by guilt from saying something unfavorable about the woman I cared so deeply about.

"Okay." He waited for more information.

"When I think about the impact of this news, about her husband's death not being an accident, per se, it's going to be explosive. Actually, that's probably an understatement." I rubbed the back of my neck, where tension was causing the muscles to ache. "Rio has so much resentment for Bas already, and she's going to see this only one way, and that is as Sebastian's fault. If someone wasn't trying to hurt him, her husband wouldn't have been caught in the crossfire. Sean Gibson would still be alive."

"Do you think she will physically act out?" Elijah asked. "As in, we need to have a fire extinguisher on hand?"

"I hope not."

"Well, you'll just have to keep a close eye on her."

"She told me to stay away from her today, before I left to come here."

"Why?" Elijah pressed. "Why would she say that to you?"

"Things have been, shit—pardon the pun—heating up between us lately. And I mean, really getting hot."

"Yeah?" he asked with a salacious grin.

"Yeah." I couldn't help but grin too, but quickly added, "Don't bother asking for details, because I'm not giving you any."

"Awww, come on, man. Throw me a bone here. I'm in the worst dry spell of my life."

"I find that hard to believe."

"I never joke about sex. Or lack thereof."

"You could walk out onto the street and get any woman— or man—you wanted. What's the problem?" I asked, happy to be on to a different subject once again.

"That's the problem. I don't just want anyone. There's only one I want. And she's proving to be more difficult to find than Jimmy Hoffa's corpse."

"Well, our buddy over there is going to be a corpse if my Blaze has her way with him when she hears this latest development. He'd better watch his back for the next few days."

"So you're going to tell her?"

"It will be better coming from me than anyone else. At least I think it will. I may have to restrain her first, though." My dick gave an involuntary jerk, and I had to shift in my seat.

"You're such a bastard." Elijah chuckled. "You had to plant that image in my head, didn't you?"

Without thinking, I punched him in the arm. Hard.

"Oww! What was that for?"

I aggressively pointed a finger in his face. "You don't think of her that way. Ever," I warned.

"Goddamn, Twombley. I didn't realize you were in so deep."

I dropped my chin to my chest and shook it slowly from left to right. After a few beats, I looked back up to see he was still rubbing his arm.

"I'm not sure I realized it either."

CHAPTER ELEVEN

RIO

Lunch?

A text from Grant.

Busy. I have to do the deliveries today.

Then meet me at my Brentwood place tonight.

No.

Blaze. Stop this.

Friendzone. Remember?

8 p.m. Don't make me wait.

Ugh. I tossed my phone down on the desk, which caused Hannah, Abbi, and Dori to stop what they were doing and look in my direction.

Thinking quickly to cover my mini-fit of frustration with Grant, I said with an exaggerated huff, "These vendors are driving me insane. Why doesn't anyone just do their job?"

"Can I help with anything?" Dori asked, heading toward me with her superhero cape flapping behind her. So I imagined the cape, but at least the image made me chuckle. But when the chuckle turned into a full-blown fit of laughter, releasing the stress from the past couple of days, everyone really began to stare.

I held up a hand, trying to get a coherent word in between gasping for air and cackling. "Sorry."

Then, just when I thought I'd settled down enough to explain, I'd picture the woman in additional superhero garb, maybe a black eye mask or hair popped high in a female version of a pompadour, and I would burst into another round of raucous laughter.

Lack of good-quality sleep—hell, any sleep at this point—torturous eating habits, and stress levels that could be measured with a Geiger counter instead of a blood pressure cuff were starting to wear me down. I would never admit it to anyone, not even Grant, but I was also starting to have periods during my day that were completely unaccounted for.

The GPS app on my phone had been getting a hefty workout since Grant Twombley took a more front-and-center role in my life. Why couldn't the man just stay in one place for more than a few nights at a time? And people thought *I* had head problems...

A quick scan of the route I could take from where I'd be downtown and his home in Brentwood gave me one distance. Then I measured the course again with a stop back here at the Inglewood kitchen to pick up Kendall. By making that one extra stop after the deliveries, I would avoid a million prying questions in the morning. Luckily, the app gave me the answer

I was hoping for. It wouldn't be that inconvenient to stop back by Abstract Catering to pick up my personal vehicle to make my drive to the west side after work.

If that was what I decided to do, at least. The jury was still deliberating whether I'd go to his place or not, and I didn't expect a decision until the very last minute.

Once the van was loaded with the lunch orders, I set off for the downtown route. It was always such a welcome relief to get out of the kitchen. Even though much of the administrative work had to be handled by Abbi or me, as the owners, I missed the good old days when the business was simpler.

Once the Edge opened its doors, our business model would change completely. We were putting those organizational meetings off until Abbi delivered the baby, though. She couldn't concentrate on much more than her overly swollen body parts at the moment, and I couldn't focus on more than my disdain for her husband. Nothing productive would get done by either of us.

A few hours out on my own, and my mood improved significantly. The fresh air helped me think more clearly, and being out among our clients helped me keep focused and level-headed. My thoughts usually only drifted when I was alone for extended periods, and I had a feeling Grant knew that. Maybe that was part of the reason he was so attentive. He really had been an amazing bolster since the accident, and I needed to remember to be patient with him and show a little more gratitude.

The mid-spring evening air was still cool by the time I locked up in Inglewood and switched cars to make the drive west to Brentwood. I had firmed up my decision to go see my friend after the last lunch order was set in front of the client, and I considered sending Grant a text to let him know but then thought it would be more fun to make him wonder if I was going to show up until the exact moment he opened his door and found me standing on the other side.

I didn't regret sleeping with him, necessarily, because... my God, it was an earth-moving experience in its own right... but I knew we couldn't go on with that sort of behavior. The more time I had away from his intoxicating presence, the more sure I became of the fact. The problem arose when I was near him. He had a magnetic pull on me when we were near each other. So I spent the entire drive from Inglewood to Brentwood mentally shoring up my walls against my need to feel the muscled planes that made up my favorite tree, Grant Twombley.

I let my eyes slide shut while I sat at a surface street red light near his place. I could already anticipate the seductive smell that usually knocked me on my ass when I walked into one of his homes. That damn delicious, sexy sandalwood and cedar mixed with mint and citrus. Fuck Chanel and all their creative olfactory glory.

Maybe it had nothing to do with Chanel at all. Maybe... it was just Grant that had this effect on me.

No, no, no. Wasn't going back down that road. Seriously. How was I already changing my tune just by getting within five miles of the bastard? I knew pheromones were a thing, but could they really be this potent? Nah. No way. This was just a plain and simple case of sad and lonely me wanting to be ravished and adored by sexy, handsome, intelligent, and attentive him.

Nothing more.

I parked Kendall in the driveway of his two-story condo,

grabbed my purse off the passenger seat, and went to the front door. A quick look at my phone showed the time at twelve minutes past eight. Well, tough shit, he'd have to deal with it. Traffic was a bitch in this town, and if he ever drove his own ass around, he'd know—

The front door whooshed open, and six and a half feet of man, wearing a body-hugging T-shirt over his very well-defined muscled body, filled the space.

Grant stood in the doorway with his hands over his head, gripping the wide, bright-white molding that framed the opening. His dark denim jeans hung low on his hips, shamelessly advertising the cut vee of muscle that led the eye right to his crotch.

My throat was so parched when I went to speak a greeting, no sound came out.

The side of his mouth kicked up in a lazy, smug grin before he said, "You're late. I distinctly remember saying not to be late."

Grant stretched one long arm out and hooked four fingers into my thick, studded, black leather belt and pulled me toward him. I all but stumbled into the foyer as he moved back from the doorframe and shut the panel behind me with a solid clap. The sound made me jump, and the motion of the door made my short hair flip up in the back.

The entire interaction made me feel like a skittish, gun-shy colt rather than the self-assured mustang I had myself pumped up to be earlier in my car. The effect this man had on me, and over me, was downright unsettling.

He moved closer, trapping me against the door with his massive body. Grant wasn't a mountain of thick muscles like some men, but with more than a foot of height advantage over me and so much lean muscle definition . . . well . . . massive seemed to be a suitable description.

"Well," I said. "Here I am. What did you want to see me about?" A snippy attitude was my best defense in this arousing situation.

"Where's your bag? You're not driving home tonight." He stroked a few stray pieces of hair across my forehead with sure fingers, lingering way too long where we touched. "You know what, it doesn't matter. I'm sure I have stuff here you can borrow."

"You keep women's clothing on hand?" I just shook my head. "You're a player's player, Grant Twombley. The king of players, really." I ducked off to the side to get away from him. The heat that was already building in my core would betray me if I didn't. I propped a hip on the arm of a surprisingly old sofa and waited for him to answer my question.

Instead, he stepped up to me, so close, his leading leg was between mine. "I meant you could wear something of mine if you had to, but I'm guessing you really have a bag in your car. You're just playing some game here."

"I don't play games, Tree. You should know that about me by now."

He reached out and cupped my shoulders with his warm, comforting palms, but I immediately shrugged out of his grip. "Friends, Grant. If you can't respect that, I'm going to turn right around and go back out the door. I can't keep doing this with you. I need your friendship right now. I value it more than you'll ever know. But if that line is too blurry for you, then I will have to go without."

He jerked his hands away from me and held them up between us in surrender. "All right. All right," he said, keeping his blue gaze pinned to mine. "For now. We can do this your way. For now."

"Do you mind if I get some water?" I asked, looking over my shoulder as I meandered into the kitchen. Even though this was one of the swankier zip codes Grant owned property in, the condo itself wasn't over the top. A modest two-bedroom place like this in this neighborhood probably sold for one and a half million dollars. There was no yard, and there was at least one shared wall with the unit next door. Grant was one of the lucky residents who scored an attached garage.

"Sit down. I'll get it for you. What kind of host would I be?"

"I don't mind making myself at home," I said but plopped down on the denim sectional. "I thought you were going to renovate this place?" I asked, looking around the room. The decor and the flooring were in desperate need of modernization.

He rubbed the back of his neck, one of the telltale signs of stress in my friend's body-language dictionary. "Yeah." He heaved a sigh and handed me a bottle of water, already having opened it. He sat down beside me, even though the entire sofa was available, and angled his tall frame toward me, resting his long arm across the back of the cushions. "I just haven't had the time to get out here with my general contractor. I could just have the interior designer I work with handle everything, but the last project she did?" He waited for my nod that I was still paying attention, and I couldn't fault him. I was really drifting off during conversations lately.

"I think I met her in Naples one day when I stopped by and you weren't home? The stunning Greek woman?" The pang of jealousy I felt that afternoon was back with the same bitter vengeance that it possessed that afternoon.

Shit. He's not yours, girlfriend.

"That's the one. Amaya."

"That doesn't sound Greek, though."

"She once told me her ancestors were rulers in the Incan Empire, in what is now Chile."

"Well, she's beautiful. Have you slept with her?"

"Do you really want to talk about that?"

"No. I guess I don't. But anyway, what did she do on the last project? It seems like you're hesitant to use her now."

"She went fucking nuts with my black card. I mean, cray-zee."

I barked out a loud laugh hearing Mr. Businessman Twombley use such teenage-girl slang. It made my heart ache and my eyes fill with unwelcomed tears. God, I was such an emotional basket case.

Immediately, Grant scooted right up against me and gathered me into his arms. And honestly, I was done fighting him off. If I wasn't strong enough to make it through ten hours without him, what made me think I could live without him in my life, physically and emotionally supporting me? Who was I trying to kid?

"Baby, what's wrong? Why do you have tears?"

"I missed you. I know that's so stupid." I buried my nose in the crook of his neck and inhaled. The immediate calming sensation from his scent covered my mind and body like an invisible veil.

"I don't think that's stupid. At all. It feels good to be missed. I miss you when we're not together, too. That's the main reason I wanted to see you tonight. I mean, would I like to be inside you again? Hell yes. Do we have some things to talk about? Unfortunately, yes. But just being in the same room with you, Rio? It calms my nerves. Knowing that you're doing okay, that you're safe and happy? That's become one of the most important things to me."

The look on his face was so earnest and honest, if I hadn't already been sitting down, it would've knocked me off my feet. It wasn't an expression I'd seen before on his handsome features, and he looked positively vulnerable. Grant Twombley wasn't a man who laid himself bare for other people and, I had a feeling, rarely—if ever—for a woman.

"But really? What made you get so emotional? Because you missed me?"

"That, yes. But—I don't know how to explain it so it makes sense." I knocked on the side of my head with my knuckles. "You know how messed up it is here."

He pulled my balled fist down from my skull and held it in his hand. "Stop saying things like that. You've been through a tough time, Blaze. Anyone would be off their game."

The tears came again, uninvited. "That's what I'm talking about. That, right there."

Grant tilted his head like a handsome, confused little puppy, so I explained further.

"You see all of me. You see everything. You see all my parts—the good, the bad, the light, and the dark. Yet, here you sit. Your heart is so brave and beautiful, Grant. You're an amazing man."

I had to embrace him after saying all of that because looking into his fathomless eyes was just too intense. He absorbed my words while I was saying them, and I knew he really heard them. Whatever he did with them from there? Well, that was up to him. But I gave him my truth, and that was all I could do. I wasn't in love with Grant. But I knew I loved him, and I could very quickly, and naturally, fall in love with him when my heart was whole again.

I would never ask him to wait around for me, put his life on a shelf while I picked up the pieces of mine and reassembled them and figured out if there was a space available for him to fit. Those were questions only he could answer. Those were his truths, and I wouldn't ask him for them, because frankly, I wasn't ready to hear them.

Grant pushed my short wild hair back from my face while he stared at me. He soothed me with his long fingers, steady movements, and sure touch. "You are the most beautiful woman I've ever known, Rio Katrina."

I nearly bugged my eyes out of my skull, having never been fond of that stupid middle name. "How did you know that?" I gasped.

He grinned mischievously. "I have my ways."

"What's your middle name?"

"Wouldn't you like to know?"

I dug a finger into his ribs, and he squirmed away. "Tell me."

"No way," he laughed.

"I'll just ask Elijah. Or Sebastian. Okay, fine, not Sebastian. But Elijah will tell me. He loves harassing you." I pulled my phone out of my back pocket to fire off a text to the other man Grant considered his best friend. I noticed I had a message from Abbigail, but I left it unread.

Grant threw his head back with a genuine laugh. It was probably the first time in two weeks, maybe longer, that I'd heard a real laugh come from him. "That he does. The bastard will sell me out any chance he gets, too. But be prepared..." Grant warned.

"What?" I asked. "Be prepared for what?"

"Making a deal with Banks always has a price. Always."

"Hmmm. Duly noted." I nodded thoughtfully but grinned all the while. I couldn't help but test out a few name combinations.

"Marshal?" I wrinkled my nose. "Anthony?"

"You're never going to guess it. Not in a million years. It's a family name, so unless Elijah spills the beans, you'll never just pick it out of thin air."

"So just tell me. If it's a family name, it must have some meaning?"

He laughed again. "Yeah, it means my mother was probably high when she picked it out and thought she'd sound regal like the princess she always wanted to be. Instead of a pauper." His good nature had totally faltered by the time he finished speaking.

I put my hand on his thigh and rubbed back and forth. "I'm sorry."

He stopped my motion with his much larger hand on top of mine. "Don't be. It's not any fault of yours."

"I know, but I should've dropped it while you were in a good mood."

"Well, we need to have a serious conversation anyway."

"Not sure I like the sound of this . . . " I let my voice drift off while I stared at him warily.

Grant sat forward on the sofa cushion and then turned to face me. He took both my hands in his and held them for a few moments, looking down to where we were joined. The whole scene gave me a terrible sense of déjà vu, and I tried to yank out of his grasp, but he just held me tighter.

Exactly like he did then, too.

"Let. Go," I said through clenched teeth.

"We need to talk about this, Rio."

"I feel claustrophobic when you hold on to me like that." I grabbed at my throat like I was being strangled by imaginary hands. "I want to stand up." I sprang up immediately when he released my hands and paced back and forth from the kitchen through the living room to the front door and back. I completed the circuit twice before he shot to his feet and intercepted me on my way past.

"For fuck's sake, you're making me batty with the pacing."

"Then I'll leave. Whatever you need to say, you can text me. Or send an email."

"I have an idea. How about a walk? Outside? The neighborhood has some nice walking trails. I know it's late, but they're all well-lit and maintained. Do you have a jacket in your car? You can borrow a sweatshirt of mine if not."

The idea didn't suck. And at least I wouldn't feel so cooped up inside this condo. "Yeah, I have a jacket in my trunk. I'm parked right on the driveway. I'll grab it on the way out."

Grant led the way, handing me a bottle of water once I zipped up my hoodie. The night was brisk but pleasant. I'd probably end up taking the jacket off once we were walking awhile.

"I'm glad we did this," he said, looking at me while we walked. "I hate seeing you panicked like that."

"It's literally the worst feeling."

"Have you always been claustrophobic?" he asked, tentatively grasping my hand to hold while we walked.

"I don't know if I'm actually claustrophobic, you know?"

He was giving me the most skeptical look when I finally met his gaze.

"I'm serious. I can ride in an elevator just fine. I've had an MRI and did just fine. I think it's more of a panic attack than anything else. The way you were holding my hands and looking at me, it took me right back to the moment you told me about—" I couldn't finish the sentence, but I didn't have to. He knew what I meant.

"Told you about what?" he pressed.

Now I was the one looking at him like he was the village idiot.

"I want you to say it out loud. Don't think it's escaped my notice, Blaze. You won't say his name. You won't say that he's dead!" Grant threw his hands up in frustration. His loud voice caused a dog to bark somewhere in the distance. "Hell, I'm not sure you sleep in your own damn bed when I'm not there with you."

"That's ridiculous," I scoffed.

"Is it? Why is there always a bed pillow and blankets stuffed behind the sofa?"

I snapped my stare in his direction. How did he even see those? Fucking Tree and that height advantage. Had to be.

Grant's shoulders dropped a few inches as he tried to relax his temperament. "It will be good for you, baby. Just take one little step at a time."

"You don't know what you're talking about," I said quietly, but there was no mistaking the amount of acid in my tone.

"Okay." He sighed heavily and yanked at his nape. "But that's sort of what we need to talk about. So I hope like hell you can deal with what I'm about to tell you. Because if you don't hear it from me, you're going to hear it from the cops. And fuck..." He looked up at the nighttime sky as if the answers he needed would be spelled out in glittering stars and moon dust. "Then Sebastian will somehow twist the shit into his own version of the facts, I'm sure."

"Just say what you need to say, Grant. Stop coddling me. I'm a big girl. I can handle the shit life throws at me."

He looked at me with one blond brow hiked almost to his hairline. "I think we both know that's debatable."

"You can be such an asshole sometimes."

He waited before saying anything else. The only sound filling the night air was our sneakers hitting the concrete sidewalk in unison.

After a few minutes, I finally broke the silence. "So the reports came back on the equipment maintenance? The reports I requested at the police station when they presented their other findings?" I looked over to Grant because he was unusually quiet. "Is that what this is about?"

He shoved his hand back through his floppy blond hair. It was longer than he usually wore it, and I kind of like it. "Yeah," he muttered.

"Well?" I stopped walking, and he had to double back to where I stood in the middle of the walkway. No one else was out for a stroll this late at night, so we had the path to ourselves. "What did they come up with? It wasn't an accident, was it?"

Again, his shoulders dropped in resignation, and it was all the confirmation I needed. None of the information came as a surprise, though. From the moment I allowed that seed to germinate in my mind, the roots had taken hold. Every new leaf that sprouted along the strangling vine of my husband's accident just became more of the foliage that adorned my topiary of hatred for Sebastian Shark.

"No, there was definitely foul play. It looks like the hydraulic lines on the forks were tampered with. They collected some fingerprints that aren't consistent with the mechanic's or the operator's, but because of the number of people on the job site and the number of people in and out of the equipment rental yard, it will be tough to nail down when and where the tampering happened."

"Right." I nodded along while Grant spoke. "Tough," I repeated.

"Whoever pulled this stunt did their homework. I've got to say, of all the shit we've dealt with recently, this one was executed in the smartest way."

My mouth hung open in disbelief while I tried to formulate a retort. "Are you actually giving props to the person who assisted in my husband's accident right now?"

"No. No. I'm sorry." He rushed toward me. "I'm sorry, baby." Then he went to wrap his arms around me—the same arms that only an hour ago, I wanted to spend the night in—but I smacked at his outstretched offer. "I'm so sorry," my friend repeated. "That was such an insensitive way to say that. And my timing was the worst. Please forgive me. You're right, I'm a total asshole."

On the path up ahead, I could see a park bench. Sitting down seemed like a great idea suddenly. I was about to camp out right there on the pavement when the seat caught my eye, so I beelined for it.

"Blaze? Where are you go—?" Grant interrupted himself and just followed me instead, tracking my line of sight to the bench. When he stood in front of where I plopped down, he cautiously asked, "Do you mind if I join you? If you need time . . . or space . . . or whatever."

I couldn't hold in my giggle. Watching a six-foot-six man flounder around in discomfort over asking a woman to sit beside her was one of the most incongruous sights to behold. Even though the topic at hand was the furthest thing from humorous, observing a socially awkward Grant Twombley would top the list every day of the week.

"Tree. Just stop. Sit down and stop acting like a schoolboy about to have his first kiss."

He let his sexy, lopsided grin spread across his full lips before saying, "At this rate, I'm never going to get to kiss you again, am I?"

"It's not looking good, no. But that's how this whole day started. Friendzone, remember?"

"I guess I was still holding out hope. But after this next conversation . . . " He trailed off, and I bolted up on the bench, sitting with my spine ramrod straight.

"What? There's more?"

"Yeah, afraid so. And unfortunately, this isn't good."

Thumbing over my shoulder, I asked, "And that other shit was?"

Grant just shrugged and then rubbed his forehead between the sides of his thumb and index finger. He looked at me with tired, weary eyes and said, "I'm so fucking tired of dealing with this man's bullshit, Rio. You have no idea." He went back to massaging his forehead again as if he couldn't look me in the eye after admitting that.

"I can only imagine. But you're an adult." I paused and put my hand on his thigh, waiting for him to raise his gaze to meet mine before continuing. "A freethinking, wildly successful adult. Unburden yourself and get away from him before he takes you down with him."

"Can I lay my head on your lap?" His voice was so small, so pure.

I chuckled, really thinking he was joking, but the pleading look in his worn-out stare told me he was serious. I scooted to the end of the bench and patted my thighs with the invitation. Now we both had what we needed. I wasn't trapped indoors, and he had a little TLC.

Absentmindedly, I stroked my fingers through his thick blond hair while we enjoyed the fresh night air. "Your hair has gotten so long."

"I know. My girl is on some pilgrimage or something, and I had to schedule an extra week and a half between appointments." He kept his eyes closed while he spoke. "She'll be back late next week."

In a nearby tree, an owl called out to its mate and then took flight when the return call didn't come as quickly as he preferred.

"Did you know that owls mate for life?" I asked quietly while stroking his hair.

"No, I didn't know that. That's pretty cool." He quietly enjoyed my ministrations before asking, "Wonder what nature's answer is to a situation like yours."

"Believe it or not, I know the answer to that too." I sighed, my heart heavy as I thought about love, life, and all the things going on between this gorgeous man in my lap and me. "At least for owls, anyway. When I was a little girl, I was fascinated by them, so I learned all the facts I could find. I was really interested in barn owls because I loved their haunting white faces. They call this time the hooting season. The males are out looking for mates before they begin nesting. Back east, it happens in the fall, but a lot of things don't follow the same patterns here in Southern California because the temperature stays relatively the same all year."

We grew quiet again, listening to the owls calling to each other in the trees.

"So, what happens?" Grant pressed, looking up at me. "If an owl's mate dies? Do they spend the rest of their life alone?"

"No," I said solemnly, but I didn't want to admit the rest. He would press for the information, though. I knew this man well enough to know that. "The surviving bird finds a new mate and begins breeding again."

"Nature has a way of making it all seem so simple, doesn't it?" he asked, turning to look up at me. "Basically, life is just about companionship and making babies."

I gave a halfhearted smile.

If only it were that simple.

Grant sat up then, brushed off a dry leaf that clung to his sleeve, and turned to me once more. "We may have a big problem, and you need to know about it in case Sebastian keeps pressing the issue."

"What do you mean? What's going on? And why do we have to keep bringing up that bastard's name?"

Grant frowned. "The night of the accident. At the Edge construction site, when I found you there, and you were—"

"Yeah, yeah, I know. What about it?" I went from serene to annoyed in record time. "Why would Sebastian even know about that? Did you tell him? Grant?" My voice went up an octave when I said his name. I gasped at the notion that he'd sold me out to that bastard best friend of his. The idea stabbed me straight through my already broken heart.

"No!" he answered firmly. "No. I didn't tell him. I promised I would protect you, and I'm a man of my word, Rio. I may be a lot of shitty things, but if I give you my word, I honor it." He stared at me for a few moments and then started shaking his head. "Christ, I can't believe you would think I'd do that to you."

"Then tell me what you're talking about, because that's the way my mind naturally connects dots. All I've ever experienced is people selling me out to protect themselves."

"Well, I haven't. I said I wouldn't do that to you, and I didn't. In fact, I just stood in front of the only man I've been able to count on for my entire life. A man I've considered my brother." Grant winced with a pained look. "The only person who has had my back, every fucking time I've needed him—and I lied to him. Lied right to his face, Rio. And I did it to protect you."

He watched my eyes with intense scrutiny, seeming to gauge my reaction to his assertion.

"That was your choice, Grant. All of it. You didn't have to come there that night. You didn't have to get involved or get Elijah involved." I stood up and paced in front of the bench but fought the urge to run off like I wanted to. Instead, I whirled around and faced him, squared my shoulders, and let him feel every ounce of my fury. "And you certainly didn't have to lie to him. Don't try to guilt me about it now."

But Grant didn't rise to my bait. Instead, his shoulders fell in resignation. When he looked up to meet my glare, his eyes were filled with so much sadness, it nearly knocked the breath from my lungs. "Is that really what you think I'm trying to do? Do you really not know me at all? After all the time we've spent together? You think I'm trying to guilt you?"

"Don't you get it?" I hissed. "You're the one who doesn't know me! I'm fucking crazy, Grant! And every day, I lose my shaky grip on reality a little more. Don't align yourself with me. I'm the loser's bet." I shook my head while I stared at him with pity.

Grant surged to his feet and gripped my upper arms so tightly, I'd probably have bruises. He gave little shakes to my shoulders to punctuate his words while he said, "You're wrong. So wrong. And I refuse to give up on you, so don't you do it either. But you need to take this seriously, Rio. Elijah scrubbed all the video footage from that night, but whatever forensics picked up from the soil on-site is showing evidence of fire, and Bas is on it like a bloodhound right now. You need to lie low and not indulge in your 'hobby' right now. Okay? Are you listening to me?"

He shook my upper body again, and I knocked his arms away. "Don't fucking touch me!" I yelled. My voice echoed off the condos that backed up to the walking trail.

"Keep your voice down before we have the police back here," he gritted through clenched teeth.

"Then keep your hands to yourself. I heard you the first time you said it. You're not my daddy, Grant. Or my Dom, or, well, shit. You're not my anything, are you?"

"I'm your friend. I care about you—so much." He looked up to the stars for a few moments before sucking in a deep breath and bringing his face level with mine again. "But I know that man better than anyone does, Rio. He will destroy us all—you, me, and Elijah—if he ever finds out we've lied to him. Please tell me you understand the gravity of this situation."

★ ★ ★

I spent the night on Grant's sofa. I refused to complicate things by getting into bed beside the man. I knew myself well enough to realize there was no way we wouldn't end up comforting one another in all the best but wrong ways. He wanted me to take the guest room, but he would just end up in that bed with me before sunrise, too. So I agreed to the couch or to drive all the way down to Orange County to my own place.

As I drove into the Abstract Catering kitchen, I tossed around the idea of putting the Seal Beach bungalow up for sale. Grant's realtor would probably be happy to sell the place for me. Sure, it needed some improvements, but the home was charming. Properties in that zip code held their value no matter what the real estate market did elsewhere.

Before I knew it, I was parking Kendall in her usual spot and digging for my keys at the bottom of my purse. I still loved this place in the early morning hours. The quiet of the kitchen, the therapeutic lull of chopping and prepping ingredients, the first smells that filled the kitchen—all things that took me back to uncomplicated days when it was just Abbi and me here.

And we were happy.

We worked our asses off every day, but we were so happy. We would chat and giggle, sing and dance around the kitchen while we cooked and acted like teenagers playing chef in our moms' kitchens. The nostalgia strangled me to the point of a near anxiety attack, so I shut the memories down, threw open my car door, and power walked across the parking lot to go inside.

I didn't need my key because Hannah was already inside, busy in the walk-in cooler loading a prep pan with ingredients for the lunch menu special.

"Good morning, beautiful!" I called out to her so I wouldn't startle her when she came out.

"Hey, Rio! Morning!" She came around the corner smiling

brightly, but her face crumbled when she saw me.

"That bad, huh?" I fussed with my hair a bit, but I knew it was hopeless. "I have a ball cap in the car. Maybe I'll go with that today." I gave a quick nod, solidifying the plan.

Hannah slid the pan from her hip to the worktop and looked at me with cautious eyes. "Do you want someone to talk to? I know Abbi can be pretty abrasive." She followed her comment with a gentle smile. "I mean, no offense. I know she's your sister-in-law, but it seems like things have been tense between you guys."

"None taken. Walk with me?" I motioned to the door and then held up my car keys. If I was going with the ball cap look, I needed to run out to my car.

"Sure thing." Hannah dried her hands on her chef's jacket, and we strolled out to Kendall.

"I just didn't get much sleep. And not because I was knockin' boots all night. I just . . . well . . . I'm having a hard time being the only owl in the nest. You know?"

"I can't even imagine," the pretty girl said while nodding. "Obviously I've only been single so far. But can I ask how long you and Sean were married?"

"Just shy of seven years," I said quietly. "We were young when we started dating, so we sort of grew up together." I popped my trunk open, grabbed the worn cap from among the pile of crap I kept in there, and then slammed the compartment shut again.

With the visor facing backward, I fingered my bangs back under the hat and wiggled it until it felt just right. I turned to Hannah for her opinion.

"Much better." She smiled cheerfully. "No one will notice you didn't sleep well now."

"Please." I laughed, but the noise sounded as bitter as it felt. "Abbigail watches me like a hawk all day. It's like she's keeping a journal about my behavior or something."

"But why? Why doesn't she just try to show some compassion instead?"

"This is her version of caring. That's why I'm trying to be patient with her. And it's ramped up about seventy-two percent with the baby Shark on board. I can't wait until that little sucker swims downstream so we can all have a little peace around here again."

We both burst out laughing at my comment, but I sobered quickly, feeling guilty for talking badly about my sister. I loved that woman with my whole heart. I truly did.

"You know I love her, right?"

"Of course I do," Hannah assured me. "You're just venting, and I get that. I have four sisters, so I know what it can be like." She rolled her eyes dramatically. "Trust me."

"Four more little golden goddesses are running around this town who look like you? Girl!" I whistled. "How has your poor daddy not had a heart attack?"

"Actually, he's had two already. But that's just from his workaholic habits and his love of fast food."

We were back inside the kitchen, and I repeated "Fast food?" and clutched my heart like she just told me my baby was ugly.

Hannah held up her hand in a *stop* gesture. "I know, I know."

We laughed again and got to work on the day's menu. The other women arrived soon after, and the usual tension that came in the door with Abbigail settled over the kitchen.

Later, while dumping a large pot of pasta into a strainer,

my tired muscles finally failed me, and I lost my precarious grip on the handle, spilling scalding hot water over my wrist and forearm.

"Motherfucker!" I bellowed but finished draining the pasta. Immediately, I turned the tap to lukewarm water, thrust my arm under it, and buried my face in the crook of my uninjured arm. I swayed my hips from side to side, trying desperately to absorb the pain with the movement, but I really wanted to scream more. The pain was so intense.

Abbi and Dori rushed to my side to help.

"Hey..." Dori soothed. "Hey, Rio? You okay? Can I see it?" she asked gently.

"It'll be fine. Just a stupid burn. Happens all the time," I said from my hiding place. I knew my face was tear-streaked, and I didn't want to see either of them at the moment.

"Sister, can I see?" Abbi whispered from my other side while gently stroking my back. Her touch felt more painful than the burn. At least it took my mind off the scald. "Let's see if we need to get you some medical attention, okay?"

Twitching away from the contact, I said, "No, Abs, it's fine. How many times have we burned ourselves? I can tell by the way it feels. Please. You guys, just back up. Let me breathe for a sec." Hopefully Abbi heard the panic rising in my voice. She knew me well enough to pick up on my cues at this point.

I watched Dori's shoes move away in my limited line of sight, but Abbigail's were still planted directly beside me.

"That means you too," I finally growled when she remained beside me. I didn't even recognize my own demon-possessed voice when I issued the warning. Abbi instantly took a step back but still not far enough. With each second that passed, the pain in my arm morphed into a rage in my gut.

So fucking typical—these Sharks. Always thinking they knew what was best for everyone. Had to take control of every situation. She was just like him now—the puppet master at every fucking event.

I stood up and shut the water off. The tender skin on my forearm was an angry scarlet. Second-degree burns— probably nothing worse. I didn't see any blisters in my quick examination. The minute the water stopped flowing over the injury, though, the agony intensified, but it just fueled my rage even further.

"Let's get you some help."

"You've been dying to say that, haven't you?" I snarled.

"What?" Abbi asked, bewildered.

"I know that's what you think. I know that's what everyone thinks," I said, backing away from her.

"Rio," she cooed. Her voice was sickening and gentle. "I meant for your arm. But if you want to talk about something else, why don't we"—she pointedly looked around the kitchen, and I followed her movement—"go outside."

"What? You don't think everyone knows I've lost it? You don't all talk about me when I'm not here? Please!" I shouted.

"Rio. Stop this. No one talks about you. We all just want to see you, well . . . happy."

"Fuck off, Abbi. Fuck you all, actually. Take your happiness and your wellness and go fuck yourself with it."

I started laughing like I was certifiable. God, that felt so good to finally say. I'd wanted to tell this woman to go fuck herself for so long. I stormed over to the desk to grab my keys and purse. I needed to get the hell out of the building before I really did or said something I'd regret.

Might be a little late for that sentiment.

But when I spun back around to head toward the door, Abbigail stood in the way. Her giant green eyes brimmed with tears, and shit you not, her lower lip actually quivered. There were times I thought the woman practiced this pitiful routine in the mirror. Was anyone really this emotional?

But fuck if it didn't work. Stabbing guilt struck me in the stomach like a bully's sucker punch. I actually clutched my unburned hand to my abdomen when one crocodile tear rolled down her ruddy cheek, followed by another, then another.

"Abbi..." I gasped. But she started shaking her head slowly from side to side.

"No. Just stop, Rio. Just...yeah...no."

"Abbigail, please, you don't understand," I pleaded. Tears filled my own eyes as my rage ebbed and regret took its place.

Dori came to stand by her boss's side, superhero cape flapping in the wind. "I think you've said enough already, Rio."

Just like that, the tide replaced my sorrow with anger again. I was an emotional typhoon. "You can go fuck yourself right out of this conversation, Dori. This is between Abbi and me." I pointed my finger right in her face, and Abbi's eyes bulged so full, it was almost comical.

"You know what, maybe you should just leave, Rio," said Abbi. "You need to get some professional help before you hurt someone...or yourself. I know things have been hard for you since my brother died—"

I burst out with a cackling laugh. "Is that what you think will fix this? Little Miss Perfect Life? Professional help? You don't have a damn clue what I'm going through. Because you've been so busy in your perfect world, in your perfect house, with your perfect fucking man." I heaved in a fortifying breath to continue my diatribe. "You, like everyone else, haven't bothered to ask or care about what I need or find out how I'm getting through this nightmare."

I pushed past her then, but at the last moment, stopped with my hand hovering over the doorknob.

Aggressively, I pointed my index finger toward Abbigail. "Your brother's gone, and it's your man's fault. Yet somehow you strut around here like a little queen, and I'm the one everyone thinks is crazy. But when your last name is Shark—or, pardon me—is about to be"—I curtseyed dramatically—"everything always comes up roses, doesn't it?"

CHAPTER TWELVE

GRANT

"You did what?" I bellowed into my cell phone, not caring that I was shouting at a very pregnant woman. The potential damage Abbigail might have caused with her "good intentions" was immeasurable. I could tell by her responding outrage and incensed tone she didn't see it the same way.

Not in the least.

"Grant, you didn't see the way she was acting today. I'm really worried about her. I've known her for much longer than you have, and I feel like I know what's best for her. I know you've grown to . . . " She paused, choosing her words carefully. "I know that you care very deeply for Rio. That the two of you have become good . . . umm . . . friends."

"There's more to it than that, Abbi." The words escaped before I could tamp them down, but I immediately decided I didn't care if she knew how completely I'd fallen for her sister-in-law.

I didn't care if the whole world knew at this point.

She made a choking sound and then cleared her throat. "Pardon me?"

I would deal with the fallout of admitting my feelings later, when Rio's physical well-being wasn't a concern. Right now, I needed to find her and help her. She would never forgive

Abbigail for doing this to her.

"Where have they taken her? Do you know?"

"Yes, of course I know," she scoffed. "Do you think I would just have her taken away to the county mental hospital or something? Be serious, Grant. I'm not some cruel and heartless bitch. I want what's best for Rio, too. I've begged her to get help. Begged her to talk to someone."

A few long moments passed over the phone line before I summoned every last shred of patience I had left. Through gritted teeth, I said, "Abbi? Tell me where she is. I'm not going to ask you again. You've fucked up royally by having her caged up somewhere, and if I don't get to her and help her, I'm afraid of what she's going to do."

"Grant, she's in the care of professionals now. I can assure you, I found the very best."

"You don't know what you're talking about..." I trailed off, realizing I wouldn't be getting anywhere with the woman. If she wasn't this stubborn before hooking up with Sebastian, she'd quickly absorbed a lot of his personality traits.

"No, I think you're the one with only half the picture here. Rio's had mental health problems most of her life. Maybe it's time for you to step aside and let her family care for her now." The condescending tone of voice she used made my vision blur to a red haze.

"Like you've cared for the past month, Abbi? Where the hell have you been since Sean's accident?" My tone was icy and bitter. The accusation hung like static over the phone line.

"How dare you..." she finally whispered.

Which made my bellow sound three times as loud. "Tell me where she is! Now!" Just as I made the demand, my phone signaled an incoming call on the other line. It was a Los

Angeles number I didn't recognize, but if there was any chance it was about Rio, I needed to take the call.

Abruptly, I hung up on Abbigail and switched over to the other call. "Grant Twombley," I rushed out.

Please let it be her. Please let it be her.

"Grant? Grant? Are you there? Is that you?" Rio sounded childlike and terrified.

"Blaze." I breathed her name more than spoke it. "Baby, I'm right here. Where are you?"

"Grant? Where are you?" She repeated my words in lieu of an actual response.

"Baby, I'm going to come to you, but you have to tell me where you are."

"Abbi is so mean. She was so mean to me today. And then these people came to my house, and they made me hold still and stuck my arm with something that made my head so heavy." She stopped talking abruptly, and I pulled the phone away to look at the display, making sure I hadn't dropped the call. "I'm so tired," she finally said.

I called Elijah from the phone on my desk. I made sure she was still on the line on my cell every couple of seconds.

"Dude, I need your help. Can you track Rio's cell phone right now?"

"Yeah, probably. What's going on?"

"I'll tell you the whole story when you pick me up out front of SE. Are you nearby?"

"I'm in the building." He chuckled. "You okay, man? You sound like you're losing your shit."

"Text me when you have a bead on her. I'll keep her on the line as long as I can, and then I'll meet you out front."

"You got it, brother. See you in a few."

"You still there, Blaze? Did you have lunch yet? Maybe I can pick you up?"

"I can't leave here. I'm trapped, Grant. I'm in prison. Abbi put me in prison. She knows I'm crazy, and she told them too."

"What did I tell you about saying that? Hmm?" I made sure my voice was gentle, almost playful when reminding her I didn't want to hear her use those self-deprecating words. "There's nothing wrong with needing some help now and then. But you don't have to be locked up for us to do that. Abbi doesn't know what you need. I'm sure she meant well, but she just doesn't know."

"Grant?"

"Yeah, baby?"

"Can you hold me?" Her normally strong voice cracked before turning to a whisper. "I don't like it here."

"I'm going to fix it. I promise. I'm coming for you, and I'll fix everything. Okay?"

"Okay."

"Why don't you take a nap until I get there? Elijah's getting his car from the parking structure, and we'll be there in just a little while. You rest. Don't go anywhere with anyone else though, okay?"

"What? What do you mean?"

"Just stay where you are until I get there." The last thing I wanted was for her to get spooked and try to make a break for it. They would either end up sedating her or transferring her to a facility with tighter lockdown capabilities. My guess was wherever she was currently must not be too strict if she was already making phone calls.

"You're such a tree. You know that?"

"You keep telling me that, so yeah."

She got quiet again, and this time when she spoke, her tone was wistful. "I'm like the owl from the other night. I keep calling out, over and over again. But my mate doesn't answer back anymore." The silent pause was even longer this time, and then finally she said, "I don't know how to move on, Grant." Her voice broke when she said my name, and it felt like maybe my heart had as well.

I was lost on how to respond. More than anything, I wanted to promise Rio that I'd be the one to answer when she called now. I'd be the man who would come when she needed help. She could grieve the loss of her husband and move on with a happy, productive life. She deserved that and had taken so many steps in the right direction to ensure that outcome.

My phone vibrated with an incoming text, so I pulled it away from my ear and took a quick look to see that Elijah had captured her location with some proprietary software he used directly from his own phone.

"Blaze?"

"Hmm?" she answered wearily.

"Elijah just sent me a text that he's downstairs. He's going to drive me over to pick you up, okay?"

"Oh, okay. I guess I'll see you later then. Bye." She disconnected the call without an inquisitive word on how I knew her whereabouts. That alone was a great indicator of how strong the sedative was currently coursing through her system.

Reina was busy at her desk when I hustled past, but I paused long enough to let her know I'd be gone for a while. "I'm not really sure how long I'll be, but I have my cell, and I'm taking my laptop in case I need to handle anything that can't wait until I get back," I explained, only slowing, not actually stopping, to rush out the words.

"Sounds like a plan," my assistant said, jumping to her feet to scurry down the hall with me. She scanned my calendar on her smart pad as we walked. "You have a one thirty meeting with your interior designer, Amaya Perez. Do you want me to reschedule that or wait and see if you are back by then?"

"Will you just tell her I'll be in touch to reschedule?" Impatiently, I pressed the down button on the elevator.

"No worries. I'll email the board of directors' agenda draft to you for approval before sending the final copy out to the members, so keep an eye out for that."

I pressed the down arrow again.

Reina arched a brow toward me. "Last thing from me… I have the reports you wanted from HR that chart overtime hours versus job-site mishaps. Where do you want those?"

Finally the elevator arrived and the doors parted to let two people off. I slipped my large hand over the door sensor to hold the thing open while I gave one last instruction to my assistant. "Can you start entering the data into the spreadsheet we created last week? Maybe do a trial on a few lines to see if the formulas work the way we wanted before entering too much info? If we have to tweak the math, we can do that when I get back or tomorrow."

"You got it." Reina put her hand on the door to keep it ajar after I pressed the button to descend to the lobby and waited for me to meet her gaze. When I did, my aide said, "Take a deep breath, please. You're not going to help anyone if you have a heart attack from all the stress before you get a chance to save the day."

After giving the young woman a genuine smile, I took an obvious deep breath and said, "Thanks, Reina. You're right. As always."

She stepped back and let the elevator close, giving one last wave before being shut out completely. I made a mental note to give the girl something extra at Christmas this year. She'd certainly been going above and beyond lately.

Elijah sat idling in the loading zone out front of Shark Enterprises. I slid into the passenger seat, and he pulled into late-morning traffic. Luckily it was one of the lighter traffic times on the downtown streets, or I would've gone mad with impatience.

"So what the hell is going on? How did she end up at this facility? There's no way she checked herself in here." Elijah started with the questions as soon as he was safely within the flow of the other cars.

"Fucking Abbigail."

"Please tell me you're kidding."

"Not even close."

"What was she thinking? Look at the web browser on my phone." He gestured to his phone in the center console between us. "I have the facility's website pulled up. I was checking it out while I was waiting for you to come down."

"Nah, I'm not going to look. I'm already really pissed. If that woman was here in front of me, I'd be worried about what would come out of my mouth."

"Can you put the address in the nav, though? I'm not familiar with that side of town." Elijah handed me his phone anyway. Even though I just said I didn't want to see the damn website, he was forcing me to look at it.

While I entered the information into his car's directional assistant, I continued bitching. "You know, Abbi and Bas both have gone off the deep end with their meddling. They think they know what's best for everyone and make decisions without thinking about the whole picture."

"I hear you, man. We'll get over there and sign her out. Try to take a couple of deep breaths, big guy. You look pale as a ghost." My friend smacked my shoulder with brotherly concern.

"You're the second person who's said that. Breathe. Fuck! I'm breathing! I'm worried—no ... freaking out is more like it. You haven't seen Rio having a full panic attack like I have. It's scary as shit."

"Then maybe she's in the right place. I mean, have you considered that? I know that's not what you want to hear right now. But if she's that unstable, are you equipped to deal with her?"

I stared out the window and watched the other cars driving by. Something about this scene seemed all too familiar. "I don't fucking know, man," I mumbled to my own reflection.

Elijah pressed a few buttons on the car's display, and an overview of our route showed that we were only about three miles from our destination.

"Is this place in the Garment District? Seriously ... "

"Well, the queen said she researched it and it was a very reputable establishment," I said bitterly. "She doesn't know a fraction of what Rio's been going through or about Rio's hobby, as she calls it. She doesn't know her sister-in-law half as well as she thinks she does. She would've never thought cooping her up anywhere was a good idea if she did."

"How did she sound when you talked to her? Was she tearing the place apart?"

"Not yet. Hopefully I can get her out of there before that starts. Whatever they have her hopped up on was pretty powerful stuff. She sounded like a five-year-old. But even that was unsettling."

Elijah swung his car into a parking space marked for visitors, and we both got out quickly but then came to an abrupt stop.

Shit. Am I really ready for this?

On paper, who was I to this woman? Why would they release her to me over the family member who had her committed to their care in the first place?

Gripping the back of my neck, I looked to my buddy. "I didn't think this through, man," I said in a bit of panic.

"What do you mean? Come on," he urged. "Let's go inside."

"Wait a second." I held up my hand to stop him, then shoved it back through my hair, gripping the strands in frustration. "I think I need a plan. What gives me the right to sign her out of here when a family member put her here in the first place?"

"Do you know if Abbi initiated a fifty-two hundred on her?"

"I don't. I don't even know what that is, dude. We didn't get into all that. I was so pissed, I just got off the phone before I really lost my shit and said something I'd regret."

"Okay, so like I said, let's go inside and talk to the people running this place and see what we're dealing with. There's a lot of bureaucratic red tape with an involuntary hospitalization, so it takes time to have one put into place. I believe a judge's ruling is even involved."

As we opened the front door of the building, I looked skeptically at Elijah and asked, "All for a seventy-two-hour hold?"

He nodded and lowered his voice now that we were inside. "Think about it. Basically you are asking them to hold her against her will because someone has determined she is a danger to herself or others. That is taking away her civil rights. It's not done without serious consideration."

"Yeah, that all makes sense."

"It's for the detainee's own protection," he continued.

"But be serious." I motioned to the lovely, well-kept building and grounds all around us. "These places are all about protecting themselves, too. I'm sure of it."

"Oh, you can count on it," Elijah agreed.

I continued to nod as we approached a counter resembling a hotel registration desk. A woman about our age smiled warmly in greeting.

"Hi. Can I help you?"

"I hope so." I smiled back because a little charm never hurt the cause. I leaned forward marginally to see the name on her badge, since she didn't offer it herself. "Pamela, my name is Grant Twombley"—I turned a bit and motioned to my friend—"and this is my friend, Elijah Banks. It's my understanding that a very dear friend of ours was brought here earlier today. Rio Gibson?"

The woman continued with her polite smile but was all business when she said, "It's a pleasure to meet you both. Mr. Twombley, was it?"

"Please, call me Grant."

"Mr. Twombley," she went on as if I hadn't spoken, "I'm sure you can understand, given the sensitive nature of what we deal with here at Clear Horizons, I'm unable to discuss any patient information with anyone other than spouses and immediate family members."

After taking a fortifying breath, I tried a different approach with the administrator. "Earlier today, I got a phone call from Ms. Gibson. She was very distressed. She said she was being held against her will in this facility. She asked me to come get her." I watched her reaction closely for any clues on how to proceed.

The woman's brows popped up toward her severe hairline. Every strand of her intense bun was pulled back and slicked into place with the bulk tied off in a knot at the nape of her neck. The hairstyle gave her the appearance of a stern prison warden crossed with a sexy librarian.

"I can assure you, Mr. Twombley, no one is ever detained here against their will without proper court proceedings."

"Well, since Ms. Gibson was just admitted this morning, and given the backlog of our state's judicial system, I'm sure a hearing was not held"—I looked at my watch to make my point very clear—"between ten thirty this morning and now, closing in on noon."

"Pamela, can you help me understand the California Welfare and Institutions Code?" Elijah asked. "Specifically, the Lanterman-Petris-Short Act?" My friend gave a self-deprecating chuckle. "It's all so confusing, you know?" His tone sounded sugar sweet, but everyone involved in the conversation knew it was anything but.

Elijah was firing a warning shot across Pamela's bow by letting her know he had been doing his homework. If she kept toying with us much longer, we'd have an attorney walking through her front doors. Possibly a camera crew too.

"Listen, gentlemen, I'm not looking for any sort of trouble. I'm just trying to do my job. And also, keep my job."

"Of course you are, Pamela," said Elijah. "But we need to see our friend, Rio Gibson. And I need you to either tell me where I can find her or show me to the room she's in. Right.

Now. Or I will have my attorney down here so fast, your head will spin. No one likes to hear about citizens having their civil rights violated or taken away completely when protocols aren't followed." Elijah bored holes into the woman with his green eyes. "Has a fifty-one fifty or a fifty-two hundred been initiated on Ms. Gibson? And who placed t he initial call? Who is doing the assessment? Has a hearing been scheduled?"

Elijah continued firing question after question at the woman, not letting her answer one before asking another. She was so befuddled by his taunting, she finally said, "Fine!" She looked around the lobby quickly and then grabbed for the pearl necklace at the base of her throat. "Please, keep your voice down. Many of our residents get agitated very easily."

"Room number, Pamela."

"Twelve nineteen. But understand, the only reason I'm telling you is because an evaluation hasn't been done yet, so technically she isn't the center's responsibility. If you're willing to take responsibility for her, then the only people you have to contend with are the ones who had her brought here."

"And who did you say that was?"

Pamela strutted in her sensible block-heeled pumps to the computer behind the admissions desk and tapped on a few keys to wake the computer.

"I'm sorry, what did you say the last name was again? My nerves have really gotten the best of me." She gave an awkward smile, and I almost felt bad for the woman. Almost.

"Rio Gibson," Elijah and I said in chorus.

"That's right. Okay, here we are." She scanned the monitor, her eyes darting back and forth across the screen. "Looks like the initiator was Abbigail Gibson, with secondary contact

Sebastian Shark. Oh, wait. That name sounds familiar." The woman chewed on the end of her pen for a beat. "I think he's a very generous donor of the center. I think his name is on a plaque somewhere around here." She looked around randomly, as if she could spot the memorial from where she was sitting.

Pulling Elijah off to the side, I said, "I'm going to go find Rio. We'll need to leave immediately, and if she's still drugged to the extent she was when she called me, I may have to carry her." He arched his brows, and I shrugged. "Not really sure what my other options are, man. But I think we need to make it quick. Bas usually has eyes and ears everywhere. I'm surprised he hasn't stormed the front door already."

"No shit. Well, what are you waiting for, man? Go get your girl."

"She's not my—"

Elijah tilted his head in doubt. "Cut the crap, Grant. We don't have time for it right now. Not to mention, I'm not buying your bullshit anymore. Just go find her so we can blow this taco stand."

I nodded once. Then again. Giving myself an internal pep talk more than anything. If I were being honest with myself, I was terrified of what I was about to find inside room twelve nineteen.

Jogging down a long corridor, I scanned the numbers on the doors until I found hers. I knocked softly and put my ear to the door. It was quiet, but I heard some movement, so I tried the doorknob.

Unlocked.

I slipped inside, turning my back to the center of the room while I closed the door as quietly as possible.

"Grant?" Rio's soft voice instantly comforted me.

Until I turned to face her in the middle of the room. I couldn't make sense of the scene before me. At least not for a few moments. Panic swelled in my stomach and thrust up through my lungs and burst out in a gasp.

"Rio?" I sucked in a lungful of air, not wanting to believe my eyes. I squeezed them shut, thinking when I opened them, it would all have been some silly trick of my imagination. There was no way I was seeing what I thought I was.

"Fuck! Rio? What are you doing, baby? What are you thinking?" I started toward her, but she held her hands up in warning.

"You shouldn't have come in this room, Grant."

"No. Come on, I'll help you clean this up. Then we'll get out of here."

"They won't let me leave. They know the truth. Hasn't Abbigail told you? I thought she would've told everyone by now."

"Move away from all of that stuff. Now." I tried using my stern, dominant voice, but Rio just stiffened her spine and stood taller.

"You don't get to tell me what to do, Grant. No one does. Because I'm the crazy girl. Oh, that's right. You haven't heard the news yet."

"What have I told you about saying that?"

"Well, it doesn't matter now anyway. Soon it will all be gone. They'll all be gone. No one will know just how sad and lonely I really am. How lost and afraid."

"Stop talking like that. Right now. Come here. I'll take care of you, baby. Come here to me."

I held my hand out to her so she would move away from

the pyre she had assembled in the middle of the room.

Instead, she struck the small flint of a matchstick on the side of its box and held it up in front of her lifeless eyes. She dropped to her knees in the middle of the room as she watched the small flame dance in the draft. The glow reflected back twice, once in each pupil as she watched the fire burn away until it snuffed itself out.

"Rio, baby. Please. Come to me. Put the matches down and come to me." I held my arms open to her, but she was too engrossed in her handiwork to pay any attention to me.

"I'm going to burn this fucking place to the ground, Grant. Then I won't have to be trapped here. No one will. I hear people screaming and crying in the other rooms. I hear them in my head even when they stop. Now they're in my head."

She thrashed her head back and forth, as if doing so would get the sound to fall out one side or the other.

"I don't want to hear that, you know?" She looked at me with curious eyes, wondering if I could relate to the misery. I nodded along in sympathy, not having a clue what the right response was.

"I have enough pain and sorrow in there already. I can't take other people's too." She knocked herself on the side of her head with the heel of her hand. She did it so hard, the thump echoed through the room. Then she did it again. And again. Each time, I felt more bile rising in my throat. The woman I was in love with was unraveling before my eyes, and I felt like my fucking feet were riveted to the floor—helpless to do anything but watch it happen.

"No! Stop it, Rio! Stop hurting yourself!" I shouted, and she finally looked up to me. I fell to my knees, mirroring her position on the floor. The only thing separating us was the pile of combustibles she had gathered from around the room.

Rio looked from me to the kindling and then back to me. "Save yourself, Grant. You're too good of a man to go down with a crazy woman like me."

I held her gaze while I promised, "I'm not leaving here without you, Blaze. I'll carry you out kicking and screaming if I have to."

In rapid succession, she lit match after match after match and tossed them onto the pile of bedding, paper, and other incendiary things. The fire flared up so fast and so hot, it was almost blinding between us.

"Rio! Rio, no!" I sprang to my feet and charged right across the pile of combustible debris that separated us. My girl was frozen in place, watching the blaze spike up higher and higher. A wild look in her eyes told me she had checked out completely. If she was getting out of the place alive, it was going to be in my arms.

I scooped her up easily, and she immediately nestled her face into my neck. I threw the door open to her room and hurried down the hall with her in my arms. Just before reaching the lobby, I spotted a fire alarm on the wall so I threw open the cover and pulled the lever down, immediately sending a blaring signal throughout the building.

Elijah saw me stalking across the common area with Rio cradled against my chest. He immediately started toward the door, and I wordlessly followed. We were securely in his car and driving out of the parking lot before either one of us spoke.

"Dude. What the hell happened?"

"Don't ask, man. Just, yeah . . . drive."

"Where to now, my brother?"

"Can you take us down to the marina?"

"As in Marina del Rey?"

"Yeah." I nodded as well and then turned to check Rio in the back seat. She already had her eyes closed. Whether she was sleeping or unconscious, I had no idea.

"Sure, but—"

"Elijah, I said don't ask."

"All right. All right," my friend acquiesced.

"And once you drop us off, I need you to do me one last favor."

"I don't think I like the sound of that, but okay . . ."

"Forget you ever saw either one of us today."

ALSO BY
ANGEL PAYNE & VICTORIA BLUE

ALSO BY ANGEL PAYNE

Misadventures:
Misadventures with a Time Traveler

Honor Bound:
Saved
Cuffed
Seduced
Wild
Wet
Hot
Masked
Mastered
Conquered
Ruled

Cimarron Series:
Into His Dark
Into His Command
Into Her Fantasies

Temptation Court:
Naughty Little Gift
Pretty Perfect Toy
Bold Beautiful Love

Suited for Sin:
Sing
Sigh
Submit

Lords of Sin:
Trade Winds
Promised Touch
Redemption
A Fire in Heaven
Surrender to the Dawn

ALSO BY VICTORIA BLUE

Misadventures:
Misadventures with a Book Boyfriend
Misadventures at City Hall

**For a full list of Angel's & Victoria's other titles,
visit them at AngelPayne.com & VictoriaBlue.com**

ACKNOWLEDGMENTS

One of the biggest joys of writing is taking the reader on a journey created from a combination of my own thoughts, daydreams, and real-life experiences. When I sat down to write the first part of Grant and Rio's journey, I knew it was going to be an emotional one, but I also knew I was diving into a pool I'd never swam in personally. So, I "took it to the streets," so to speak, and was overwhelmed by the responses I received from so many readers who were willing to share their stories with me.

Without the help of the following very brave women, Grant and Rio's story would not have been possible: Betsy Way, April Antolich, Amy Bourne, Rheanna Kay Clark, and especially Michele Mucciolo. These women shared personal, emotional, and raw details that helped guide me through writing the story you find in this book.

I hope I've done their experiences justice, and I hope my interpretation of Rio's situation is just as authentic, heartbreaking, and gut-wrenching as theirs were when they shared them with me. I can't thank you all enough for being so brave.

With love and gratitude —Victoria XO

I couldn't begin to comprehend a project like this—so intense and insane—without an amazing partner to share the

wild ride. Victoria Blue, you are my hero and my inspiration. Thank you for your emotional bravery, your daily courage, and your heart of gold. You're an incredible woman!

Cannot say enough thanks to my family, for putting up with the insane hours and providing your unwavering support. Tom and Jess, you are my rocks. My heart. My soul.

My love and gratitude to my awesome family: Mom, John, Sue, Audrie, Jim, Gina, Brian—and my sweet pooches, LaaLaa and Claire, for holding me up on all the hard days.

So many thanks to my small but mighty army of friendship love: Carey Sabala, Cynthia Gonzales, Shayla Black, Jenna Jacob, Jodi Drake, Nelle L'Amour, and Cheryl Stern. I love you amazing ladies.

Fathomless and boundless gratitude to our Waterhouse Press team! Fearless leaders Meredith Wild and Jonathan Mac . . . editing GOD Scott Saunders . . . and the funny, fearless, utterly beautiful support team: Robyn Lee, Haley Boudreaux, Keli Jo Chen, Amber Maxwell, Kurt Vachon, Jesse Kench, Yvonne Ellis, Jennifer Becker, and Dana Bridges. Not a day goes by that we don't rave to each other about how blessed we are to have all of you in our world!

So thankful for the Payne Passion force! You are all my special family and my guiding light. So many thanks to Martha Frantz for keeping the train chugging in our Facebook group— and to my epic kid for keeping me well-versed on Instagram and Tumblr!

—Angel

ABOUT ANGEL PAYNE

USA Today bestselling romance author Angel Payne loves to focus on high-heat romance starring memorable alpha men and the women who love them. She has numerous book series to her credit, including the action-packed Bolt Saga and Honor Bound series, Secrets of Stone series (with Victoria Blue), the intertwined Cimarron and Temptation Court series, the Suited for Sin series, and the Lords of Sin historicals, as well as several standalone titles.

Angel is a native Southern Californian, leading to her love of being in the outdoors, where she often reads and writes. She still lives in Southern California with her soul-mate husband and beautiful daughter, to whom she is a proud cosplay/culture con mom. Her passions also include whisky tasting, shoe shopping, and travel.

Visit her at AngelPayne.com

ABOUT VICTORIA BLUE

International bestselling author Victoria Blue lives in her own portion of the galaxy known as Southern California. There, she finds the love and life-sustaining power of one amazing sun, two unique and awe-inspiring planets, and four indifferent yet comforting moons. Life is fantastic and challenging and every day brings new adventures to be discovered. She looks forward to seeing what's next!

Visit her at VictoriaBlue.com